GRAVE STONES

For recently engaged Detective Inspector Joanna Piercy, a murder is the last thing she wants to deal with. Especially one with as dark a back story as that relating to calculating landowner and farmer Jakob Grimshaw; a man who managed to make enemies of all his neighbours and what little family he still had. One thing is certain: Joanna has a tough job ahead of her.

GRAVE STONES

GRAVE STONES

by

Priscilla Masters

Magna Large Print Books
Long Preston, North Yorkshire,
BD23 4ND, England.

British Library Cataloguing in Publication Data.

Masters, Priscilla
    Grave stones.

    A catalogue record of this book is
    available from the British Library

    ISBN   978-0-7505-3169-6
    1\16

First published in Great Britain in 2009 by Allison & Busby Ltd.

Copyright © 2009 by Priscilla Masters

Cover illustration by arrangement with Allison & Busby Ltd.

The moral right of the author has been asserted

Published in Large Print 2010 by arrangement with
Allison & Busby Ltd.

Magna Large Print is an imprint of Library Magna Books Ltd.

Printed and bound in Great Britain by
T.J. (International) Ltd., Cornwall, PL28 8RW

Who else could I dedicate this to but Henry, my beloved grandson?

Chapter One

Sunday, 16th September

Pools of rain trickled down the limestone wall, licking its way over lichen and mosses, filling up crevices before spilling onto the mud, liquefying it further. It treated the usual and the unusual alike, rivulets coursing towards the barns, the cowshed, the door of the farmhouse, which stood ajar. Everything was damp and dripping, covered by a moving sheet of water which almost drowned an ant scurrying frantically to find its lost tribe. A slow worm slept in almost the one warm, dry place, between two stones, protected from the elements by an overhang; the Scarlet Pimpernel had closed her petals and the lichens and mosses flourished. Finally the ant was reunited with the rest of its kind and they marched in grim and narrow formation across the drab colours: the pale grey of the limestone, the sopping green of the moss. The only hint of colour was in the splashes of another, brighter hue, which had once been scarlet but was now changed to blurred and watery flecks of rust-red. Specks of it spattered the wall, a larger patch on the ground mixing with the mud and something else that had once been human tissue. Brain tissue: thinking, loving, hating, knowing – finally fearing – brain tissue. A person's personality, character and memories, now carelessly spilt over the ancient stones. It could think no more. As the batter of rain continued, the pattern changed, too, becoming less defined while the wall stood motionless and imperfect. For like a damaged row of teeth, something was missing, spoiling the line. The copestone was still near, lying at the foot of the wall, almost touching the still shape on the floor as the rain continued its rinsing of the scene.

About nine hundred miles away Joanna Piercy was lying on a striped velour beach towel that had been carefully laid over a wooden slatted sunlounger to keep the gravelly sand from sticking to her body. She was reading – or trying to read – a paperback while Matthew chattered and attempted to distract her. Finally, in desperation, he grabbed the book and held it aloft, like a trophy.

'Matthew.' Joanna made a vain attempt to snatch the book back. She was laughing. 'This is so unfair.' She put her hand out again to attempt recovery but Matthew was tall; his arms were long and he wasn't going to give it back. He held it away from her, his face both merry and challenging.

'Come on, Jo,' he said, bending over her now, grinning. 'How can you possibly lie there reading when the sea is so inviting?'

She glanced over his shoulder at the sparkling water. He spoke the truth. The sea did look beautiful. Cool and clean and bright. She made another swipe at his hand – and missed again. 'The book's exciting,' she protested. 'The heroine has just been shot and I can't bear–'

He stood up before her, tall, tanned and slim, hands on his hips, black swimming trunks, honey blond hair, bright green eyes and that wonderful eager, inviting expression. It was too much. She abandoned the idea of reading – for the next hour at least. Matthew was right. It was time to frolic.

She sat up, fastened the halter-neck strap of her bikini around her neck, peeled off her sunglasses and jumped to her feet. 'I'll race you,' she said and before he had a chance to respond ran helter skelter down the beach,

Matthew in hot pursuit.

They had finally given in to the terrible English 'summer' weather and escaped to Spain – Mojacar, in Almeria, the south east corner where both the Moorish influence and the sun were at their strongest.

Joanna felt happy. Ecstatically happy. She had felt like this from the moment she had stepped off the plane. After days and days of heavy skies and thunderous rain at home the Spanish sunshine had dazzled, the colours seeming almost too bright for her eyes. On that first afternoon she had squinted up at the bluest of skies, the whitest of walls, the brilliant reds of the geraniums in their terracotta pots decorating the balconies, and felt as though a giant weight had rolled off her chest. All towns in England can seem dreary at times under leaden skies but the incessant rain in the Staffordshire town of Leek, the malicious floods that had drowned parts of the country and the persistently cold temperatures had seemed to leak her happiness away, making her disgruntled and irritable. Something her colleagues – particularly Korpanski – had both noticed and commented on. She'd felt a certain dissatisfaction with her life, feeling she was simply treading water as the years slipped by without really going anywhere. So when Matthew had suggested they take a break she had gladly agreed. They'd spent a fruitful hour on the Internet, hiring a small apartment near the town of Mojacar and a jeep for the duration. They had spent their days sunbathing, swimming in the sea and reading paperbacks and the evenings strolling hand in hand through shops and restaurants.

Like her, Matthew was in buoyant mood.

The sand here was coarse and gravelly and hot underfoot; the beach shelving steeply making the rollers high and powerful, their breaking over the beach providing the perfect background music. They ran straight into the waves, hardly pausing as the surf hit their knees then their chests. They were both good swimmers and enjoyed the challenge of a fearsome current. Matthew bent his head towards her, eyeing her with lascivious amusement. 'I hope you didn't pay more than fifty pence for that scrap of a thing you're wearing.'

'Why?'

'Because there isn't more than four square inches of material in it.'

'It's the latest thing,' she said unperturbed, 'and I'm not even telling you how much per square inch I paid, Matthew Levin. It's none of your business. I shall get a lovely tan and be the envy of everyone back at the station.'

'I sincerely hope not,' he said. 'If you start flashing your white bits I would fear for your morals.'

In the flippant holiday mood she was in she was tempted to stick her tongue out at him. Instead she dived underneath the waves, tasting the salt water against her lips.

At that very moment, Detective Sergeant Mike Korpanski was queuing up to go on Oblivion at Alton Towers. And as he watched a car of previous passengers scream, white-faced, and disappear into the black hole, he wasn't absolutely sure that this was where he wanted to be. But Ricky was tugging at his arm, coaxing him and pleading, without realising that his father, for all his toughness, was not relishing testing his response to G-forces.

The trip to Alton Towers was an annual treat that he and Fran promised their children. Normally they enjoyed it. But this summer, queuing in the cold and rain, it didn't seem much like a treat to him. For two pins he would have vanished into one of the restaurants and left Ricky and Joss to their own devices. But he was a father and so he grinned at the pair of them and was about to be hurled into Oblivion.

Less than ten miles away in the town of Leek, Queen of the Moorlands, the rain had stopped, luring Hilary Barnes out of her house on the Prospect Farm Estate with a basketful of washing, looking up at the sky, willing it to hold off raining just long enough for the sheets to dry. As she pegged the laundry to the line she sniffed the air cautiously. *That smell.*

She used the rotary line, holding the plastic pegs in her mouth and pinning the clothes neatly in rows, socks paired together, a line of knickers, a couple of shirts, all the time eyeing the overcast sky with a malevolent challenge.

You dare rain – again. She felt like shaking her fist at it – or taking a deep breath and puffing the clouds out of the way like the portrayal of the North Wind in a child's picture book. But it was no use. The sky remained obstinately heavy and grey, threatening to soak yet another line of washing, without even a glimpse of blue. Not even enough to make the fabled sailor's trousers.

She sniffed again, screwing up her face. It is sometimes hard to know whether our memory stores smells, retrieving them at inopportune times. Was it there, in the air, or simply remembered, a chemical flashback? Hilary paused, hardly daring to breathe. Should she get the drains checked again? Was it worse? She breathed in tentatively and believed it was. This was not her imagination but an invasive, pervasive stink, which was fouling the air all around. She put an experimental hand over her nose and mouth and gave a sharp sniff. At the same time her eyes drifted towards the bottom of the garden. The boundary of her house and all the houses on this side of the Prospect Farm Estate was a dry stone wall, beyond which was probably the most decrepit farm in the whole of Staffordshire. Her lips tightened. Ignoring the fact that the farm had been in existence more than two hundred years before the estate – or development – as the brochure had called it – she could not understand why the council could seem to do nothing about Prospect Farm itself. The animals looked skinny and emaciated, covered in sores; the yard was nothing but a quagmire – particularly after all this rain. The entire place was a breeding ground for flies and rats. She'd seen a large, brown rodent scuttle from her wheelie bin only last week. Sometimes she fancied the filthy spillage actually seeped beneath the stone wall to pollute her own garden. There were certainly brown patches on the lawn nearest the wall. The barns were dangerous, about to collapse, with gaping holes in the roof. The house was – her eyes narrowed in disapproval – a disgrace. Broken windows, doors falling off their hinges, peeling paint. It was a tribute to nothing but neglect. It was hard to imagine that it could ever have been anyone's pride and joy. Certainly not now. She pursed her lips.

And as for Grimshaw. She practically shuddered as she pictured the farmer, bent with arthritis, in navy dungarees, hardly acknowledging her greetings. The question was – what was to be done? Her eyes slid over her garden fence towards her next door neighbour's house.

Ten years ago Jakob Grimshaw had started selling off small pockets of land around his farm. A portion of field here to a local farmer, a larger sliver there to a couple who had a daughter and a pony but nowhere to keep it. As he had sold the land a local property developer named Gabriel Frankwell had watched and plotted for his own share. He stepped in at exactly the right moment, bid for and bought a parcel of land, obtained planning permission for nine houses with suspicious speed and employed architects to maximise his profit. Finally he had built the Prospect Farm Estate: nine luxury houses, all five-bedroomed, three-bathroomed, double-garaged and individually designed. It was common knowledge that Frankwell had banked on procuring the farm itself and finishing the job before retiring to Rio de Janeiro, where he had a twenty five year-old mistress named Lucia, but old Grimshaw had proved stubborn – quite a thorn in his flesh – and the deal that would have secured Frankwell his final million had proved tantalisingly out of his reach. He, as sharp a wide-boy as existed, had been thwarted by someone he considered a simple Stafford-shire farmer. Frankwell was humiliated and furious but he too was stubborn, persistent and sometimes, when the stakes were high, he could also be patient. It had been these qualities that had lifted him out of his native Liverpool estate to the position of one of the wealthiest men in Leek. While waiting for the farmer to cave in he had sold seven of the houses, given one to his ex-wife, Charlotte, as part of their divorce settlement and lived in the ninth while it was on the market.

Next door to Hilary Barnes, Frankwell was nibbling his lip. It was sheer bad luck that the housing market had crashed at the very moment that he *needed* to sell the final property quickly. Frankwell was a man who did not like to be thwarted and he imagined the farmer laughing behind his back, which added to his fury. His patience was wearing thin now – partly because he needed to be with Lucia and partly because he was uncomfortable with the proximity of the neighbours, who never missed an opportunity to voice their disappointment with their purchases. Almost every time he put his nose outside the door one of them would complain. It was wearing him down, depressing him. Then there was his ex-wife, who could be vindictive and unpredictable at times. One never quite knew with her. One day she could be saccharin-sweet, the next spiteful and sour enough to turn the milk, as his daughter had wittily said. In fact the first reason was the most pressing; Charlotte and he had usually managed to see eye to eye. They were both practical realists. But he did not exercise the same control over the other reason for wanting to move. Lucia was due to give birth in five weeks' time. Nothing would stop this and he had decided early on that he wanted to be present at the birth, which had surprised even him. He certainly hadn't wanted to be at Phoebe's birth; neither would Charlotte have wanted him there. But the relationship with Lucia was different in every single detail from his relationship with his first wife. He loved Lucia with a sentimental, maudlin absorption that made him putty in her hands. He had a feeling this child would be a son and that his future life with sweetheart and son would achieve perfection, the zenith of his entire existence. For the first time in his tricky life he would live in financial security and tranquillity. He simply needed a bit more money. Frankwell ground his teeth. It all depended on two things: selling this final property and acquiring the last three fields that belonged to Grimshaw's farm, the farm building itself and selling it all on with planning permission, which he had already secured by way of a little palm-greasing. Friends in the council offices were to be nurtured. Frankwell peered through his patio doors, scowling at the decrepit barn. That eyesore, he thought angrily, was why none of the viewers had translated their obvious admiration of the house into a firm offer. With the property market being so much tighter now, people wanted perfection. Odd how he'd bought the land (cheaply) and built the houses without realising just what a problem it was. But it had hit him right in the solar plexus the second he actually lived in one of his own properties. He had quickly realised that, while the farm and its traditions initially appeared pretty, almost like a Victorian pastoral painting, the reality was something else: cow byres bred flies, animals left excreta, everything either smelt or made a noise. Instead of revelling in the rural idyll – as he had promised his buyers when they needed subtle persuasion – the inhabitants of the estate resented the farm and blamed him for its problems. Worse, Grimshaw had turned stubborn. The last time he'd spoken to him the farmer had grimaced with his toothy grin. 'If I sell that to you, *Mister* Frankwell, I'll have no farm left. It'll be the end.' There had been a note of mockery in his tone. Malice sparkling out of the pale eyes.

Frankwell ran his fingers through his hair. He couldn't afford for this final part to go wrong. He didn't want to fall at the last jump. He didn't take failure well. To cheer himself up he conjured up the vision of Lucia to comfort him. But he could only seem to see her standing, hands on hips, thick black hair a storm cloud around her face, mocking him. She was not comforting him but taunting him instead.

He opened his eyes, glared at the crumbling wall and the wrecked farmhouse beyond. *That* had been the biggest mistake of all. *It* was responsible. *He* was responsible.

Hilary had finished pegging her washing out and mercifully the weather had remained dry. She turned away from the wall to return to her house. But after two steps she frowned. Something was not right. It wasn't *just* the smell. It was quiet – too quiet. There was none of the usual farmyard activity. She could not hear any of the normal everyday sounds – the dog, Ratchet, barking or growling. There was no rattle of the chain he pulled after him.

It was not natural. Why was he so quiet?

She listened, her face tensed, her head on one side, the pupils of her eyes small and sharp. She was an intuitive and inquisitive woman. The cockerel was quiet too. And the sheep and the cows. Even the pigs. She peered across towards the farmhouse, frowning.

Were they all sleeping? The farmer too?

She knew then that it was all too still. And overlying the abnormal torpor there was

24

that unpleasant, rotting smell. Already she had a sense of foreboding. *It* was not right. Nothing was right.

She went inside, closing the door behind her.

But even though she closed every single window in every room of the house she could still smell it permeating her luxury home. The scent of rotting meat.

She knew exactly what it was.

Korpanski gripped the restraint that fitted tightly over his chest. Would Ricky despise him if he squeezed his eyes shut? He tried to laugh it off. 'What a laugh, hey?'

Ricky looked at him curiously and slipped his hands in his. 'Aren't you just a *bit* frightened, Dad?'

This is the dilemma of a father. To be honest and confess he was, sharing this with his son and making him feel normal for experiencing fear? Or bluff it out, deny any cowardice, bolster up the male ego and shrug it off. Which one?

Korpanski had no more time to make a decision. He saw Fran and Jocelyn way down below them. Managed a weak wave. And then...

He thought his heart would stop. He could

not breathe. The air rushed passed him. Beside him his son shrieked in terror as they dropped. Vertically. He felt sick. And then they were in the black hole, braced against the final jolt which came out of the unknown. And out again in the fresh, cool air.

And then it was all over. Korpanski sucked in a deeply relieved breath. He heard the click as the restraints were released. He lifted it up, grinned shakily at his son. 'Great,' he said. 'That was absolutely *fantastic.*'

His wife and daughter were waving, Jocelyn dancing towards them. Fran met his eyes and gave a small, cynical, sideways, lopsided smile. He might have fooled Ricky, she was saying, but he hadn't fooled her, not for a second.

'Careful,' Matthew said, gripping her arm. 'There's a big wave coming.' He dived underneath it as she stood her ground, feeling the surf crash against her body. She felt dwarfed by the power of nature. Breathless, exhilarated, gasping for air, Matthew surfaced, clenching his right hand into a fist. 'Look what I found,' he panted triumphantly, 'on the sea bed.' His hair was sticking to his head, seawater streaming down his face. He held his hand towards her then curled the fingers back, one by one, until Joanna could see what he held. 'Oh, Matthew,' she breathed. 'Matthew.'

It was a ring, a single black pearl, set in a hoop of silver studded with diamonds. She stared at it speechlessly before looking up at him and reading the mix of amusement and anxiety in his face while the waves continued crashing around them. But she was oblivious to all but the man standing in front of her and the object in his hand. He was smiling that ever-hopeful smile.

'I hope you don't expect me to go down on one knee,' he said. 'I might just drown.' He paused, his gaze focused on her. 'I think you know what I'm saying, Jo.'

'No. You don't need to go down on one knee,' she said, standing against him, brushing his lips with her own. 'I understand.'

He moved even closer and took her left hand. 'I take it that's a yes, then?'

For answer she slipped the ring onto her finger, put her arms around his neck and stood, looking up at him, oblivious to the surf smashing around her legs.

We can all ignore the surf breaking around us but it is still there. Energetic and furious, it can still bruise us.

Together they walked out of the sea. Matthew took hold of her hand and gazed down at the ring. 'It's a Tahitian pearl,' he said eagerly, as they walked up the beach. 'I wanted something unusual – different.'

'It is that,' she agreed.

'It's set in white gold. The pearl,' he continued, 'is between nine and ten millimetres and...' he was grinning with more confidence now, 'is AAA quality. That,' he carried on speaking quickly, continuing the teaching session as they walked over the coarse dark sand, 'means that it has been graded for lustre, surface quality, cleanliness and something called nacre, which is the amount of pearl which covers the piece of grit, the initial flaw which gave rise to such beauty.' He cradled her left hand in his then lifted it to his lips.

'I have to give you this, Matthew Levin,' she said. 'You certainly do your homework.' It was typical of him that he would think, research and then buy. All before asking her. 'It's lovely,' she continued. 'And so unusual.'

It was so him.

Matthew nodded. 'I thought a black pearl was somehow right for a detective inspector.' His grin was wide and warm. 'Sinister, beautiful, mysterious.' His light grin robbed the words of any cliché. 'Unpredictable, Jo, just like you, with a bit of grit at your centre.'

'Should I be insulted?'

He shook his head.

'Oh Matthew,' she said, pulling his face down to hers. 'I do love you.'

'I know,' he said comfortably, tucking her arm inside his.

She touched the pearl. 'And after all that studying,' she mocked, 'if I'd said no?'

He was silent and instinctively she knew the answer.

It would have been the end. He would not have asked again but had risked all on that one throw.

She would not ask that question again. Ever.

The ring felt strange on her finger but it was a perfect fit. 'How did you know my size?'

'And you're supposed to be the detective?' he mocked.

She looked at him even more carefully, studied the tousled hair the colour of damp sand, which he wore a little shorter these days, a little tidier; the bright green eyes that could hold such warmth but more often than not held a very straight, uncompromising message. Matthew could be a very stubborn man, which was easy to read in his face – from the firm set of his mouth to the square angle of his jaw. Many times she had watched the full, generous lips tighten. She reached out and touched the smooth cheek, remembering. Their love had stood many tests; one a wife, two a daughter, and three her career, which was always a threat side by side with Eloise. Yet in a way it had been these tests that had constructed their love.

Stone by stone.

She twisted the ring around on her finger, the band feeling strange in her hand. All beauty comes at a price. An oyster spoilt by a piece of grit, a relationship so easily spoilt in the same way. And yet from that irritation was formed a stone of such depth and beauty. This ring and its significance might mean many things to Matthew but it could ultimately cost her a sacrifice. She was well aware that they had a lot to talk about before they tied the knot – and not just the trifling details of a wedding.

'We should celebrate tonight,' she said. 'We have a lot to talk about.'

Always sensitive, Matthew's face changed to become suddenly strained. He pressed his index finger against her lips. 'One step at a time, Joanna,' he said quietly. 'Let's not spend the evening talking about how high some of the fences are that we need to jump.' He frowned. 'Let's just enjoy the moment as a romantic interlude.'

'Enjoy the moment,' she echoed, ignoring Eloise, the house, her career, his yearning for a son. As they reached their sunloungers Joanna was aware of the fact that they were a different couple from the one that had left them.

This had changed everything.

The Korpanski family were on their way home, relaxing in a pub in Ipstones, a small village between Alton and Leek. Korpanski was downing a pint of Rudyard Ruby, a beer brewed locally in Cheddleton. Fran had offered to drive for the rest of the day as a reward for his bravery earlier on. He only wished he could eradicate the amused look in her eyes every time she met his eyes. Why do wives read their husbands so completely when *every man wants to be a hero*.

Ricky was telling his wide-eyed sister how terrifying it had been – the climb that seemed to go on for ever, the fall into the unknown, the jolting, the screaming, the terror, the speed. He pulled his face out of shape with his fingers inserted into the corners of his mouth to illustrate the effect of the G force. Satisfyingly, his sister's mouth was wide open with admiration.

8p.m. Mojacar

Something must have appeared different about them that night because the man with a guitar serenaded them, the gypsy in a flamenco dress gave them a rose without asking for any Euros and the waiter who had served them each night since their arrival offered to take a picture of them together. And so they froze onto the screen of Matthew's digital camera, a newly engaged couple, heads close, smiling into the lens.

Riding on the back of that was the next hurdle, something she had pushed to the back of her mind. Matthew wanted another child while she didn't want any of her own. But Matthew's daughter, Eloise, was almost grown up and he felt he'd missed out on years of her childhood because his marriage had broken up. Eloise Levin was currently doing her A levels and had been having long discussions with her father about medicine as a career. Something even worse had been whispered: Eloise was talking about applying to Staffordshire University. It was a well thought of, new medical school, with a growing reputation. Its buildings were, according to Matthew, first class, its facilities equally so. He should know. He taught Pathology there. Joanna had overheard the telephone conversations with his daughter without voicing her own, private objections.

That would mean that Eloise would be living very close to them at best. At worst...

Joanna stared into the corner of the restaurant, watching a skinny black cat scavenging beneath a table. She couldn't bear to face it. Surely, *surely* Eloise wasn't thinking of living with *them?* But a quick glance at Matthew's face seemed to tell her different. There was an unnerving set to his jaw. Perhaps he thought that if he and Joanna were engaged or married she would be less likely to object to Eloise's presence. Joanna's eyes lingered on Matthew's face and she remembered something else.

In the last few months he had started to find their cottage too small. He wanted to move into the town, preferably into one of the large Victorian houses that lined the Buxton road. But she loved Waterfall Cottage. She loved living in the quiet moorlands village where they had finally moved more than a year after Matthew had left Jane, his first wife, Eloise's mother. Waterfall Cottage had been their first home together. A romantic love nest. She didn't want to move. She almost sighed and handed Matthew the black pearl back. But something stopped her.

It was all or nothing now. And she couldn't bear the thought of nothing. It was later, much later, as she was getting ready for bed, pulling the ring off her finger, that Joanna started to count the complications. There would have to be a wedding. Where? What sort?

In number 3, Prospect Farm Estate, Charlotte Frankwell was sitting in shell pink satin lingerie, painting her nails. She had allowed them to grow long and had filed them straight across into sharp, deadly weapons. Now she was applying white French nail varnish to the tips and admiring the effect, splaying her fingers wide in front of her. When the scent of something unpleasant wafted through the open window she stood up angrily and slammed it shut, careful not to damage her nail varnish, and turned back scowling. An expression that would have made her ex-husband disappear quickly.

When she had accepted number 3, Prospect Farm Estate as part of her divorce settlement, she had not expected a *real farm*, with real *smelly* animals in her back yard. She wouldn't have minded little moos and baahs but the smells could be simply atrocious. And that scruffy, rude man in his disgusting clothes. Did he ever wash? Charlotte doubted it. Whenever she saw Farmer Grimshaw tending to his animals in the farmyard that backed right on to her garden, she studiously ignored him. Her mouth tightened. Added to that, Gabriel was *practically* her next-door neighbour; there was only creepy old Mostyn in his shiny black suit between them when she'd hoped he'd be far away in Rio by now with his pregnant little gold-digger juvenile delinquent, leaving her free to pursue other goals. This was not ideal.

Her eyes narrowed and her orange-painted mouth curved. Friends said Charlotte Frankwell had about the most unpleasant smile in the human race. It held malice and spite, cruelty and vindictiveness, and no mirth at all.

Next door, in number 5, Peter Mostyn was sitting at his computer, attempting to make sense of the accounts in front of him. Once he had paid the mortgage and standing orders he had little enough left. Then Carol got her claws into his last pennies. That solicitor she'd hired to handle the divorce was a bloodsucker. A criminal. Mostyn clenched his jaw. Did he want him to starve? Didn't he realise that Carol and her paramour had *plenty* to live on? They didn't need his money. His anger bubbled up. How was it that a wife could abandon her husband for another, richer man, rob him of his children and still bleed him dry? There was no justice in this immoral world. He flexed his fingers and wished they were fastened around the bastard's scrawny little neck. He leant forward to peer again at the screen. He was in trouble. He simply wasn't managing his finances. He'd have to put the house on the market and buy somewhere cheaper. He heaved a great long sigh. He loved this place. It was so good for when the children came over for the holidays. It felt old-fashioned, traditional and peaceful. He too caught the waft of something unpleasant in the air but, unlike Hilary Barnes, it meant nothing to him. The physical smell merely mingled, unrecognised, with his bitterness and anger and lay there, rancid and oily, at the bottom of his heart. How much would the place fetch? £400,000? £425,000? With a bit of luck. It had not been a good investment in spite of the assurances Frankwell had given him. The property market had been anything but healthy lately and Leek wasn't exactly Mayfair with its still exploding house prices.

He wandered into the kitchen to flick the kettle on, his eyes scanning the room with some appreciation. All done to the highest specifications. He'd give Frankwell that. Handmade units, granite surfaces, built-in appliances, bathrooms aplenty, separate bedrooms for all three offspring. Once he had taken up residence he had never wanted to move again. But now, with his financial situation so dire, his pleasure in the place was turning as sour as his life. The more he liked it the worse it would be to move. 'Bloody Carol', he muttered, filling his mug with boiling water and spooning in powdered milk and coffee. And all for the man Carol had left him for, the one he called 'that Simmonds chap', who was fifty if he was a day, hugely overweight. *And* made of money. So why did she want all of his? Spite. It had to be. It was a travesty of justice. That was what it was. Mostyn sipped his coffee, his eyes peering over the rim suspiciously. Carol and

Simmonds were clever. They lived together but were wisely avoiding tying the knot. He could appeal but that would be more expense. Every time he rang the solicitor he seemed to see the man's finger hovering over the time clock, totting up the pounds. The last bill had been over a thousand pounds. Just for a few letters.

Carrying the mug of coffee he returned to the study and peered again into the computer screen. Solicitor's bill. He hadn't put that on the accounts. So that was why he was overdrawn – again – at the bank. It was no use asking for another extension to his overdraft facility. He wouldn't be able to pay it back unless...

Mostyn's face narrowed to grow sly and cunning, his eyes dark and unfathomable.

He had a secret.

When he had bought number 5 he had brokered a very smart deal. He had bought the field on the far side of the farm from old Grimshaw for a snip of a price. It was a good-sized field – an acre and a half – and to further the masquerade that it still belonged to Grimshaw he'd allowed the farmer to continue grazing his cattle on it. He would bet on it that no one knew it no longer belonged to the farm. He had to hold back the smirk when Frankwell boasted about expanding the estate, swallowing up the farm, building a further fifty houses on the fields where sheep and cows now grazed. In Mostyn's mind he imagined the small, select development expanding to a larger estate, which would turn his field into a building plot and raise the price accordingly. All it had needed was planning permission, which Carol, with her customary lack of confidence in his financial acumen, had grumpily assured him would never be granted. 'It's Green Belt,' she'd said when he'd confided in her. 'It's yet another pig in the poke from Mostyn Estates and Co. You're wasting your money, Peter.'

He'd encouraged her to believe this was so right through the divorce settlement but actually, through a business acquaintance in the Planning Department of the local council, he knew different. Leek was short of houses. Overspill from the Potteries had soaked up every available dwelling and people liked the quaint town with its picturesque streets and mock Victorian buildings. Prices had continued to creep up even over the last year, when the rest of the property market had stagnated. And with the flood plains being no good for building on, mutterings were being made about the need to build on Green Belt. After all – Prospect Farm Estate itself had been built on Green Belt. Why shouldn't it expand? And without the farm itself, the estate would rise in value.

Unconsciously, Mostyn rubbed his palms together. If he could only manage his finances until the children had finished school he would be all right. His father was elderly, his mother dead. Being an only child he would inherit all. So the dismal figures on the screen were simply a symptom of a *temporary* cash flow problem. And then he had his piece of land. There was only one thing that stood in the way of an excellent profit there. The farm. When he had bought the field he had realised that if the estate were to be expanded the farm would stand in the way. The only access to his field was through the farmyard, which was why he had been able to buy it so cheaply. Even he, with his optimism, knew that no planning permission could be granted unless the farm was also sold as building land. The far side of the field was bordered by a brook. If only Grimshaw could be persuaded to sell up the road could curve around, finally ending in his field. They could even keep the duck pond as a feature. But the last time he had talked to the farmer Grimshaw had looked bemused. 'Sell my inheritance? No way, sir. That farm is all I have left of my family tree. My old bones belong here. No doubt Judy'll sell up after I'm dead. I can't do much about that. She despises farming. She's no interest in the land and all it can yield. Oh yes. She'll sell up for sure after I'm dead, squander it all on high living, a smart car and some foreign holidays, I'll be sure.' His face had grown even meaner. 'She only wants money, that girl. Greedy, she is. Money's all she's ever been interested in – even as a little girl. Always wanting more of everything: food, toys, presents, a bigger horse, a smarter bedroom.' The old farmer looked weary. 'I couldn't keep up with her demands. Not on a farmer's salary. It weren't possible.'

Mostyn had shrunk away from the defeat in the old man's voice. The pale eyes had fixed on his face with a sneer. 'This farm'll be gone afore too long, dunna you worry. Your investment will make good.' He'd stomped back into the cowshed leaving Mostyn to wonder. *When* would his investment make good? The farmer might live for years. Sometimes he wondered whether Grimshaw had made a monkey out of him, that his stupidity and simplicity were a front and really he was laughing at him. At all the inhabitants of the Prospect Farm Estate and their mean little tricks: leaving gates open, chucking weedkiller over his fields, leaving plastic bags to blow over the wall knowing that they were potentially lethal to his animals, fishing line strung across the gateways when no one from Prospect Farm fished, as far as he knew. But none of their tricks irritated Grimshaw as much as his farm annoyed them. So he had the last laugh.

Mostyn had turned around and returned to his house, reflecting. The old farmer spoke the truth. He would never leave. He might be getting on a bit – well into his seventies – but these moorlands folk were tough. He might last for years. On the other hand... As for the daughter, again Grimshaw spoke the truth. He couldn't imagine Judy the witch going in for farming. Whenever she visited her dad it invariably led to a blazing row. She'd ask for money. Scream, more like, and Grimshaw would dig his heels in. Mostyn could remember plenty of incidences of raised voices, shouting, fury followed by the little red car skidding back down the farm track, anger spilling out of it.

Judy wouldn't want to do anything with

the land except sell it. She'd want to take the money and run. Mostyn put his fingers over his mouth and chewed his nails as he stared into the computer screen, willing the figures to dance across the columns and produce something a little more healthy. He typed out a few figures – an optimistic top price for the field – and watched all the DR in the bank statement turn magically to CR. Credit. If Grimshaw was out of the way he could realise his investment quickly and bingo. Mostyn snapped his fingers cheerily. Problem solved. He smiled, saved his workings out and switched the computer off.

The wall was in darkness. Clouds drifted shadows across the stones, a field mouse scuttled along its foot, a bat flew towards it, suddenly rising in the sky to clear the top, a hedgehog foraged around its base. From far above a barn owl scanned the stones for its evening meal and spied the field mouse. It swooped. The spattered stains were almost invisible. Inky black against grey.

Leaning against the wall is something strange and foreign. Farmers do not, as a rule, lie motionless, in their own yards, for hours, days at a time, right through the night.

Steven Weston was standing at the window, frowning at the scene. He didn't like being made a fool of. You'd think with his training to present things well he would have realised. But he'd rather liked the outlook onto the farmyard, been seduced by Frankwell's oily blurb. He dropped the muslin curtain with a curse. *He* who *wrote* the bloody stuff for a living, had been taken in by someone else's spiel. Which made him hate Gabriel Frankwell even more. Kathleen had mocked him as they'd viewed it. 'Didn't you realise,' she'd said in that condescending tone she habitually used when addressing him (only him, he'd noticed; she kept that special tone specifically for him), 'farmyards are smelly places; they breed flies and animals are noisy. We could have bought no end of places for the price we paid for this. I told you you were being a fool.'

Along with Frankwell his wife was good at making him feel a fool. Which was why he'd taken up with Faria. She made him feel something else. Something quite different. Subconsciously he straightened his shoulders, puffed out his chest, flexed his muscles and drew in a long, deep breath. He morphed into someone powerful, sexy, interesting. Fascinating. He fished his mobile phone out of his pocket. As he'd thought, the little envelope icon was flashing a message at him. *'He's out 2night!!?'*

He tapped one back. *'What time?'*

She must have been keeping an eye out for his response because her reply was almost instant.

'8'

He tapped back a quick, *'C u then.'*

Before deleting all messages.

Then he smiled. She was hot stuff.

Chapter Two

Tuesday, 18th September. 10a.m.

Joanna looked at her suitcase, which seemed to have shrunk over the holiday, and wondered how on earth she would fit it all in. On the other side of the room, Matthew was more successful. He had already fastened the huge bottle-green *Berghaus* rucksack he'd had from his student days.

'I don't suppose you could squash in a couple of pairs of shoes?' she asked hopefully. 'These wedges take up an awful lot of room.'

He opened the top, gave her a severe look and held out his hand. 'I don't know why you have to bring so many pairs of shoes,' he grumbled. 'Surely hiking boots and one pair of evening shoes is enough?'

'Oh my word,' she said, mocking. 'One day engaged and we're already having a domestic about shoes?'

Matthew took a sideways look at her and burst out laughing. 'Do you know how good it feels,' he confessed, 'to see that black pearl on your finger?'

She looked down at it. 'Yes, I do know,' she said. 'It feels good to me too. I love it. It's so special. Thank you.'

'Come on then, give me the shoes.'

'Thanks.'

'My pleasure, my lady,' he said, still grinning. The holiday levity was staying with them both. She wondered how long it would last when they were home and she was back to work with its irregular hours and stiff demands.

10.30 a.m.

The smell was worse. Kathleen Weston knew it. She didn't care what her husband said. It wasn't simply an obsession or her imagination. It was worse. She could even smell it on the pile of washing she'd just ironed.

'Steven.'

He looked up guiltily. 'Darling.'

Now it was her turn to look suspicious. Why would he call her darling? He'd stopped calling her that years ago. She narrowed her eyes and gave him a sharp look. Intuitively, she knew that particular word was well-oiled. It had slipped out without him even thinking. She put a finger on her chin. Now what could that mean? She knew about the lustful looks he'd given that belly dance teacher who lived at the end of the road. The one who exposed her rather plump midriff between low-slung jeans and crop tops and wiggled her backside like a randy grasshopper.

The witch, she called her privately. The wiggling witch.

But now looking at her husband's face, startled because he'd realised what he'd said, she changed the epithet to whore. Wicked whore. Well, she thought. The whore had better look out because she had her in her sights.

Kathleen Weston was a deeply vindictive and vengeful woman. She was patient too. It was a potentially lethal mix.

'The smell,' she repeated tightly.

'What smell?' But his face betrayed him. Steven Weston was a poor liar, which was lucky for his wife because it kept her informed of what he was up to. She stared back at him, waiting.

'I think it's coming from the farmyard,' he said finally. 'An animal must have died or something.'

Even as he said it he could have bitten his tongue off. She would be bound to want to investigate. He watched her, knowing. He should have remembered her love of animals. This tough, brittle woman was as soft as marshmallow where animals were concerned. He'd seen her cry when stories came on the television about dogs or cats being neglected. She'd driven into Leek once to take an injured hedgehog to the vet, had sobbed uncontrollably when she'd hit a rabbit with her car – even though it had bounded straight back into the hedge. He'd watched her free flies from spiders' webs and then worry what the spider would eat for lunch. She'd stopped the traffic once to retrieve a dead cat from the middle of the road. Her love of animals didn't stop there. She spent three days a week helping at the animal charity shop in Stanley Street. In contrast, her toughness towards the human race was little short of Draconian. She was for hanging, castrating, flogging, cutting ears off. All her pity was focused on the animal world.

'You think an animal's died?' Her face twisted in alarm.

He twitched.

And as he had looked at her, she now studied him. A thin, worried, guilty face, thinning hair – just like his father. Bowed shoulders, which made him look years older than his early forties. Fast on the heels of these observations came a further thought. *What the dickens did Faria Probert see in her husband?*

Sex? Was the woman a sex maniac?

Faria's husband, George, was equally as unexciting as Steven. In fact there was little to choose between them. Maybe the explanation was that Faria was simply addicted to bland, middle-aged men. In spite of herself, Kathleen smothered a giggle, turning it into a cough. Perhaps Faria had a secret source of Viagra and turned these unexciting men into something else. The thought conjured up images too funny to contemplate.

Kathleen frowned and looked again at her

husband. Yes, there were traces of the man she had fallen in love with – honest, hardworking, affectionate and loyal. Steven had had all these attributes together with a soft, sweet, private smile. But the years had intervened cruelly. Perhaps if they'd had children their marriage would have entered a second stage. But she had failed to conceive. How was it that it was *she* who had failed? Why didn't they say that *he* had failed to impregnate her? But that was never the way. It had been *she* who had earned the looks of pity while *he* had merely smirked and said jauntily, 'Not for want of trying,' which had earned sniggers from both men and women.

Her lack of a family had, in turn, isolated them from their friends, who never quite knew whether to chat about their own offspring or pretend they didn't exist. But the very worst thing about being childless was that they were exclusively together. In an undiluted form. Like too strong a cordial they'd needed water. As it was they had each other – or no one. But perhaps now he did have someone. Someone who was as fertile as rich farmland. Kathleen shivered and felt suddenly very alone. She plunged her hands deep into the pockets of the zip-up sweater she was wearing with jeans faded at the seams and reflected. Perhaps her love of animals was nothing short of an outlet for the love she would have lavished on children. She couldn't help a weary sigh. She'd mentioned the word adoption to Steven only once. He had looked horrified. 'Bring up some whore or drug addict's kid?'

So she'd dropped the subject but felt her insides twist with grief at the thought of the thieving, fertile Faria, who had five children – and a lover – as well as teaching belly-dancing.

How did she find the time? The energy?

She looked up to see Steven eyeing her uncomfortably and the silence between them grew thicker.

'The worst thing about holidays is the hours wasted hanging around at the airport,' Matthew grumbled. 'Why do we have to be here three hours early?'

He knew the answer, of course, as did everyone. The spectre of terrorism was enough to make travellers obedient to the rules. From removing their shoes at the security check to not taking liquids on board, putting lip-glosses in their suitcases and spending three fruitless hours at an airport. People stuck to the rules.

Joanna looked up reluctantly from *Second Shot*. 'Actually,' she said, 'I don't mind the hanging around. At least you can't drag me off to the sea for a swim and I can read my story in peace.' She waved the book around. 'In fact,' she said, 'I quite welcome the interlude once I'm holed up in a nice little corner with a good book.' She bent her head then lifted it. 'Why don't you go to the bookshop and find yourself something to read?' she said pointedly.

'I've got my sudoku.' He pulled the book out and licked his pencil with intent.

Joanna bent back over her novel.

Minutes later Matthew stood up again. 'Want a coffee, Jo?'

She almost threw the paperback at him until she read the glow in his eyes, pleading. Reluctantly she inserted a bookmark, tucked the novel inside her bag and stood up.

Shit – she'd just been at the point where Charlie Fox was walking right into the enemy's house. The book was as hot as a roasted chestnut.

Together they sauntered towards the coffee shop. Joanna tucked her arm in Matthew's, gave him an amused kiss on the cheek. 'You can buy,' she said. 'Make mine a large cappuccino.'

He bent his head and kissed her.

Finally it was Kathleen Weston who investigated – alone. The thought of an animal suffering or even dead haunted her so she couldn't concentrate on anything else. It was no use expecting Steven to accompany her. He'd suddenly remembered 'an important appointment' for which he needed to go to the office, urgently.

She walked slowly down the garden, making each step count, listening to the silence that wrapped her in the cold, damp day and seemed all the more sinister under the heavy sky. Now Steven had voiced his opinion she was apprehensive. What if a cow was slowly rotting in the September sunshine – or a pig? What if it was Ratchet, the dog. She smiled. Ratchet was a hound with a snappy foul temper; it was difficult to feel any affection for him. It had always amused her and once Steven too that old Grimshaw had probably named his dog after the scary Nurse Ratched in *One Flew over the Cuckoo's Nest* without even knowing it. This was just one of the casualties of the broken relationship. Since his affections had shifted towards Faria, nothing amused them both, at least – not at the same time.

She'd reached the wall. And now she was so close she could not think how she could ever have wondered what the smell was. It was so obvious. She remembered seeing people on the TV covering their noses and mouths with scarves after 9/11. At the time she had wondered why then assumed it was because of the dust thrown up by the collapsing towers. Now she knew. It wasn't only the dust. It was the scent of rotting body parts.

It was then that she noticed something else; one of the copestones was missing from the top of the wall. And now she wondered why she had not noticed it before. It drew the eye as surely as a missing front incisor.

Dry stone walls are not made for climbing, which is why all through the Staffordshire moorlands the farmers are careful to maintain the stiles for the ramblers, discouraging them from clambering on the stone walls and destroying the environment. Once a dry stone wall starts to crumble it soon dissolves back into its natural state – a pile of stones; as Kathleen was quickly realising. She put her foot in a crevice between two stones only to feel her foothold immediately start to rock. She put her hands on the top, clambered up and watched the stones scatter behind her. She had started a small avalanche. Even when she was astride the wall she could both feel and hear the stones shifting. And the smell was overpowering.

She glanced across at the farmhouse, only partially visible behind a huge oak tree the roots of which had lifted the concrete in the yard. The house had a look of careless neglect, with peeling paintwork and moss smothered brickwork. It had not been touched for years – merely inhabited. Boards had been put over windows broken by a few young vandals from the town. The panels of reeded glass in the door had cracked, and it stood ajar. Yet it didn't appear to be inviting entry, rather daring it. Challenging.

Kathleen could see no animals, hear no sounds, spot no movement. Which was odd. The farmer had cows, two Tamworth pigs and a dog. So why were they all quiet? She knew they were not out in the fields. Only the sheep grazed in the far field. In fact, now she thought about it, she hadn't seen any other animals on the farm for more than a week, which was in itself curious. The cows had not been in the fields, grazing as they should have been. The fields had been empty except for the sheep. Strangely so, she now thought. She shifted her weight uneasily, frowning at the oddity of the situation. She had not even heard the dog for some time.

'Hello,' she called.

Silence met her. Not even an echo replied. She shouted louder. 'Hello. Hello. Mr Grimshaw. Hello. Are you there? It's Kathleen Weston, your neighbour. I wondered if you were...'

The words 'all right' seemed suddenly fatuous.

She looked straight down, beneath her, realised her foot was within inches.

The wave of nausea washed over her almost before she had assimilated the cause.

Sometimes our eyes see things seconds before our minds do.

Then she retched and was sick, thus sullying the crime scene.

She staggered back to the house, and dialled 999.

In the moments immediately before the call, Korpanski had been feeling virtuous. He was catching up with the inevitable paper work, tidying up loose ends, when the telephone rang.

Detective Constable Alan King took the call, his long arms reaching right across the desk, bony elbows projecting like old-fashioned traffic indicators. He listened. 'Put her through,' he said, without consulting Korpanski. King listened for a few more minutes before covering the mouthpiece. 'Sounds like there's a body, Sarge.'

Korpanski felt the hairs start to prickle at the back of his neck. 'Where?'

'Prospect Farm.'

Korpanski frowned. 'On the estate?'

'No, Sarge, on the farm.'

'Natural causes?'

King shrugged. 'She didn't get near enough.' He spoke again into the mouthpiece. 'Just you wait where you are, Mrs Weston. Someone'll be with you in a few minutes.'

He put the phone down, stood up, recalling the hysterical words. *I think rats... Something's... He's...*

Korpanski saved all the data on the computer. 'Who's reported it?'

'A neighbour. From number 1 on the estate. She says she thinks it's the farmer.' He looked almost apologetic, 'and that he's been lying there some time.'

Korpanski stood up then, revealing his

entire, bulky, six-foot-four frame. 'Well, we'd better get out there then, hadn't we, see what's what.'

He took Timmis and King with him, blue light flashing, siren screaming, racing along the Ashbourne road out of the town. A back-up car with a couple of WPCs and some uniformed officers kept up with them. As Korpanski drove he remembered. The odd thing was that he knew Prospect Farm quite well. When he was a kid, growing up in Leek, he had sometimes walked out to the place, just outside the town. He even remembered the farmer, a crusty old thing even then, and the daughter, who had been at the same school as him; a sly little girl who watched her classmates' mischief without comment then whispered in the teacher's ear. She had been a plain girl, insignificant, stick-thin, short on friends, always making a nuisance of herself wanting to play. He wondered what had happened to her and tried to remember her name but failed. The last he'd heard she was nursing somewhere in Stoke.

There had been a wife too but he didn't know what had happened to her. She hadn't been around for years and he couldn't even remember what she'd looked like. The daughter must not live at home because the farmer lived alone these days. He'd seen him once or twice around the town on cattle market days, wearing the same blue cotton dungarees and tweed coat he had favoured years before, tied around the middle with orange nylon baling twine.

Korpanski screamed through red traffic lights, cursing as an aged driver in a Morris 1000 seemed paralysed before the kerfuffle and straddled the crossing, finally moving forwards so the squad car could inch through.

Korpanski resumed his dragnet of information about Prospect Farm and its inhabitants. About ten years ago the farm had shrunk as houses had encroached on its land, emphasising its scruffiness. Korpanski winced. Fran would have loved to have lived in one of the executive-type dwellings but the houses on the estate were out of the pocket-range of a mere detective sergeant. All the same, Korpanski had witnessed the area's progress through the years with interest. Each time he'd found himself in the area, he'd driven round the estate, dreaming, noting that the contrast wasn't simply manifested by the buildings; the gap between the yuppie types who inhabited the mock-Tudor houses and the crumbling farm seemed to be widening.

And now this.

He took the turn sharply into the Prospect Farm Estate, screeching to a halt in front of Number 1.

Kathleen Weston was waiting for him in the drive. He saw a distressed woman in her forties, dressed in a zip-up sweater and faded jeans. Her face was green, her arms wrapped tightly around her, hugging herself as she rocked to and fro on a pair of trainers. Korpanski waited as the second car pulled up behind him. This, he thought, with a touch of wry humour, needed a woman's touch.

And Piercy was missing until tomorrow morning. Korpanski smiled to himself. She'd be furious at missing all the drama. He made a sudden face. Because for that matter, Levin was away, too. The most important thing to ascertain now would be cause of death. Natural causes, they could all go home. But if there were any grounds for suspicion... Well – no problem. He could manage this one for the first twenty-four hours at least. Korpanski gave a little grin of confidence to himself. Even up to Inspector Piercy's standards.

He climbed out of the car. 'Mrs Weston?'

She nodded.

'You rang us?'

Again she nodded. The two WPCs stood either side of her, ready for hysterics, but Kathleen Weston looked calmer now, keeping herself tightly reined in for the police presence.

'I think it's the farmer,' she said in a tense voice, lifting haunted eyes to his face. She would not forget what she had seen even when she closed her eyes. It was as though the scene had been painted on the inside of her eyelids. 'I think he's been dead a while. The smell,' she said, her eyes flickering along the road as she tried to keep them open. 'I've noticed the smell for a few days.'

'Let's take a look, shall we?' Korpanski shot a meaningful glance at WPC Dawn Critchlow. However brave Mrs Weston was being he knew this pale, dead fish look of shock. She took the hint and moved towards Mrs Weston. 'Come with me.'

Kathleen Weston led them through a tall oak gate into the back garden then glanced ahead to the wall, which was the boundary between her land and the farm. The first thing Korpanski noticed was the irregularity caused by the missing copestone. The second was the smell.

They call it the smell of death.

Korpanski and DC King left Dawn Critch-low to care for the shaken woman and walked carefully up the garden path, taking note of the orderly garden and the lavender hedge, which did little to mask the scent. He carried on, towards the boundary, took one look over the wall and, mirroring Kathleen Weston's response, almost threw up.

The crumpled figure of the farmer lay propped up against the stones, almost tucked beneath them. His chin had dropped forward onto his chest, presenting the back of his head, and his legs were stretched out in front of him. Korpanski could see only too clearly the terrible damage done to the back of the skull and took in, within seconds, the entire bloody scene around him: the cope-stone, lying innocently nearby in the mud; the wall spattered with blood, hair and a nasty, dried-up jelly-like substance that he took to be brain tissue. And Mrs Weston was right. The fingers had been nibbled, prob-ably by rats. He spoke over his shoulder to Alan King. 'You're going to have to summon a full forensic team,' he said. 'It's either one hell of a coincidence that the stone fell on the exact spot where unlucky old farmer Grimshaw decided to have a picnic or else the poor guy's been bashed over the head and we've got ourselves a murder scene. Either way we'll need the police surgeon and some shelter.' He backed away from the wall. 'A couple of uniformed had better start house-to-house and interview anyone who's at home this side of the road. Leave the other side till later. And try and contact the daughter for identification, will you?' They walked together back up the path, nodding to Dawn Critchlow as they passed her, supporting the stricken woman. 'We'd better make our access route up the farm track. That'll leave this area relatively clear.'

Within an hour the farm was sealed off, as were the back gardens of the houses that backed onto the farm. A team of officers was interviewing all the inhabitants in the odd numbers of Prospect Farm Estate and Doctor Jordan Cray, Matthew Levin's locum, was examining the body.

'Can you say how long he's been dead?' Korpanski asked hopefully.

Cray turned to face him. 'Somewhere around a week,' he said. 'There's been quite a bit of rodent and insect activity. It might be worth summoning a forensic entomologist. Do you know when he was last seen alive? Family?'

Korpanski shook his head. 'There's a daughter,' he said. 'I think she's now a nurse somewhere in Stoke. They're trying to locate her.' He was practically hopping from one foot to the other. 'But I don't think they were close. There was a wife but no sign of her for a number of years. Can you tell whether it was homicide or accident?'

Both Cray and Korpanski looked at the copestone. 'Almost certainly the ultimate cause of death was multiple skull fractures due to this stone coming into contact with the poor man's head, which I suppose in a very unlucky life *could* conceivably be an accident. But,' he said, picking up one of the dead man's bagged hands, 'there are defensive injuries. And more than one blow. The poor guy was trying to protect himself from an assailant. He was felled and probably slumped against the wall. Then our killer probably dislodged that thing from behind, delivering the fatal injury.'

Korpanski nodded and looked around him.

As a crime scene it was a nightmare. Soft mud left impressions – until the rains came again and again and washed them all away. There were even animal footprints. Little paws, bigger ones. They had sniffed, licked, nibbled and walked away into the night, having sullied his crime scene.

'Sir.'

He jerked in response to the urgency in DC King's tone, following the detective's tread with a feeling of foreboding.

The body of a black and white Welsh Border collie was stretched out on the concrete area near the front door of the farmhouse. The dog lay rigid, a feeding bowl just within reach of the chain that fastened him to the wall via a ring on his collar. Korpanski wasn't a great dog lover. As a uniformed policeman on the beat he'd been bitten too many times to feel much affection for the animal. But he did love Border collies. Partly because his grandmother had owned one and partly because he saw the breed as the equivalent of policemen. Black and white, hardworking and loyal in a bouncy, energetic sort of way. Working dogs. He hunkered down on his meaty thighs and stretched out a hand. The dog was stiff and cold, its mouth open, saliva and vomit nearby.

When he stood up again he felt angry.

'There's more,' King said quietly. 'Animals in the sheds.'

Korpanski didn't want to see it. He felt upset about the dog. 'Call a vet,' he said brusquely.

Mark Fask, the civilian scenes of crime officer, was taping off access corridors, marking the stones and organising a search of the farmyard and house, while the police photographer was taking pictures of the body, the wall and the dog.

Having made a pot of strong tea Dawn Critchlow was 'chatting' to Kathleen Weston. 'So tell me, when did you last see the farmer?'

'A week, ten days ago. I can't remember precisely.' Her face was blotchy but the colour was returning. The tea was working.

'Would you like me to call your husband?'

An expression close to distaste crossed the woman's face. 'Don't bother,' she said dryly. 'He'll be home when he's finished his *work.*' The last word was uttered with a note of mockery, a fact which Critchlow squirreled away.

She glanced around the kitchen, taking in the cream units and black granite tops, and unwittingly echoed Korpanski's thoughts. 'Nice place you have here.'

Way beyond the pocket of a WPC.

Mrs Weston looked around the room as though surprised at the comment. 'Yes,' she

66

said, frowning, 'I suppose it is.'

Dawn Critchlow struggled not to roll her eyes at the mega-sized kitchen absolutely *stuffed* with units, which opened onto an *enormous* conservatory that housed not only an *eight-seater* dining table but also a soft and comfortable-looking sofa, which she would simply *love* to sink down into at the end of a busy day. WPC Dawn Critchlow's husband had been a garage mechanic on the Ashbourne road but the garage had closed last year. He'd tried to open a car repairs business on his own and had ended up badly in debt. The only job he'd been able to find since had been as a shelf-stacker in the local DIY store, which was not only poorly paid but which he hated. However, he had no choice but to take what was offered. They'd remortgaged their tiny terraced house twice and only by the skin of their teeth avoided having it repossessed. To make up the short fall in their finances, she volunteered for all the overtime she could get, which made her permanently tired. Sometimes she dreamt of living in a house like this. And then she woke up.

She sighed. She didn't mind folk living in wonderful houses but she hated it when they didn't appreciate how lucky they were.

'How long have you lived here?' she asked Kathleen chattily.

Something passed across the woman's face. 'Five years,' she said tightly. She could have said five unhappy years but instead she followed up with, 'We bought it new.'

'And do you like it here?'

Korpanski used to say that WPC Critchlow must have a degree in getting information out of people. She was a natural at the art. They didn't even *know* they were being interrogated.

'Not really,' Mrs Weston returned frankly.

'Any particular reason?'

'The smell,' Kathleen said.

'That's only been for the last few days – surely?'

Kathleen Weston took a deep lungful of air then wrinkled her nose as though her breath was tainted. 'No – I don't mean that. Yes, that's new. The place was – I don't think he looked after his animals properly,' she said. 'They were dirty, neglected. I never saw him clean out a barn or a shed. The cows and pigs were without water, sometimes left inside in hot weather.' Her voice became impassioned. 'He wasn't fit to look after animals.'

Whoah. *Animals' Rights,* Dawn Critchlow thought. She knew the sort.

Next door but one, PC McBrine was having more success with Peter Mostyn though instinctively he didn't like the short, balding man with the shiny suit, the evasive eyes and the over-willingness-to-help syndrome, who smelt too strongly of an identifiable Lynx deodorant. *Africa.*

'Anything I can do to assist the police.'

Mostyn was irritating him already with his pasty face and sweating forehead.

'Just answer my questions, sir,' McBrine began formally. 'How long have you lived here?'

'Six years.'

'Alone?'

Mostyn's face leaked anger. 'Not at first,' he said.

McBrine simply raised his eyebrows.

'I came here with my wife. She left me three years ago. For another man. We're getting divorced.'

McBrine almost sniffed it in: spite, jealousy, hatred, financial problems.

'Any children, sir?'

Mostyn dropped the play-acting and scowled. 'I don't see what that's got to...'

Which confirmed McBrine's supposition. He smiled.

'Three,' Mostyn said tightly. 'They spend a lot of time here.'

'I bet they like it, with the farm.'

The simple comment softened Mostyn's face to something proud, paternal, almost beatific. 'My daughter, Rachel, does particularly,' he said. 'She rides the pony sometimes.'

McBrine smiled in fake empathy.

'But my son, well...' he held his hands out, palms uppermost. 'I don't think it makes any difference where he is,' he said. 'As long as he's hooked into his video games. And my youngest daughter, Morag – well – she's quite young. Only four.'

'When did you last see the farmer, Mr Grimshaw?'

Mostyn looked vague. 'I haven't a clue,' he said.

'Might it be worthwhile asking your daughter?'

Mostyn shrugged. 'Possibly. But I really don't think–'

'When was your daughter last here?'

'She was here the weekend of the eighth and ninth. She left on the Sunday evening.'

'And your son?'

'Was here the same time.'

'Did your daughter ride that weekend?'

Reluctantly, Mostyn nodded very slowly. 'Yes,' he said, 'she did.'

'On the Saturday or the Sunday?'

'Both days.'

'We're going to want to speak to her.'

Mostyn looked wary.

'Naturally, as her father, we'd expect either you or your wife to sit in on the interview.'

'Ex-wife,' Mostyn said, but he looked mollified.

DC Danny Hesketh-Brown, next door, was having a pretty tough time of it. His problem was that his eyes were very blue, his hair dark, his features regular, and he was six-foot tall with an athletic bearing. Women were drawn to him like the proverbial bees to a honey pot.

Charlotte Frankwell opened the door to number 3 and gave the policeman one of her winning smiles.

He brandished his ID card in front of her nose and she invited him in. She sat opposite him at the kitchen table, leaning forward to display an impressive and possibly fake cleavage. What Charlotte didn't know was that in spite of his appearance she was wasting her time. Hesketh-Brown had one man and two women in his life: one an intelligent and attractive wife, Betsy, who was a teacher in Tunstall, in the Potteries; the second, his daughter Tanya, who was six months old; and the little man, Tom, a sturdy six-year-old who already had a plastic policeman's helmet that he practically went to bed in. And the tiny baby and his wife were the only women likely to be in his life for the foreseeable future.

However, for all his morals, Danny Hesketh-Brown was a man and he hadn't missed out on the skinny jeans and white see-through shirt. And Charlotte Frankwell wasn't wearing a bra to restrain those bouncing breasts. Had he been available she would have been a very tempting proposition. Hesketh-Brown sighed. Time was... Then he remembered the kisses that had sent him off to work that morning and felt ashamed.

'There's been an accident at the farm,' he began awkwardly.

'What sort of accident?'

'The farmer, I'm afraid.'

'Oh.' She seemed unconcerned. 'Coffee?'

'No thanks.'

She seemed not to have heard him decline the offer, clip-clopping into the kitchen on pink stiletto mules and absent-mindedly filling the kettle. She turned around then to face him in an almost choreographed move and he wondered why such an attractive woman who didn't look over thirty felt she had to be so obvious – wearing blatantly seductive clothes and an awful lot of makeup. She concentrated on spooning deliciously scented ground coffee into a cafetière and filled it with boiling water. 'Well, the farmer's old,' she said. 'I guess it was bound to happen sometime.'

Hesketh-Brown hesitated. Grimshaw must have seemed ancient to her but all the same this was a callous response. Even if an expression of sympathy was sometimes a formality, he would still have expected it. He had to remind himself that Charlotte Frankwell wasn't aware of the circumstances of Grimshaw's death. He let her carry on believing that poor old Grimshaw had met with an accident. Too early to start promoting the official line, anyway. Until the post-mortem was completed, *nothing* was certain.

Charlotte poured the coffee and they sat around the kitchen table, Hesketh-Brown's mind busily memorising details. Charlotte Frankwell wasn't wearing a wedding ring. There was a brand new Merc C 350 parked in the drive, which the last time he had run a fantasy price check had been retailing at £32K. And she had a child. A daughter. He'd seen a pair of small, pink shoes in the laundry beyond the kitchen, which fairly obviously didn't belong to Ms Frankwell. How the hell could she afford to live in a place like this? Rich parents? He narrowed his eyes. He didn't think so. She didn't have the polish of boarding or finishing school.

He sat back in his chair. Must be divorce, then, Danny, my boy, he thought, and felt pleased with himself for sorting out an answer.

'When did you last see the farmer, Mrs Frankwell?'

Apart from raising her eyebrows at the 'Mrs', Charlotte simply looked bored. She carefully studied an intricately painted fingernail. 'Oh, I don't know,' she said impatiently.

'Well, your land backs on to his.'

She shot him a look of scorn. 'Unfortunately,' she said. 'Fairly typically of my ex-husband – almost my entire view of the dilapidated farm is taken up with a barn that's falling down and a cowshed that isn't much better.' She gave a wry smile. 'Perhaps Gabriel hoped I'd be out in the garden one day and the bloody things really would collapse on me.'

'Sorry?'

'The entire place,' she said, 'stinks like a sewer. I wouldn't have come here if I'd known. And I'll be selling up very soon. Moving to Spain the second I've sold. Put my darling daughter in boarding school. Preferably one with very long terms and short holidays.'

All of a sudden Hesketh-Brown didn't find Ms Frankwell at all attractive. In fact she looked downright ugly. He looked around him. 'But it's a nice place,' he said. 'You're lucky to be able to afford it.' *At your age.*

Her eyes narrowed. She knew exactly what he was thinking.

How?

And she deliberately didn't tell him.

'Yes,' she said coolly. 'It is nice, isn't it?'

Danny was getting fed up with this game. 'So you don't know when you last saw Mr Grimshaw.'

She looked up then and he caught a gaze of her amazing blue eyes heavily fringed with what he suspected were false eyelashes. 'No.'

He stood up then, leaving the barely touched coffee on the table. 'And you haven't noticed anything suspicious around the farm?'

'Like what?' She pursed her lips.

This woman, he thought, is dangerous.

He had the feeling he was playing a game involuntarily. But far from seducing him, this woman was annoying him. 'Well then, if you can't help...?' He left the phrase open, the ball firmly and squarely in her court.

'Sorry,' she said – without regret.

He gave up and left without saying anything more.

They were up in the clouds. Joanna was still sneaking a few pages of her book while Matthew, without enthusiasm, was struggling with the sudoku. 'One of the difficult ones,' he muttered.

She took no notice. Charlie Fox was facing her antagonist.

The airhostess came round with the drinks and Matthew eyed the small bottles of champagne. 'Why not?' he said. 'Why ever not?' He bought two and then confided in the woman in the seat next to him. 'We've just got engaged.'

The woman, plump in a cream T-shirt encrusted with sparkly stones, was fulsome and generous in her congratulations. Joanna stared out of the window at clouds that looked like soft sand, as though you could run through them, sinking only ever so slightly. Matthew flipped the cork out of the champagne, poured her one and handed it to her. 'To us,' he said.

'Yeah,' echoed the woman in the cream T-shirt.

Joanna took a long sip and acknowledged that she wasn't looking forward to flashing her black pearl at Korpanski. She almost dreaded his response.

Korpanski, meanwhile, down on the ground, was enjoying directing the investigations and already anticipating bringing Joanna up to date. 'Have we got the next of kin yet?'

'We've just located her. She's on her way from the Potteries.'

'Sir,' PC Timmis had got as far as the barns and was swinging the great door open.

Dreading what he would see Korpanski gave in, stomped towards the barn himself and peered inside.

Chapter Three

Later that day

They drank their champagne, yawned through the usual announcements about turbulence and duty free, then it was, 'Return your seat to the upright position.' Joanna peered out of the window. Manchester looked its usual grey, half smothered in a damp, chilly looking fog, the airport impersonal. They stood up and reached for their hand luggage in the overhead rack, and it suddenly hit her how different things were from their outward journey. She might simply have slipped the ring on her finger but the reality was that it meant so much more than that. She knew that tacitly she had agreed to a wedding; and that was the first of the list of problems.

Joanna Piercy had always been unlike other little girls. Encouraged by her father, she had been a tomboy, the son he had not had, disappointed with two daughters. She simply hadn't ever had the dream of being princess for a day in a cloud of white chiffon, to the sound of church bells and bridesmaids in pink. But her mother and her sister would want exactly this. They would try to persuade her towards the traditional. Not a beach wedding barefoot in Bali or a simple civil ceremony in a hotel or registry office. That would be battle number one.

Next she would be, in title at least, stepmother to Eloise. She drew in a deep, sighing breath. Eloise, sharply intelligent, openly hostile. Theirs had been an uneasy relationship from the first. Matthew's daughter blamed Joanna for the break-up of her parents' marriage, and though Matthew had sworn the relationship had been damaged before they had ever met, Joanna had certainly been at the very least the catalyst for the split. Problem number two.

Thirdly, Matthew had never made any secret that he wanted another child. When she had had a miscarriage the year before he had grieved – more than she had, which in turn made her feel guilty and wrong-footed. It wasn't only that Matthew wanted a child. His desire was more specific than that. Like her own father, he wanted a son. The trouble with that particular wish was that it was something not even the most devoted wife in the entire world could possibly guarantee.

She filed behind him along the aircraft aisle and felt a moment of sheer panic. She actually moved forward to touch his arm and tell him that it was all too much. She could not go through with it. She bumped into his rucksack and took a step back before lecturing herself. This was silly. 'Get a grip, Piercy,' she whispered, knowing that she could not imagine a life without Matthew Levin at her side.

So...

She did touch him then, reaching forward so he turned his head and brushed her lips with his own.

Sealed with a kiss.

Roderick Beeston was the vet the police invariably used in cases where animals were involved. Familiar with both large and small animals, he had looked at dog bites, neglected animals, poisoned dogs, victims of road accidents, deflected a man-eating Alsatian and so on. His talents were useful to say the least.

At three in the afternoon he turned up in a battered Land Rover, looking every inch the country vet. Green wellies, a Barbour oilskin, corduroy trousers. Ignoring the rain that tumbled incessantly from the sky, he strode towards Korpanski, his hand already held out. He gave Korpanski's outstretched hand a vigorous shake. 'Hello, Mike,' he said. 'What have we got here?'

'Not sure, really. The farmer's been bashed over the head and there are some dead animals around. A dog...' They both turned as Korpanski indicated the stiff body of Ratchet. 'And there's more,' he said. 'In the barn. A couple of cows, some pigs.'

Roderick Beeston looked serious. 'And Grimshaw's dead, you say?'

Korpanski picked up on the note of enquiry in the vet's tone. 'You knew him?'

'Yeah. Not well.' Beeston gave an open, friendly grin, brushed some of the curly black hair out of his eyes. 'These moorland farmers don't like paying my bills but I've been here a few times. He had a problem with some sheep a couple of years ago. Nasty case of Footrot. We had the devil's own job getting rid of it. Just when we thought we'd won, another damn ewe would start limping. Poor old Grimshaw. He was one of those people who seem to have no luck. And now this. Well...'

He returned to the Land Rover, slipped on a pair of latex gloves, removed a large black bag from the back and approached the body of the dog, unmistakably long dead.

'Dear, dear.' Roderick Beeston sniffed at the dish. 'Looks like poison,' he said, fingering a sliver of foam around the dog's mouth. 'Probably barbiturates. He would have just gone to sleep. Dogs are easily disposed of with a dose that would simply ensure a human a good night's sleep. Poor old thing. Not the nicest of hounds. These old farmers' dogs know their place and guard their area with what could be called aggressive vigilance. Had my trouser leg in his teeth a couple of times.' He patted the head of the dog. 'Not any more though, eh, Ratchet? I'll take him with me, Mike, do a post-mortem and let you know.' Together, he and Mike loaded the body bag into the car. Ratchet had not been a large dog but he was surprisingly heavy. 'I can do an analysis on this stuff but at a guess it is simply barbiturates.'

'We'll want to run our own fingerprint check on the dish first,' Korpanski warned. 'It just might give us the break we need. Who knows?' He slid the dog dish and contents into a plastic sleeve and sealed it before spooning some of the dog's vomit into a second bag and sealing that too.

'OK, but I'd like to do an analysis on the stomach contents,' Beeston said, 'if it's all right with you. And I can titrate the doses of whatever was in Ratchet's dish, if you get your guys to pass it on to me when they've finished with it.'

Korpanski nodded and the vet straightened. 'So what else?'

'In the barn.' Together they rounded the farmhouse and opened the barn doors wide to peer inside. It was like a scene from a Doré engraving of Hell. Animals' skinny bodies were strewn around the barn. All dead. There was a stink of death around the entire place, heightened by the gloomy interior. Beeston bent down to study a black and white cow, lying near a calf. The cow's brown eyes were sunken, wide-open, appealing for something. 'My initial guess is dehydration,' he said.

Appealing for water, then.

They walked to the back of the barn where two pigs lay. Beeston bent over one, touched its flanks. 'Still alive,' he said, crossing to a large bucket of water and carrying it back, sloshing over the barn floor, to splash on the animal's head. The piggy eyes flickered; its tongue lolled out. The vet continued trickling water into its mouth. 'It might just make it,' he said, 'but the other one,' he glanced briefly across, 'she's obviously had it.' He sighed. 'Lovely pair of Tamworths, they were. Grimshaw had them for years. Had one of his few pieces of luck last year with a really big healthy litter from this pair. I gave him the name,' he added cheerily, 'years ago, when Grimshaw bought him because of the red colour. This is the boar. Old Spice. Judy named the sow. Posh.' He turned around, full of merriment and mischief. 'Get it? Posh Spice? One of the few amusements his daughter contributed to the farm.'

Korpanski smothered his grin.

'You see, if the animals were shut in here,' Beeston continued, 'even though the weather was cool, they would have needed to drink. Lots.' He scratched behind the pig's ear then stood up. 'This is a bad business, Mike,' he said grimly. 'I don't know how much you can tell me about what's happened to Grimshaw...' He accompanied the probe with a frank, enquiring grin. 'Bashed on the head, you say?' He waited for the detective's explanation.

'It looks like murder,' Korpanski said awkwardly. He hated breaking protocol and was uncomfortably aware that whatever it *looked* like they didn't *know* – not for sure.

'We haven't done the post-mortem yet. It's later on this afternoon. But it has to be homicide.'

'Poor man,' Beeston said, then, looking around him, 'I wonder why on earth anyone would want to kill Grimshaw.' Then, 'No Inspector Piercy?'

'She's on holiday till tomorrow.'

'This'll bring her right back down to earth with a bump.'

'Sure will,' Korpanski agreed.

'I'd better go up the field and just make sure the sheep are OK,' Beeston said, 'then I'll come back and look after Old Spice.' Korpanski watched him open the five-barred gate and stride up the field, the vet's purposeful step underlining his feelings.

It seemed an age before their luggage came through on the carousel, Matthew's battered green rucksack and her huge black suitcase. Next came the trip back to their car, in a van laid on by the parking arrangement. And then there was the matter of locating Matthew's BMW. They heaved their luggage into the boot, started up and joined the traffic out of Manchester.

The post-mortem was arranged for four

o'clock. It was a grim afternoon, chilly enough to warn of the approaching winter.

Korpanski and PC Timmis parked in the lot outside the anonymous brick building, the scene of so many dramas played out under the white arc lights angled over a mortuary slab.

Doctor Jordan Cray was already in his scrubs, gloved-up and waiting.

There followed the usual procedure, the cutting off and bagging up of the clothes to be examined by the forensics team, the weighing and measuring of the body before the initial examination and taking and labelling of samples – blood, hair – giving them to the scenes of crime officer. The entire body was x-rayed and the pictures displayed on a computer screen.

Next came measurement of the injuries, the external damage done to the head and the rest of the body, photographing the injuries with a rule next to them. It would all be needed as evidence, finally to come before the courts and the coroner.

Then it was time to begin, starting with the head. The mortuary attendant used the Stryker saw to remove the skull cap while Cray made comments as he worked.

'Fragments of bone embedded in the

brain,' he muttered. 'Fractures of C1 and C2.' He looked across at Korpanski. 'He had more than one potentially fatal injury. The high spinal fractures would have rendered him quadriplegic, unable to either move or breathe. And the extent of the skull fractures – they're embedded deep in the brain. Death would have been quick and, looking at the copestone, I'd say that is your murder weapon.'

Korpanski nodded.

It was an hour later that Jordan Cray was documenting his findings.

Cause of death: respiratory failure due to extensive skull fractures particularly in the occipital area, together with cervical spinal fractures which caused fatal and irreparable damage to the Circle of Willis.

Then he described the sequence of events, as he saw them, to the detective. 'What happened was this,' Jordan Cray said slowly. 'There was a fight during which Mr Grimshaw tried to protect himself.' He indicated the injuries on the under side of the victim's forearms, then held up his own to illustrate his opinion. 'I think the weapon then was something like a baseball bat, judging both by the marks and the fact that there's no debris in the wounds. One of these blows was forceful enough to break his left ulna. This is typical of a defensive injury.' He crossed to the x-ray screen and traced the bones with his forefinger. It didn't take five years in medical school to see the displacement of the smaller of the two forearm bones.

Cray moved back to the body and continued. 'Our victim fell backwards, indicated by bruising and lacerations on the sacrum and lumbar region of the back. I think he probably fell against the wall. This happened shortly before death. You saw the green stains on the clothing? I think if you consulted a botanist he would confirm that the moss was the same. And then when our victim is hurt and helpless on the floor, our killer sees his or her chance and topples the copestone right on our victim's head, fracturing two cervical vertebrae.'

Korpanski felt queasy. 'Oh,' he said, seeming to taste the formalin on his tongue even though the air exchange was turned full on.

'I'd say that did it.' Cray finished with a flourish of satisfaction. 'And incidentally, Sergeant Korpanski, I removed a rose thorn from Grimshaw's right palm. That should give you some clue to the location of the initial assault.'

All this time, back at the farm there was activity. The copestone had been removed to the laboratory for DNA analysis. The entire wall and murder scene had been photographed from all angles, an arc light illuminating the darker areas. The fingertip search of the scene was ongoing, as were the disposal of the animals' carcasses and the search of the farmhouse.

Roderick Beeston had taken Old Spice to his surgery and was drip-feeding the animal.

Hesketh-Brown had moved to the other side of the road and was interviewing more inhabitants of the Prospect Farm Estate.

Amongst them was Hilary Barnes.

He'd found her in the garden, secateurs in her hand and a weed bucket at her feet. He flashed his card and asked her whether she'd noticed anything out of the ordinary.

She looked him up and down before replying as though her answer somehow depended on what type of person this detective was.

'I was dead-heading my roses when I noticed some flies,' she said. 'Nasty big bluebottles. There have been more of them recently, as well as a particularly offensive smell.' She looked severely at Hesketh-Brown as though it was all his fault.

'Have you noticed anything else?'

The woman looked at him now with wise eyes and a touch of humour.

'Apart from the police cars screaming round the place, do you mean? Or the house-to-house interviews going on across the road all afternoon? What specifically, Constable?' Her mouth actually twitched.

So she'd actually read the ID card.

'There's been an incident,' he said carefully.

'So I gathered.'

'At the farm. I'm afraid the farmer's had an accident.'

'An accident, Constable? Do you mean he's fallen off the haystack or turned his tractor over?'

Hesketh-Brown felt hot. There was no fooling this woman, was there?

He hid in the cloak of protocol. 'I can't tell you any more than that, Mrs Barnes. When did you last see Mr Grimshaw?'

Hilary Barnes thought for a minute. 'Certainly not in the last week,' she said. 'Before that...' Her face was taut in concentration. 'I think probably about a fortnight ago. He was driving his tractor very slowly along the road. There were quite a few cars behind him getting very impatient.' Again that touch of wry humour.

Hesketh-Brown gleaned nothing more from Mrs Hilary Barnes. He moved next door.

Korpanski had fiddled for a while with a phone. He was torn. Joanna wouldn't want to come home and walk straight into a murder investigation but she would play merry hell with him if he didn't tell her as soon as he could. Tomorrow, he argued, surely, would be soon enough, but he could picture her frown when she asked, sarcastically, when, exactly, *had* he planned on telling her. In the end he deferred the decision. Front desk had told him Grimshaw's daughter was sitting outside, waiting to speak to him.

Joanna and Mike were stuck in a queue, fuming alongside a hundred other motorists. A lorry had shed its load on the M6 causing tailbacks, they heard, when they tuned in to the local radio station. Matthew came to a halt, put his hazard lights on and slid his hand into hers. 'Back with a bump,' he commented good-humouredly. Joanna nodded and put off switching her mobile back on, feeling that for now she, too, was still in holiday mode. The minute the phone was on she would be back in the swing of things. Work, her mother, her sister. She could almost hear their overexcited shrieks when she told them about the engagement. She eyed the phone in the bottom of her bag with malevolence and left it switched off.

Judy Grimshaw had changed beyond all recognition and yet the shell was the same – colourless, nondescript, thin rather than slim, shoulders hunched and rounded. Glasses that gave her a goggle-eyed look. But what Korpanski observed had changed most about her was an unattractive and cynical twist to her thin lips emphasised by a strange choice of deep orange lipstick, which made her mouth look like a garish gash. Korpanski surmised that life had not treated Judy Grimshaw as well as she had anticipated when they were at school together. She had always worn the air of a woman who was *going places*. How often do these people lead ordinary lives, doing mundane jobs, living within a few miles of their birthplace? He glanced at her wedding-ring finger and noticed not only was it bare but there was no tan line or little bump where a wedding ring had been recently.

'Hi, Judy,' he said. 'Remember me?'

'Mike?' Her expression moved swiftly through pleasure and embarrassment, settling into tight-lipped anger.

So she did.

'What's happened?'

'Let's go somewhere more private, shall we?'

She nodded and followed him down the corridor to an empty interview room, where they both sat down. 'I'm sorry, Judy,' he said. 'I'm sorry to have to break it to you like this.'

She watched, curious, silent and unafraid, waiting for him to speak.

Korpanski swallowed. 'I'm afraid it's your dad. He's met with an accident.'

Her pale eyes met his and her mouth twisted even more out of shape. 'An accident? What sort of accident?'

'It looks like murder. I'm sorry.'

She brushed the apologies aside. 'Don't keep saying you're sorry, Mike. What's happened? Tell me.'

'He was found on the farm – near the wall that borders the estate.' The mouth, which he now thought ugly, twitched but she stayed silent, leaving the entire burden of speech with him.

'There isn't a nice way to say this, Judy. He's dead. His head had been smashed in.'

She was uncomprehending. 'Who by?'

'We don't know yet.'

'Of course,' she said sarcastically. 'It's a bit soon for you to have made an arrest.'

'We just don't know, Judy.' He could hear the defensive tone in his voice. 'Put it like this: there isn't anyone obvious.'

'Was it theft?'

Had circumstances been different Korpanski might have chortled at the question. From that pathetically poor and neglected farmhouse? What would anyone steal? The family silver?

He tried to say it nicely. 'I don't suppose there was a lot to take.'

'Not the thousands of pounds he kept in his mattress?'

'Sorry?'

Judy Grimshaw crossed her skinny legs encased in faded jeans. 'Come on, Mickey, surely you've heard about farmers who don't trust banks.'

He hated being called Mickey. It had been a schooltag, a mockery of his Polish father who had always had trouble speaking the

Queen's English though no problem at all fighting for King and country through the Second World War. The teasing had also been one of the reasons he worked out at the gym three times a week. If he didn't want to be called Mickey then he wouldn't be. His height had helped. Six foot four inches topped most men.

He eyed Judy Grimshaw and couldn't decide if the money-under-the-mattress yarn was simply that or the truth. He settled on blunt confrontation.

'Did he?'

She shrugged. 'I don't know. I hardly went near the place.'

Korpanski nodded. It fitted in with what he'd already been told.

'Can I see him?'

'If you want to, I can take you to the mortuary. We need–'

'Identification,' she supplied.

Concern about the state her father was in must have leaked into his face because Judy gave the ghost of a smile. 'It's all right,' she said. 'I'm a nurse. Remember?'

'Yeah, but surely it's different – being your dad and all.'

'I've seen it *all* before,' she said wearily.

'OK. But before we go, I have to ask you,'

Mike said, 'if you know of anyone who had a grudge against him? Anyone who might want him dead?'

The second ghost of a smile. 'Apart from the inhabitants of the estate who paid grossly over-inflated prices for an exclusive view of the scruffiest farm in Staffordshire?'

If only police too could hide behind the phrase *No comment*.

Korpanski felt the muscles in his neck stiffen. He stood up and led her out to the parking lot.

During the journey he made an effort at conversation. 'Married, are you?'

'Divorced.' She almost spat the word.

'Kids?'

'A daughter.'

'And your mum?' He remembered a thin woman with untidy hair and a worn face, who always wore an apron around the farm so that once when Judy was in the choir he hadn't recognised the woman attending a school concert in a black skirt, smart green box jacket and high-heeled black shoes as her mother.

'Ha.' There was venom in the expletive. 'My mother? Left Dad years ago. Having a fine old time with her lover. Spain, London, New York. You name it.'

She turned and looked at Korpanski. 'She was young when she met my dad. Just nineteen. Fell pregnant with me practically straight away. Had all these illusions about being a farmer's wife. She didn't know how hard farmers expect their wives to work in this part of the world. Years later, when she'd milked and got up at dawn day in, day out, stunk of animals all the time and catered for all the farmhands, she finally saw the light and moved out. Met another man.'

She sat back, folded her arms, pleased with herself. 'Had a lot of sense, my mum.'

Korpanski struggled to find something to say.

'Do you see much of *her?*'

The mouth distorted. 'Not since the day she left. Too busy making up for lost time to get in touch with her daughter.'

'I'm sorry.'

'Oh, don't be.' Judy's face was hard and bitter. 'I prefer to think of her living it up at the high spots of the world rather than drudging around on that blighted place.' There was something brave about the words that didn't quite ring true.

Again Korpanski could find no suitable response. He almost shrivelled in the face of so much venom. He knew he should be asking a significant question but it had slipped out of his mind. He was stuck, which gave Judy the opportunity to take the lead, eyeing him as he drove. 'You always were a hunk,' she said. 'Look after yourself, don't you, Mickey?'

She put her hand over his on the steering wheel.

'I'm married, Judy,' he said, keeping his eyes fixed on the road ahead.

The hand slid away slowly, back to her lap. 'Yeah, well,' she said, 'so was my husband when he took up with...' She held her fingers up. 'Now, was it four or five different women? Not always in succession. He liked more than one at a time. It fed his ego when I wasn't enough.'

Korpanski was glad when they arrived at the morgue.

In his time, Korpanski had watched plenty next-of-kin identifications. He had never seen one without some form of emotion – sorrow, grief, anger – some sign that there had once been a connection between the dead and the living, the person who was deemed to be close enough to the deceased to tick the box of next of kin. Judy Grimshaw (he must find out her married name –

or rather the name she went under these days) stared down at her father. 'That's him,' she said, then pulled the cloth back over his face and walked out. Korpanski watched her. Not a muscle had twitched for the old man. Even he felt more sympathy for the old farmer now.

He was glad to drop her back at the police station to pick up her car and find himself alone, back in his office.

He rang the team of scenes of crime officers.

'Found anything?'

'Nothing further of significance except that the mattresses in all the bedrooms have been ripped apart. Probably with a knife. Your assailant must have been in quite a mess. Foam and horsehair and stuffing all over the place. One of my lads had an asthma attack and has had to go home.'

'Any money there?'

'Little cash box in the sitting room, forty pounds in it. Nothing else.'

Korpanski put the phone down and wondered then if Judy Grimshaw's story was true. Surely, surely people didn't really hide money in mattresses these days? Korpanski allowed his mind to wander. In these days of Internet banking, holes in the wall and credit cards? Surely not.

Or had someone merely *thought* there would be money there? Plenty of people know there doesn't have to be *real cash* – just the storybook kind that villains believe in. And act on. The Chinese whispers that feed legends. And at some point, in one person's ear, legend becomes fact.

In, this case it might be difficult sorting out fact from fable.

Korpanski came to a decision. He'd put it off long enough. He checked his watch. A little after six. He picked up the phone and dialled. 'Hi, Jo,' he began, when he was through to the landline answer phone.

6.40 p.m.

It was around half an hour later that Matthew and Joanna finally dropped their luggage onto the floor of Waterfall Cottage, Joanna feeling the familiar sinking feeling we all have on our return from a dream holiday. Back to the nightmare. She had sometimes wondered whether it is better not to have escaped in the first place because, however humdrum it is, we all have to return to our daily lives.

Bills.

The washing.

A leak?

The answer phone flickering. And that was before they a) checked their mail, picked up their emails and switched on their mobile phones and b) told anyone that they were engaged.

There were eight messages. Joanna pressed the play button.

Eloise. 'Hi, Dad. Just wanted to tell you I have an interview next week at Staffordshire University Med School.' She was already picking up the abbreviations that mark the chosen few from the rest of the populace. 'Just wondered if I could stay with you the night before. Dad,' her childish voice rose an octave, 'I'm so excited. Well – excited and nervous. Anyway, hope you've had a great holiday. You did the right thing getting away. The weather here's been foul. Love.

She didn't need to leave her name. Our nearest and dearest don't.

Joanna's mother was next, reminding her not to forget her nephew's birthday. 'You *are* Daniel's godmother, Joanna.' No *hope you've had a nice holiday* or anything pleasant or civilised, Joanna noticed, and she hadn't forgotten Daniel's birthday anyway. She pressed delete.

There were a few more, Tom and Caro inviting them out to supper. 'They had some *great* news.'

And lastly: 'Hi, Jo.' Korpanski's gruff voice. 'Hope you've had a good holiday. No need for you to worry. Everything's under control. But I thought you'd want to know right away there's been a murder. Old farmer bashed around the head round about a week ago. Out at Prospect Farm. No one in the picture yet. Cray's done the PM. Cause of death: head injury caused by one of the stones from the wall. Heavy old thing. Some animals involved. The vet, Beeston, suspects the dog was poisoned and the animals probably died of thirst, basically. One pig seems to have survived. Name of Old Spice. I'll buy you a drink if you can guess the name of his wife.' A dry chuckle before he continued. 'Anyway, see you tomorrow.' A pause. 'Umm – I'm looking forward to having you back.'

Joanna looked at the ring on her finger and touched the black pearl, smooth as milk, an omen. A murder investigation. Straight back into the thick of it. Late nights, broken dates. Total absorption and commitment. And Eloise coming to stay next week. She looked across the room at Matthew. His mouth was straight.

She lifted her eyebrows and held her hands out in a what-can-I-do? expression, and Matthew's face didn't change a bit as he dialled Eloise's mobile.

Chapter Four

Wednesday, 19th September. 8.30 a.m.

Joanna felt frustrated. She'd been looking forward to getting back on her bike after the holiday. Autumn was such a colourful time to ride through the moorlands and the nights would soon be drawing in, the clocks going back and the pleasure of her morning and afternoon trips to and from work would be diminished.

But now there was a major investigation. And she'd carried out enough major incident cases to know that time was of the essence. No meandering around wobbling on a bicycle like an old-fashioned Plod. The public expected something much more snappy. Also, she might need to use her car during the day. So she reluctantly left her cycling shorts in the drawer and picked out a straight black skirt, black shirt, a scarlet jacket and medium-heeled black shoes. She gave a regretful glance at her paperback, which was sitting on the chair. Charlie Fox would have to suspend activities until things quietened down a bit. She glanced out of the window. The day looked dull but it felt warm so she didn't bother with tights. She always laddered them anyway and her legs were quite brown. She slipped the pearl ring on her finger and wondered what Korpanski would say. He could be unpredictable but, of course, distracted by a major investigation, which he had handled for the critical first twenty-four hours, he probably wouldn't be in the slightest bit interested in her personal life.

As she brushed her hair she reflected – one good thing about returning to work at full speed was that it was the perfect excuse for delaying telling her mother and sister about their engagement. *'Too busy, Mum.'* She mouthed the words.

She and Matthew had a quick breakfast before loading the dishes into the dishwasher. She kissed him goodbye and left.

Her Honda started the first time like the

great little workhorse it was and she was in the station within fifteen minutes, parked in one of the protected lots. Cycling in would have taken her a lot longer. Even discounting the necessary change and shower.

From the moment she walked in it was easy to tell that things were far from normal. For a start, there were clusters of officers talking in the hallway. She greeted them before going straight to her office to find Korpanski already at his desk. And that, in itself, was out of the norm.

'Morning,' she said lightly. 'Thanks for the message.'

Korpanski stood up, his eyes glowing a welcome. 'Great to have you back, Jo.'

'I'd like to say it's nice to *be* back,' she said dryly, 'but it isn't.'

'You look well,' he commented. 'Tanned. Happy.'

She planted a box of chocolates on his desk. 'Little pressie,' she said, 'from España.'

'No need to ask if you've had a good time.'

She shook her head.

'Or what you've been doing with yourself. Judging from your tan, not a lot more than sitting in the sun.'

She giggled. 'Not *only* that,' she said.

Now was the ideal time to tell him, while

all his attention was on her, but Mike moved on quickly.

'I've arranged a briefing for nine thirty.'

'Which just gives you time to fill me in.'

'Yeah.' He paused.

'I gave you the bare details on the phone. Farmer's name: Jakob Grimshaw. Age: sixty-three. Lived alone–'

She interrupted. 'No wife? No family?'

'One daughter lives and works in Stoke, wife either divorced or separated. She went her own way years ago.'

'Go on.'

'Last seen alive for certain on Sunday, 9th September, just over week ago. He kept himself to himself. Neighbours started noticing a smell a few days back. One of them, a Mrs Kathleen Weston, went to investigate. The odd numbers of the Prospect Farm Estate back on to the farm. The boundary is the dry stone wall. Grimshaw's body was found propped up against it. The copestone was found near the body with traces of skin, hair and brain tissue on it. Forensics are analysing everything but I can you their findings without the benefit of a microscope.' Korpanski gave one of his mirthless smiles, lifted by a twinkle in his eyes. Joanna smiled back. 'The even numbers of the estate back onto fields. The neighbour, Mrs Weston, from number 1, climbed the wall to investigate the smell and the flies and found the farmer's body collapsed against it.'

'Right,' she said. 'Post-mortem findings?'

'Cause of death was a head injury caused by the copestone from the top of the wall.'

'I know what a copestone is, Mike.'

He grinned at her. 'I missed your acid wit, Jo.'

She was tempted to punch him but he was doing a good job. It was more appropriate to listen.

'As I said, the head injury was caused by the copestone making contact with the back of his skull.'

'It could have been an accident.'

Korpanski shook his head. 'Defensive injuries: a broken arm, bruising. He fell against the wall and hurt his back. Then there's the poisoned dog.'

She raised her eyebrows. 'Indeed.'

'I mean the dog had been poisoned deliberately but the other animals died accidentally. They were shut in the barn without water. If the farmer's body had been discovered earlier they might have survived – like the pig.'

She smiled. 'Well there's some good news then.'

He looked at her uncertainly, unsure how to take this. She smiled again, reassuringly, and he nodded.

'How many houses actually border the farm?'

'Five.'

'Have you any suspicions if any of them might be responsible?'

He shook his head. 'Nothing obvious, Jo. According to the house-to-house comments, the inhabitants of the entire estate felt that the farm was scruffy and it devalued the property, but you don't murder someone because your property's devalued.'

'You might if– Are any for sale?'

Korpanski shook his head. 'No boards up, anyway.'

'Right.'

She felt suddenly self-conscious, as though her ring was huge and would be noticed instantly. It felt hot and conspicuous on her finger.

Ten, nine, eight... He'd notice it in a minute. Seven, six, five...

But Korpanski's attention was all on the case.

'There is one thing,' he said. 'The guy who built the estate lives in one of the houses. He's divorced and his ex-wife lives a couple of doors away.'

'Really? That sounds interesting. So he hasn't sold the final property?'

'No.'

'We'll interview both him and his ex-wife. Nothing like a divorcee to spill the dirt, is there, Mike?' She thought for a minute, then asked, 'What about the farmer's daughter?'

Mike practically shuddered. 'Judy bloody Grimshaw,' he said. 'She was at school with me.'

Joanna couldn't resist teasing him. 'Not a schoolboy crush, Mike?'

'Not likely. You want to see her.'

'Well – is not being a beauty and being a schoolmate of yours likely to make her guilty?'

Korpanski grinned. 'Much as I'd like to say yes, she was probably at work anyway.'

'We have an alibi to check then, don't we, Mike? I take it she'll be the beneficiary?'

He nodded. 'Probably. If the wife doesn't surface.'

'And this farmer's daughter – is she married?'

'Divorced, apparently.'

'Right.'

'A partner?'

Korpanski shrugged.

Joanna nodded. 'It's early days yet. But it might be worth talking to both her and her ex. As I said – nothing like a bit of spite to flush out the truth. There is one other significant fact that I haven't had time to go and look at for myself. Mark Fask is doing the scenes of crime bit and he said that all the mattresses had been slashed.'

Joanna waited.

'Grimshaw's daughter said there was a rumour that her father kept money there.'

'Not under the mattress, surely?' But whether the story was true or not they both knew rumour could create sufficient motive. When Korpanski simply turned his dark eyes on her she continued with a sigh. 'Well – at least it gives us a potential motive apart from the posh housing estate, though neither appears a valid reason for murder.'

'Exactly.'

'Right – let's get on with it.'

'After you.'

That was when his eyes landed on the ring. They widened. 'No,' he said. 'I don't believe it.' He looked at her, confused.

'Congratulate me, Korpanski.' She hadn't meant for it to come out so sharply but the truth was that she'd dreaded this moment.

'Sorry,' he said quickly. 'Congratulations,

Jo. No need to ask who the lucky man is.'

'No,' she said shortly, before bursting out. 'Well, you might sound a bit happier about it, Mike.'

'Why should I be?' He was at his truculent worst.

She glared at him. We all have our own perspective on events.

He planted himself in front of her. 'Does this mean a big life change?'

Again she shook her head. 'No,' she said emphatically. 'It does not.'

'And does Levin know this?'

Bloody Korpanski, she thought irritably. Why did he invariably put his finger right on the throbbing pulse of a problem? The truth was that they hadn't really discussed this aspect of their engagement – or any other aspect for that matter. She frowned.

'Come on,' she said. 'We can grab a coffee on the way.'

All briefings are the same, she reflected; interminable reading out from notebooks of irrelevant and frankly boring detail. The truth was that she was itching to get out to the farm, catch the *feel* of the murder scene, make her own observations, rather than rely on Korpanski's and the officers assigned to the case. She wanted activity, to be involved, to speak to the main protagonists herself, size them up, get their measure and decide why Grimshaw had met with such an end.

So she listened with half an ear, ran her eyes down the diagrams and scenes of crime photographs, memorised the names and felt the old restlessness.

An hour later, she and Mike were heading out of Leek, along the Ashbourne road, towards Prospect Farm.

The day had brightened and the trees were beginning to show the first tinge of autumn. She sat back and let Mike drive, her Wellington boots in the back of the squad car. She'd worked on farm crime scenes before and was familiar with the hazards.

They passed the neat 'development' with its individually designed, generously sized homes and tidy lawns to the front. 'Did you say nine houses, Mike?'

'Yeah.'

'Why stop at nine, I wonder,' she mused. 'Does Gabriel Frankwell have plans to build more?'

Korpanski shrugged. 'I don't know. We ran a check yesterday. There's no current planning permission application in that area. He lives in number 7 but he was out all day yesterday,' he said, 'so we haven't spoken to him yet.'

'Then keep your fingers crossed he's around later,' she said. 'I shall be interested to meet these people myself.'

The entrance to the farm was only a couple of hundred yards beyond the estate and Joanna was immediately aware of the contrast. A gate, rotten and hanging drunkenly almost off its hinges, a dingy farmhouse beyond, reached by a muddy track. She was glad of the wellies.

Police tape had been stretched across the gate and it was easy to see the activity of the scenes of crime team. White-suited men were everywhere, looking like busy spacemen. To the left of the farmhouse, against the wall, stood a white forensic tent.

They left the car near the road and walked towards the scenes of crime team, squelching noisily through the mud.

Fask greeted her warmly. 'Good holiday, Jo?'

'Yeah,' she said. 'Very good. Thanks.' She glanced towards the wall. 'Shame for me to have missed some action but Korpanski here has filled me in. I'll look at the murder scene first, I think. I'll start from there.'

They stood outside the police tape, staring down at the wall, Joanna noticing everything. The missing stones told their own story; the assault and then the neighbour scrambling over before climbing just as hastily back to the safety of her own garden, starting a land slide of smaller stones. Her eyes took in the jumble of moss-covered lime-stone rocks, the numbered wooden pegs sticking out of the ground, marking where samples had been removed, shallow impressions where earth had been scooped up ready for the geologist's analysis. After a while she turned away and followed Korpanski in the direction of the farmhouse.

'The dog was lying here.' He indicated the spot on the concrete yard where Ratchet had been so pathetically stretched out. The spot indicated by white marks and a round impression where the dog's dish had been. To one side lay a small bouquet of wild flowers. Joanna eyed them and faced Korpanski with a question in her eyes, which he deliberately misunderstood.

'I bet you any money it's Mrs Weston,' he said uncomfortably. 'She's a real animal lover.'

'And how the hell did she gain access to the scene of a crime?'

Fask intervened. 'We only had one guy here last night,' he said. 'And her house backs onto here.'

'Hmm.' Her disapproval needed no other expression.

'Have you heard back from Beeston about the dog?' Joanna enquired.

'Not yet. He said it would take a couple of days.'

Joanna nodded.

'Shall we take a look inside next?'

They walked into the parlour of the farm-house. Parlour seemed an appropriately old-fashioned word for it – damp, undecorated since the nineteen forties, ancient flowered wallpaper – dirty cream and faded pink – a baize covered table with the remains of more than one meal on it. It spoke of a lonely, empty life with no pretence at tidiness or civilised cleanliness.

Joanna recalled a silly rhyme she had chanted as a child, *Will you walk into my parlour? said the spider to the fly.*

She shook her head. Being fanciful was not going to solve anything.

Fask was a civilian scenes of crime officer, with a talent for being able to mop up every single piece of forensic evidence from a crime scene. He was a good-looking guy, short, about five-foot-six, built squat and muscular like a Welshman, with very dark brown hair heavy eyebrows and a spreading paunch.

He greeted Joanna warmly; they had worked on many cases together and had a good working relationship. 'Where was it you went, Jo?'

'Mojacar,' she said. 'Southern Spain.'

'And she's come back engaged,' Korpanski put in.

'Engaged?' Fask looked shocked. 'Well I never.' Then added quickly, 'Congratulations, Inspector. Does this mean you'll be retiring from the Force?'

Joanna tossed back her thick hair. 'Not a chance of it,' she said.

'You and Levin are going to be a busy couple then.'

'Like plenty of others,' Joanna said calmly, walking on.

The bathroom was downstairs. Joanna had glimpsed it through a half-open kitchen door. Blue linoleum, a white bath with a stained plastic curtain round it, a toilet and a square sink with a tap that dripped with an irritatingly irregular beat. No modernisation here. She returned to the kitchen and ran gloved hands over the blue and cream cabinet, remembering. When she had been a child, her grandmother had had an identical piece of furniture; tall, with a glazed top and a tray which dropped down to form a work surface. They must have been the height of fashion in postwar Britain. How many of these must there have been in existence? She smiled and recalled her grandmother buttering a hot cross bun for her, gnarled hands, an elusive scent of lavender. She looked around and knew no modernisation had taken place in the entire house since the war. The forensics team had been busy here. She could see marks everywhere. She left them to it, knowing that some of the evidence collected could answer some of their questions. The process of digestion, together with the advancing mould on the plates linked to samples of stomach contents, might further help to pin down the date and time of Grimshaw's death.

The sitting room was very small, with an old television set perched on a cream-painted kitchen chair and a two-seater sofa of brown leatherette. In the corner was a door that led to a narrow staircase. As soon as she set foot on the bottom step, Joanna was aware of the intense search that had taken place here. Feathers, foam and cotton had flown everywhere, creating an unpleasant air of fustiness. Halfway up, she turned to speak to Korpanski. 'Someone,' she said, 'must have walked out of here looking like the victim of a Northern Ireland Sectarian Campaign.' When he looked befuddled, she laughed. 'Tarred and feathered,' she said.

She reached the top. Upstairs there were three bedrooms, all of similar size and shape, small with slanting ceilings and windows so dirty they hardly let in the light of day. Each held a double bed and they had all been subjected to the same assault. Grubby pink blankets were strewn all over the floor and the mattresses had been ripped apart. Feathers were everywhere, a few still airborne, meandering aimlessly in the breeze that blew in through the poorly fitting window frames. Her eyes settled on the torn covers of the mattresses and she wondered: had they contained money or not? Was this a crime with the simplest of motives – robbery – or something a little more devious?

She held a feather in her hand. 'Is this a blind, do you think, Mike? Meant to divert us from the true motive for the attack.'

'If there was a motive,' Korpanski responded glumly.

She couldn't argue with the comment. So many crimes these days *were* motiveless or had such a weak reason – 'I thought he was dissing me' or 'I asked for summat, nice, like, and he wasn't playin', so I thought I'd kick 'im around a bit.' Or, increasingly often, 'Sorry, mate, can't remember. I'd been on the pop, see?'

She sighed and hoped this wouldn't turn out to be one of those crimes.

'Who, out of our likely rogues' gallery, is out at the moment?'

Korpanski had already thought this one through and had searched the computer before he'd gone home the previous night.

'No one that would do this sort of crime, Jo. Not local, anyway. No one who's out. If this is someone from around Leek, they're new to murder.'

'That's what worries me.' She swivelled round to peer beyond the houses towards the winding track that led to the Ashbourne road. 'But as the farm is invisible from the main road, I'd be surprised if it was one of our little visitors from Manchester or some other hotbed of villainy.'

'So?' Korpanski held her gaze steadily.

'Something else strikes me,' Joanna said,

wandering out of the bedroom and back down the stairs, out again into the damp, grey day. 'If the entire assault took place where Grimshaw lay, our killer was taking a bit of a chance. The farmyard is clearly visible from at least two of the estate houses – number 1, the Weston's home, and number 3, which is where Mrs Frankwell lives, according to your plan.'

Korpanski nodded.

'The cowshed obscures the view from the other houses on that side, numbers 5, 7 and 9, unless someone was in the garden and they are open plan.'

'They're all fenced in,' Korpanski replied.

'As I recall from the briefing, your last definite sighting was from the little Mostyn girl, Rachel,' Joanna continued, rounding the yard towards the cowshed. 'And when his body was discovered, Grimshaw had been dead for about a week.' She grinned at Korpanski. 'Right so far?'

He nodded.

'I take it we're working on the assumption that Grimshaw died round about the 10th, 11th, or 12th of September.'

Again Korpanski nodded in agreement.

'I suggest, then, that we concentrate our inquiries, initially, on those dates, and spread out if we don't seem to be getting anywhere.' She took a step back. 'I just want to ask Mark Fask something. Oh, and Mike, let's have another briefing early tomorrow morning, say eight a.m., and get our team to focus on those dates.'

Fask was coming out of the cowshed.

'Do we know where Grimshaw was *first* attacked?'

'Interesting, that,' he said. 'There was some blood near the back door, which I've sent for analysis.'

'Isn't that where the dog was?'

'Ratchet, God rest his soul, if dogs have one,' Fask grinned, 'was fastened on a chain. The pool of blood we found, mind – not a splash or a spray, nothing that could travel – was three feet beyond the reach of Ratchet's chain. I would almost bet my next month's salary that the blood is Grimshaw's – not the dog's. We've also found blood at the back of the barn and cowshed, as though he was trying to escape his assailant. My theory is that he was pursued past numbers 5 and 3, ending up at the back of the garden of number 1.'

Joanna felt her mouth drop open. 'Now I see how it happened.' She looked at Mike. 'Incredible. A prolonged and violent attack

– in full view of two houses, within shouting distance of another seven. Very risky for the assailant unless he could be absolutely sure none of Grimshaw's neighbours were at home that day. Which suggests that either it was not a premeditated attack or that our killer was very familiar with the daily routine of the inhabitants of The Prospect Farm Estate. Grimshaw was first hit near the back door, then pursued round the back of the barns. He was the victim of a prolonged and violent assault then later thrown against the wall and the copestone smashed down on his head. It's possible he staggered towards the wall hoping for help from his neighbours – then he fell and the murder weapon was to hand.'

'What could you tell from the ground, Mark? Footprints?'

'Unfortunately,' Fask said, 'there's been a week of heavy rain. We got no definition of footprints at all.'

'Hmm,' Joanna said. 'Right then, Mike, time to chat to the neighbours.'

She replaced her muddy wellies with her clean shoes and they drove back down the farm track, out onto the Ashbourne road and into the estate. Like many developments of a similar size in the middle of the day, the road and houses appeared deserted.

Except for the last but one house on the right, a smart, three-storeyed residence with a huge pillared portico. Right in front, parked as showily as an advertisement car, was a plum-coloured Porsche Boxster with an ugly scrape along its length.

They looked at each other. 'Interesting,' Joanna commented.

'Well, at least it looks like Frankwell, the builder, is in. He wasn't around all day yesterday.'

They parked outside and approached the door, listening for a moment. It was surprising how much you gleaned from covert surveillance – snooping, in other words. But inside all was silent, so Joanna knocked.

The man who opened the door quickly, as though he had been watching them walk up the drive, was dark-haired and slim, with an oily, continental look. Joanna caught a strong waft of sweet, almost feminine, aftershave. He flashed white teeth at them, particularly Joanna.

In return she flashed him back a smile and her ID card.

His eyes flickered across it. 'So, what can I do for you, Inspector?'

Surely, surely he must have realised some-thing *was going on?*

'May we come in?'

He tried to resist. 'It isn't really a good time...' But Joanna was rarely refused. Frankwell met her determined gaze, realised this was not a polite question, gave up and stood aside to let them enter.

Inside it was obvious that Gabriel Frank-well was busily packing up. There were boxes everywhere. Joanna faced him. 'Moving house, Mr Frankwell?'

'Well.' His smile and palm-showing was *almost* disarming. 'I built these houses, you know. I ... umm ... I never really meant to *live* here, you understand. It's a stop-gap.'

So one of these houses was for sale in spite of there being no board up. Interesting, Joanna thought. 'I see. So do you have a buyer for this one?'

Frankwell showed his eager, business-man's instinct.

'Almost,' he said. 'Why don't you come into the sitting room?'

The room was lovely, ticking all the boxes: pale colours, a soft-looking ivory leather sofa, abstract prints over a contemporary coal-effect hole-in-the-wall fireplace, con-servatory beyond with fine views of an open field peppered with sheep, and to the right, the back of Grimshaw's cowshed, looking almost pretty smothered in a pink climbing rose. Far enough away to look quaint. Interestingly there was no view of the farmhouse, Joanna noted. Frankwell had kept the best place for himself. And now he was selling it. 'Very nice,' she said appreciatively.

Frankwell looked as pleased as though he had just made a successful sale.

'So where to next, Mr Frankwell? Where are you moving to?'

Frankwell looked slightly sheepish. 'Actually,' he said, 'I've got a girlfriend in Brazil. Rio. She's pregnant, due soon, and I really want to be with her.'

'So you're *anxious* to sell,' Korpanski put in, picking up on Joanna's thought processes.

'Yes, I am.'

'No more property development, Mr Frankwell?' Joanna mused.

'I've got some plans,' he said, 'but if you don't mind I'll keep them to myself.'

And *at last* he asked the question. 'So, what *is* all this about?'

'Did you realise there was some activity at the farm yesterday?' Joanna glanced pointedly at the distant view.

Frankwell looked puzzled. 'I wasn't here all day,' he said. 'I had a meeting with the bank manager about transferring my assets to Brazil. Then I went to sign some documents at the estate agent's.'

'And later on?'

'I spent the evening with my daughter, Phoebe,' he said. 'I'm going to miss her when I've gone so naturally I'm anxious to spend as much time as I can with her. We went to see a film at Festival Park then went out for something to eat. It was quite late when we got back. I took her back to Charlotte's.'

'Your ex-wife?'

Frankwell nodded. 'Yes.'

'You don't find it a problem living so close to her, on the same housing estate?'

'No. I elected to so I could spend plenty of time with Phoebe.'

'Before jetting off to Brazil and your new family.'

'Yes. Anyway – yesterday. I was tired. When I got back, I telephoned Lucia and we spoke for about ten minutes. Then I went straight to bed. You can verify most of that, I'm sure.' He threw the challenge down like a leather gauntlet and Joanna nodded. Frankwell promised to be a worthy adversary.

'I'm afraid the farmer's been found dead,' Joanna said. 'Murdered.'

Frankwell did a double-take. 'No,' he said. 'Old Grimshaw? No.' There was something like panic in his voice. 'It can't be. When?'

'Some time during the past week, we think,' Korpanski said carefully.

Frankwell went chalk white. 'I don't believe it,' he muttered, not addressing either of the two detectives. His head shook from side to side. 'This is not a coincidence.'

'Sorry?'

Frankwell's eyes were almost hooded, dark brown and slightly almond-shaped. Joanna decided he must have some oriental blood in him. There was something about the extreme darkness of the hair, his face shape and the olive tone to his skin.

'Nothing,' he said firmly.

'You can't shed any light on Mr Grimshaw's death?'

'No,' Frankwell said – even more firmly.

'When did you last see him, Mr Frankwell?'

Frankwell's brow furrowed. 'I haven't a clue. Not for sure. It's probably months since I last spoke to him.'

'What about?' Korpanski this time.

'If you must know I wanted to buy another

field from him. I've left some access between here and the Barnes's house and should get planning permission for another five houses. I wouldn't need to build them – just get outline planning permission. The deal would have financed a few good years in Brazil, just until I get my feet under the table there.' He gave a cheeky grin and Joanna smiled back innocently, as though she was genuinely interested. 'So did he sell?'

'He said he'd think about it. I imagined that any day now he'd let me know.' His eyes flickered towards the window.

And Joanna smelt the proverbial rat. 'Just a field, Mr Frankwell? Sure you weren't trying to persuade him to sell the farm itself?'

Frankwell's flash of temper was as sudden and violent as a summer storm complete with lightning. 'He wouldn't sell me the farm,' he said, 'however much money I offered him. He was as stubborn as a mule.' He gave a disdainful shrug. 'He told me he'd live and die there.'

'Really?' Joanna and Korpanski exchanged glances. It was Joanna who made the comment. 'Prophetic.'

She let the word sink into the air before embarking on her final questions. 'Just for the record, Mr Frankwell, have you any idea where you were on the 11th and 12th of September? The Monday, Tuesday and Wednesday of last week,' she added helpfully.

'Not a clue.'

'Do you keep a diary?'

He nodded and the two detectives waited while he left the room to retrieve it. They looked at one another. Joanna lifted her eyebrows while Korpanski made a similar noncommittal face.

Frankwell returned. 'Monday I was here,' he said. 'Tuesday I was in London until late and Wednesday of last week I was packing here all day. My daughter spent the evening with me and I cooked.' He looked pleased with himself.

Joanna got to her feet. 'Just for interest,' she said casually, which might have fooled Frankwell but certainly didn't Mike Korpanski, 'why was Grimshaw so determined to hang on to the field? I imagine you would have given him a good and fair price for it?'

'Generous,' Frankwell said. 'Believe me. He wouldn't have got a better price from anyone for that poxy bit of land. It is less than two acres.'

It was Korpanski who asked the next question. 'So what was he doing with the field?'

'Stubborn old fool was keeping a few sheep

on it. Sheep. More trouble than they're worth. He'd had no end of problems keeping sheep a couple of years back. They all had rotten feet or something. Don't know why he was continuing with them. No one would have given him a better price for that bit of land,' he said again. It was obviously one of Gabriel Frankwell's bandwagons.

They walked outside then, Frankwell keeping up with them as though he was anxious to see them off his property. 'Nasty bit of damage to your car,' Korpanski commented.

Frankwell's face darkened. 'Some people,' he said, 'see a nice car and feel envious.'

'And which house does your wife live in?'

'Ex-wife,' Frankwell corrected quickly and tried to turn it into a joke. 'I'm not intending bigamy, Inspector. Number 3.'

'Next door but one? That *is* very close.'

'It's not a problem,' Frankwell insisted.

'What complicated lives some people lead,' Joanna said gently.

Frankwell shot her a suspicious look, which Joanna bounced back innocently.

They left then, and noticed that while they had been inside number 7, a silver Mercedes had appeared outside number 3. 'Let's go and visit the ex-wife, shall we, Mike? See what she can corroborate.'

Chapter Five

Charlotte Frankwell opened the door to them instantly in response to Joanna's hard knock, leading rise to the suspicion that she had been keeping an eye on them through the window. She was a polished product, Joanna realised quickly. Manicured nails, shining strawberry-blonde hair, neat size-ten jeans and three-inch stilettos. Such women had always fascinated Joanna. How did they keep it up? To never have wild hair, be caught without make-up, slumming it in slippers and a shabby dressing gown?

Charlotte appraised her right back, gave a cursory glance at their ID cards, swiftly ran her eyes over Korpanski and addressed Joanna. 'Let me guess,' she said shrewdly, fixing her with a stare of expertly made-up very blue eyes. 'You're here about poor old Grimshaw, aren't you? I heard he'd been murdered. Bashed over the head,' she said with relish. 'How awful. Right on my door-step too.'

'That's correct, Mrs Frankwell,' Joanna

said formally. 'We wondered whether you might be able to shed any light on the crime.'

The pupils of Charlotte's eyes became very small and clever. 'In what way?' she asked silkily.

'Well – for instance – when did you last see Mr Grimshaw?'

Frankwell's ex-wife was no fool. She spent just the right amount of time thinking about it.

'I've been thinking about that since your officer asked me. I think it was... Look why don't you come in?' She asked the question with a charming flash of dazzling teeth. 'I shouldn't keep you chatting here on my doorstep, should I?'

She led them into a large state-of-the-art kitchen, terracotta tiles on the floor, cream units, black granite tops and a splash here and there of red in the wall tiles. Joanna approved. It was three times the size of her kitchen in Waterfall Cottage. They sat round a large, rectangular Victorian oak table. The feel of the room was surprisingly relaxed and comfortable.

Joanna's respect for Mrs Frankwell notched up an inch.

Charlotte reopened the conversation. 'You asked me when I last saw Mr Grimshaw.'

Both Korpanski and Joanna nodded.

'I think it was some time over the weekend before last.' She gave a swift upwards glance at a wall calendar. 'The weekend of the 8th and 9th of September. Probably the Sunday. He was talking to the little Mostyn girl. She's crazy about horses and she was riding his little pony.' Her perfectly lipsticked mouth curved into a smile. 'He has a soft spot for little Rachel. Probably the only human being he was fond of,' she reflected. 'When his daughter came to visit it was nothing but a slanging match. Noisy, too. Judy is no shrinking violet.' She gave Korpanski a frankly flirtatious look. 'When do *you* think he died, Sergeant Korpanski?'

Joanna smiled inwardly. Mrs Frankwell had memorised Korpanski's name. She just loved it when women embarrassed him.

Mike flushed. 'Almost certainly some time on the Monday, Tuesday or Wednesday of that week,' he answered woodenly.

Mrs Frankwell looked appalled. 'And he's lain there, dead, all this time?'

'This is what we suspect.'

Charlotte's eyes looked horrified. 'Just the other side of my wall? It could have been *me* who found him.'

They couldn't deny this.

133

'You didn't notice the smell?'

Charlotte wrinkled her nose. 'There's *always* a smell here. It's a farm.'

Joanna smiled and left Charlotte to take the initiative. 'I expect you've been talking to my husband?' her question was directed at Joanna.

'Correct.'

The mouth curved again. 'I daresay you thought him pretty fanciable.'

Not my type, Joanna thought, but wisely made no comment.

Without waiting for a response, Charlotte continued. 'Then let me disillusion you, Inspector Piercy. My husband would do anything to further his own ends and desires. He pleases himself.'

'Does this have any bearing on the crime, Mrs Frankwell?'

'Who knows?' she said airily, with a wave of her small hands. 'He's certainly been very keen to extend the estate – or at least make some money by buying up a field full of sheep and selling it on with planning permission for more houses. Nice little killing that. He would have made a cool two hundred thousand simply by changing the use of the land, not laying a single brick or digging an inch of foundations. You have to hand it to

Gabriel, he's clever and he would have sat it out except for *leetle Lucia.*' She managed the Romanic lilt with the talent of a character actress.

Joanna smiled. 'Hardly a motive for murder.'

Charlotte Frankwell merely lifted her eyebrows. 'You think not, Inspector Piercy? Well, perhaps you should remember a few things. My husband is unscrupulous and determined. He is also very greedy and a liar. Put these observations together with the fact that Mr farmer Grimshaw is extremely stubborn and fond of his small-holding – the shrunken farm – and you have a potentially fatal combination. Plus,' she said firmly, 'Mr Grimshaw is not quite as naive as he appears. He's not above playing tricks just as dirty as my husband's.' She looked pleased with herself for getting this in. 'Notice his car, did you? The Porsche; his pride and joy. Nasty, nasty scrape on the side.'

Joanna felt almost nauseated with the woman's malice and waited for Charlotte's punchline.

'Of course quite a few of the lanes here are very narrow, aren't they?' A stare from the cornflower blue eyes didn't quite give the desired innocence to the comment.

'Gabriel drives far too fast. And of course tractors take up rather a lot of room, don't they?'

'Did your husband report the incident?'

The blue eyes flashed onto Korpanski. 'No, Sergeant. He didn't.'

'So it was amicably settled,' Joanna asked.

'What do you think?' Charlotte asked.

The two police officers could well imagine; anger and fury meeting Grimshaw's bland smile, which probably masked utter glee at the damage done to his adversary's precious car.

Joanna leant forward. 'Let me get this quite clear, Mrs Frankwell: are you making an allegation against your husband? Are you saying that you think he's responsible for this crime? That he murdered Jakob Grimshaw to get his hands on the land?'

'*Ex*-husband,' Charlotte Frankwell said coolly, 'and all I'm saying is that if I was you, I would consider him very carefully as a suspect.'

Perhaps it was her very coolness that made Joanna shudder and decide to bring the interview to an end. She stood up. 'Thank you very much,' she said. 'You've been most helpful.'

'The pleasure's *all* mine.' She was like a

little cat. Eyes narrowing, curving smile, practically purring as she lapped up a saucer of cream.

Her face was almost serene as she closed the door behind them.

Half an hour later, Joanna and Mike were holed up in a local pub, tucking into a bar meal and a pint each of shandy. 'Well,' she said, 'what do you make of that one?'

Korpanski was silent for a minute. 'I don't know,' he said. 'She must know her husband, his faults and virtues and what he's capable of. But on the other hand, perhaps she's simply being bitchy, wanting to spoil it for her husband and his new family.'

'She didn't strike me as particularly bitter,' Joanna observed. 'She seemed more pleased to be rid of him, as though she had other fish to fry.'

Korpanski grinned. 'Don't underestimate the female of the species,' he said. 'Deadlier than the male.'

Joanna joined him laughing. 'So you say. Personally, I think that's one of those nasty little clichés.'

As she studied the humour in her colleague's face she reflected how much Korpanski had changed since his sullen, resentful, early days. She hadn't seen him smile like this for at least the first year. Then, slowly, as they had worked together, he had mellowed – perhaps she had too – and out of those changes had emerged this comfortable, companionable, loyal friendship.

Her mobile phone tone interrupted her thoughts. It was Matthew. 'Hello,' she said.

'Jo? Where are you?'

'Holed up in a pub with Korpanski,' she said, 'having just interviewed a black widow spider.'

'Sorry,' he apologised stiffly. 'I just wondered if you would be free tonight?'

'Oh, Matthew,' she said. 'With a murder investigation ongoing? No chance. Why? Was it anything special?'

'Caro's been in touch,' he came back. 'She seems keen to have a night out together.'

'What about Saturday?'

'OK,' he said. 'I'll ring her back and see how she's fixed Saturday.' He paused and Joanna sensed he had more to say.

'Also, I thought you might like to know I went over the Grimshaw post-mortem with Jordan. He's done a great job. I didn't really have anything to add except that from the first blow to his death was probably ten to fifteen minutes. There's substantial bruising around some of the defensive injuries to the forearm.' He paused. 'I don't know how that fits in with the crime scene.'

She frowned. 'Neither do I. I'll have to go back there, Matt, with a couple of stand-ins, and see how it could have happened.'

Matthew Levin tucked his last phrase in as though it was a casual after-thought, had she not known better. 'Oh, by the way. You haven't forgotten Eloise's interview is next Wednesday and Thursday, have you? It is OK if she stays with us Wednesday night, isn't it?'

Coward, she thought. He'd asked her over the phone, knowing she would not be alone and therefore unable to give vent to her true thoughts. Then she went deeper and explored why. Matthew wasn't a natural coward at all. This was simply something he would always shrink from – putting his daughter and his now-fiancée face to face.

'Fine by me,' she said, imitating the casual tone Matthew had affected.

He rung off then and Joanna made a face at Mike.

'Remind me to work very late next Wednesday,' she said and immediately felt disloyal to Matthew – even to Eloise, her about-to-be stepdaughter.

She felt her mouth stiffen. Miss Eloise Levin was a very difficult young woman, a lethal mixture of utter devotion to her father and plain dislike for Joanna.

They finished their lunch and Joanna felt fidgety, as though something was unfinished – unsatisfactory.

'We should go back to the farm,' she said. 'Matthew thinks the assault on Grimshaw was quite sustained. He mentioned ten to fifteen minutes.' Again she frowned. 'That's a long time, Mike. I find it hard to believe that *no one* saw *anything.*'

Korpanski nodded.

She paused, allowing her thoughts to sink in, move forward and conclude.

'Three houses back onto the murder scene: Mostyn, whose little girl used to ride Grimshaw's pony; Charlotte Frankwell and the Westons. I suggest we return to Charlotte Frankwell's, even if it's just to rattle her cage a bit. I'd like us to go over her exact movements on the three critical days. Is it really possible none of these people saw anything?'

As they walked back to their car she recalled something else that had struck her as odd.

'Mike,' she said slowly. 'Did you notice that all the curtains to number 4 were closed?'

'Not really, Jo,' he said.

'Do you know who lives there?'

Korpanski consulted his Filofax. 'A Mr and Mrs Parnell,' he said.

'Who interviewed them?'

Again Korpanski consulted his trusty Filofax.

'Alan King and Dawn Critchlow.'

'What did they say about them?'

'Mr Parnell was away on business. Mrs Parnell was a bit weird.'

She gave him a keen look.

'In what way?'

Korpanski shrugged. 'Didn't say. Just that something struck them as not quite right.'

Joanna let out a long, whistling breath. 'Someone else we should visit then.'

As she might have expected, Charlotte Frankwell had her answers off pat. She'd been at work on all three days in question; her daughter had been at school, then either in an after-school club until five o'clock or out with her father. 'For all his faults,' she said grudgingly, 'Gabriel is genuinely fond of Phoebe. She'll miss him when he goes.'

Joanna was quick to pick up on the regret in her tone. 'You'd probably prefer him not to go so far away?'

Charlotte Frankwell frowned. 'Of course I would. Phoebe simply *adores* her father. She was *heartbroken* when I broke the news that he was going away and that she wouldn't be seeing so much of him in the future.'

Joanna had an uncomfortable glimpse of a child bereft of an adored parent and felt a slight twinge of guilt.

'Where do you work?' she asked quickly.

'In a small dress shop along St Edwards Street. Top Hat.'

'Who with?'

'Mostly on my own but the proprietor pops in and out through the day. It happens to be quiet most of the time except Saturdays – and we're closed on a Sunday.'

Joanna tucked the fact away. 'But you're not at work today?'

The comment seemed to irritate Charlotte Frankwell. 'I'm owed some holiday,' she said haughtily. She squared her shoulders and faced Joanna with a bold stare. 'Are you saying *I'm* a suspect, Inspector?'

Joanna was tempted to quote the Clouseau line: 'I suspect *everyone* and I suspect *no one.*' But it would have been inappropriate and would probably lead to a complaint of levity in a serious case.

'The evenings?'

'I was in on my own during the evenings.'

Joanna nodded. *No alibi, then.* But from what Matthew had said, the assault on Grimshaw had been sustained. Looking at the forensic evidence of the blood spots, the progression towards the wall where he had finally died would have taken him past the backs of three houses. For somewhere around fifteen minutes there would have been prolonged shouts and screams. If, as Joanna suspected, Grimshaw had headed towards the wall hoping to attract the attention of one of his neighbours, he would have made sure he made a noise. As much as possible. On the other hand, this was the sort of housing estate that's deserted from nine to five – a ghost town during the working day. An ideal time for murder. Not so the evenings, when people might be in their gardens or have windows open and either see or hear enough to call the police.

In broad daylight then.

'Do you mind if we take a look at the bottom of your garden?'

Charlotte shook her head then gave a swift glance, for the first time looking upset. 'He was there, wasn't he? I've seen the little white gazebo you've erected. So near,' she mused.

Neither of the two police could deny it. It was a fact, which Charlotte was too shrewd not to recognise. She shuddered. 'It could easily have been me who found him,' she said, 'or worse – it could have been Phoebe.' She actually paled. 'She's just ten years old.'

She then looked up again, her face stricken. 'I suppose as he was lying so near my property I'm a suspect?'

It was Korpanski who found some sympathy for her. 'Not exactly, Mrs Frankwell,' he soothed. *You* don't have a motive. Besides, he was actually behind the Weston's part of the wall.'

The comment seemed to make Charlotte smug – arch, even.

'Right,' she agreed. 'Come on then.'

Even from her patio doors the police activity was all too obvious. Joanna could hear voices and police radios, see arc lights and a lot of people walking around purposefully. Then there was the white tent, the cars, the general air of busyness.

Charlotte slid open the patio doors and they stepped outside.

Approaching the murder scene from the

opposite side it seemed different. A mirror image of the view she had taken in earlier. But Joanna noticed other things, too. The cowshed looked huge from here, dwarfing the farmhouse to its right. From this angle, the farmhouse appeared less run-down, less ramshackle. Prettier. Almost quaint. The yard that surrounded the house looked picturesque, with the oak tree spreading shelter over almost its entire span. As she and Mike walked up the garden path with Charlotte two steps behind, she was aware of this new approach to the murder scene, the curving path, the neatly clipped sides of the lawn, a climbing rose ambling its way lazily over the wall. As she stood and studied this reverse angle, she began to realise how many blind spots there were. The back door to the farm was hidden, the area between the farmhouse and the barns, the far side of the barn. Perhaps the killer had been safer than she had thought.

She made a mental note to visit the Weston family in number 1 before the day was out. She wanted to assess the view from their garden in the daylight too.

The longer she stood and gazed, the less like a crime scene the vista appeared. She was almost lost in the scene. Until Korpanski touched her arm and broke into her thoughts.

'Jo,' he said softly. When she turned she realised she could have stood there, eyeing the farm for hours. There is something tranquil and timeless about a farmyard. Even when it is both devoid of animals and is a murder scene.

They left Charlotte Frankwell and returned to the farmhouse. Mark Fask met her at the gate, red in the face and obviously angry. 'We've had a bit of trouble with Grimshaw's daughter,' he said. 'She seems resentful of the fact that we're doing such a thorough search of the farmhouse.'

Korpanski gave a grunt and an apologetic shrug in Joanna's direction. 'That's her all right. Told you she was tricky.' Joanna looked along the track to see a slim woman in her forties, dressed casually in cargo pants, olive green sweatshirt and wellies, striding towards her. Even from thirty yards it was easy to see she was angry too. Her wellies slapped through the mud, splashing it behind her. 'Are you Inspector Piercy?' she called when she was ten yards away.

Joanna admitted that she was.

Grimshaw's daughter reached her. 'Is all

this...' she waved her hands around, 'really necessary?'

Joanna was already irritated. It was hard to believe they were investigating the murder of this woman's father. 'Sorry?' she said bluntly. And anyone who knew Joanna Piercy at all – let alone well – would have recognised the steeliness and hostility in her voice. All the warning signs of an approaching storm.

Judy Grimshaw looked at Mike, who spoke for her. 'This is Mr Grimshaw's daughter, Judy.' He sounded apologetic, as though it was somehow *his* fault that she was so angry.

Joanna gave the woman another chance and held her hand out. 'Detective Inspector Joanna Piercy,' she said with a pleasant but bland smile, 'Leek police. I'm the senior investigating officer in your father's murder case. I'm glad to have met you.'

But Ms Grimshaw didn't bother returning the civilities. 'Is it really necessary for your little terriers to go right through every single cupboard and drawer of my father's house? What on earth do you think you're going to find?'

'We don't know, Miss, Mrs–?'

'My married name is Wilkinson,' Judy

Wilkinson snapped.

'Mrs Wilkinson. I would have thought you would have wanted to unearth *anything* that might lead to the apprehension of your father's killer.'

'I don't think this,' she waved her hands at the activity all around, 'will lead you any nearer his killer.'

Joanna simply regarded the angry woman without replying. The truth was that she wanted her removed from the crime scene before she exploded. She wanted to re-enact the actual murder, and that wasn't possible with Grimshaw's daughter looking on. Even if she hadn't been a difficult, stroppy cow. This was tiresome.

She looked at Mike, knew he was reading her thoughts exactly, and hoped he would come up with some solution. But he simply stared ahead, as though trying to block out the mini drama.

So it was up to her. *Thanks, Mike,* she thought.

'It's intrusive.' Judy Wilkinson carried on the tirade. 'An invasion of human rights.'

Yeah, yeah, Joanna thought, trying hard not to roll her eyes heavenwards.

'Mrs Wilkinson,' she said, dragging out the last ounce of her politeness. 'We have our job to do. We also need to isolate the crime scene for the afternoon. I wonder... Do you think? Would you mind?'

The farmer's daughter gave Joanna a sour look. 'It's all right, Inspector,' she said. 'I have to be at work anyway.'

Phew, Joanna thought, slightly surprised that she had not taken compassionate leave.

Once Judy Wilkinson's little red car had shot off down the road they could proceed with the reenactment of the actual crime. She used Korpanski as the farmer and Hesketh-Brown as the perpetrator, with Mark Fask timing the action.

Fask was at his best doing this sort of thing, threading forensic clues through post-mortem evidence and working out the sequence of events.

He stood at the back door. 'I think our perpetrator began the attack here,' he said. 'This is where there was a large pool of blood and some fresh splintering on the back door frame. We found blood on some of the splinters and underneath, where the wood had been broken. They were consistent with the baseball bat injuries. I thought it was likely that it was during this initial assault that Grimshaw's arm was broken. We found traces of blood going down the path and towards the cowshed. It's possible that Grimshaw was thinking of barring himself in at this point. If that was what was in his mind, it's possible that the broken arm made him unable to lift the bar.' To illustrate his thesis, he pushed open the bar that held the barn doors together. 'It's quite stiff and heavy and our victim would have been weakened by the attack.'

Joanna nodded. So far it was making sense.

'We found spots of blood in many places in the yard,' Fask continued, while Mike and Hesketh-Brown 'slugged it out'. 'Particularly behind the cowshed.'

They moved behind and took the path Fask was suggesting. 'Concealed from the estate,' Joanna observed.

'Just a theory, Jo,' Fask continued, as they moved around the back of the cowshed, 'but there is a pink rambling rose here. Dr Cray removed a rose thorn from Grimshaw's hand. There are also a number of blood spots here. I wondered if Grimshaw was shouting by now, trying to make his way around towards the wall and attract the attention of the people whose gardens back on to his land.'

Joanna rubbed her chin. 'It's possible,' she

said slowly. Her eyes drifted across to the dry stone wall, the boundary between the two civilisations. Old and new.

She stood at its base and peered over at the row of houses with their neat garden furniture, tidy flowerbeds and immaculate lawns. There could hardly be a greater contrast. So now she was looking at the correct, rather than the reverse angle. The way Grimshaw must have looked at it in his final moments. She was silent as she collected her thoughts. Then she studied the spot where Grimshaw's body had been found and marvelled. It might have been slumped against the back of the wall but it was only a few feet away from the Weston's house and Charlotte Frankwell's garden. The killer had taken a risk.

She turned and looked back at the farm.

Something was...

'Tell you anything, Jo?'

'Not sure, Mike. Not sure.' She met his dark gaze. 'I know one thing. To understand this crime it is necessary to stand both in the farmyard and the neighbours' gardens.' She smiled. 'Come on, Mike, let's go and interview the Westons.'

Steven Weston was at home alone, looking distinctly uncomfortable to see them. Joanna wondered what he had been doing. She could see no book out, no computer on; the TV was switched off and the radio was silent.

'Mr Weston?' He looked nervous. He was a thin-faced, ferrety-looking man with small, pale eyes and a nervous tick in the corner of his right eye. He peered around the door, nose and right eye twitching. 'Hello?'

Joanna went through the repetition of who she was and what she was doing there. He stretched out a big hand warily. 'Yes, they said you'd probably want to talk to me.' They followed him into a sitting room with a brown leather corner sofa and a large plasma screen TV.

'It was my wife, really. Not me. She noticed the smell.' A nervous, silly smile. 'She's always had sensitive nostrils.' Sillier than the smile was his giggle. Joanna *hated* men who giggled. She felt her toes grow cold.

'When did she first mention the smell?'

'I don't know.' Weston waved those big hands around. 'Some time in the week, I expect. I can't remember precisely.' His glance was constantly shooting back to the window. Once or twice he pulled his sleeve up clumsily to glance at his watch.

The answer was soon apparent.

'Better that she tells you herself.' Another glance at his watch. Less surreptitious this time. 'She'll be home in a bit. Any time now. The shop closes at four thirty. She doesn't usually work on a Wednesday but one of the other helpers is on holiday and they don't like people to be there on their own. Safety, you know.'

Right on cue they heard a car pull up outside and the door slam, footsteps treading the path, a key in the door. Then Kathleen Weston stood before them.

She was a plump woman, tall and big-boned, with penetrating dark eyes, and a fury of fading red hair. She wore no make-up and exuded an air both of power and of motherliness. Joanna and Mike stood up and introduced themselves. Joanna eyed Mrs Weston. There was something familiar about her. Some retained memory of an event in which this woman had taken part. She frowned, irritated that her power of recall had temporarily deserted her.

'It was a good job I did investigate,' she

said. 'I wish I had sooner. Maybe then some of the animals might have survived. I can't bear the thought that, had I just peered over the garden wall, some of the animals might not have died.' She looked up. Her brown cow eyes were brimming with tears. 'How is Old Spice?' she asked.

Joanna looked helplessly at Korpanski. 'Last I heard, he was doing all right, Mrs Weston.'

'Oh good,' she said.

'Anyway,' she said, 'I put it off but then I had to look. I'm glad I did or poor old Jakob would have lain there for ever.'

Not for ever, Joanna thought, but for a lot longer, and she wondered what difference it would have made. Another day ... or two?

'When did you first notice the smell?' Joanna asked.

Kathleen thought for a moment, dug into a capacious handbag, consulted her diary then focused her eagle gazes on Joanna. 'I was at work on the Tuesday,' she said slowly, glancing down at her diary. 'Last Wednesday, a week ago, I had my hair done. I don't remember noticing a smell then. But when I came home from work last Thursday I did notice something. It got stronger, you know? Does that help you?'

'I think so,' Joanna said. 'I think you're probably one of the few people who can give us any sort of clue as to when he died.'

'It must have been in the early part of last week,' Kathleen said. 'Bodies don't smell straight away.'

Of course. She was an animal woman. No fool.

'We'll probably want to interview you again,' Joanna said. 'Is there anything you want to add?'

The Westons exchanged a glance and both shook their heads.

Joanna left them her mobile and direct dial number and they left.

When they were safely back in the car she gave vent to her feelings. 'So tell me more about Old Spice.'

Korpanski grinned. 'He's a particularly handsome Tamworth boar.' He gave Joanna a sly, sideways look. 'I suppose he's a widower now. Poor old Old Spice.'

'Yes. An innocent victim. A bystander to our crime. Shame he can't talk to us and give us a few clues.' She and Mike smiled as she handed him the phone. 'Well, even if he can't talk to us we'd better find out how this princely boar is.'

Chapter Six

'The pig is doing fine,' Korpanski said in a voice almost quivering with merriment. 'The vet's fed him and watered him and he's going to be all right. He's letting Old Spice stay at another farm in the district, where he'll be well looked after.'

'Not lodging with our Judy, then?'

Korpanski made a face. 'Being as her address is some tiny little town house, I don't think so. The neighbours might complain.' They both chuckled at the vision of a neat suburban house with a pig snorting and foraging in the garden.

The levity about the pig made them both feel better and Joanna promised herself a visit to see Old Spice.

It was almost six o'clock by the time they were ready to call on number 4 Prospect Farm Estate. As they got out of the car, Joanna studied the house. Even from the outside, it had a different air around it. Silly, Joanna thought, but it felt distinctly cooler.

It was as though what sun there was simply didn't reach this property.

She frowned and tugged Korpanski's sleeve as they approached to draw his attention to an upstairs window. They both looked up. All the windows were shrouded. But in this central window there was a small, twitching gap in the curtains. A woman was watching them. She looked pale-faced, with long grey hair and staring eyes.

Joanna told herself not to be so silly. This was a modern house in the middle of a small housing estate, yet it alone had an air of mystery; it appeared sinister and mysterious. But apart from the drawn curtains, the face watching them from the window and the sunless state of the house, it was hard to see why it was infused with such an air of intrigue.

She watched the two people approaching the property, knowing already that they were detectives. The woman, who exuded life – health, strength and vitality – and the large man who walked at her side. She resented their presence. She didn't like visitors. She descended the stairs slowly.

Joanna got a shock when Mrs Parnell opened

the door, even before she'd got around to knocking. She stared at her thinking what a bloodless, Gothic creature she was. Somewhere in her forties, she was dressed from head to foot in black, in trousers and a polo-necked sweater. There was only one bright spot of colour; a thin slash of red across what passed for a mouth.

Morticia, Joanna thought. Morticia Addams.

'Yes?'

Even her voice was strange, flat and distant.

Joanna was even more taken aback.

'I know who you are,' 'Morticia' said. 'I don't need to see your identity cards. I knew you would come.' She ignored Joanna's outstretched hand. No, not ignored. She knew it was there but looked at it with distaste, disgust, as though it had been covered in slime and bypassed it. Even Joanna looked at it and wondered why it was so repulsive to this odd woman.

'Excuse me,' 'Morticia' said as she walked back into the house, leaving Joanna and Mike uncertain whether they should follow. Hesitatingly, they did.

The interior of the house was equally bizarre: dark red walls, doors stained mahogany. They walked through a long hall lined with gilded mirrors, wondering where she had disappeared to. They heard the sound of running water ahead.

She stood framed in the doorway and led the way into the kitchen, surprisingly modern in white. No other colour but white. Clinical white. White walls, white units, white worktops, even a white, tiled floor. The stark, bright white of an operating theatre. It was a complete contrast to the rest of the house.

For once Joanna was lost for words. She couldn't decide what sort of woman Mrs Parnell was: eccentric, affected, simply odd or stark staring completely barking mad. Her inability to get a handle on her interrogatee stopped her asking the first question.

Luckily for her, Teresa Parnell took the lead.

'I expect you're here about the poor dead farmer,' she said in her pancake voice.

'Yes.'

'You know he polluted the atmosphere?'

Again Joanna felt at a disadvantage. 'Sorry?'

'He was filth,' Teresa said. 'Filth.' Her eyes swept round the operating theatre room.

'In what way?'

Joanna looked around the kitchen for clues as to this woman's character. There were no jugs or kettles, weighing scales or any of the other paraphernalia of a normal working kitchen. She found only one clue. The sole ornament. On the wall hung a print of Christ tearing open his garment to expose his bleeding heart.

Teresa Parnell got up without a word and began washing her hands. Methodically, like a surgeon, in the way that Joanna had watched Matthew scrub and glove-up for a post-mortem. She watched, fascinated, as the woman rubbed her palms, hands, up and down the fingers, not missing the thumb, a careful rinse and drying off thoroughly with a towel.

Mrs Parnell seemed to find nothing strange in breaking off a conversation purely to wash her hands.

'He was...' Her pause seemed to go on for ever. 'Malodorous,' she said. 'And evil gives off an odour.'

Joanna and Mike exchanged uneasy glances. This woman ought to be on medication or an inpatient in a mental hospital – if there were such places any more.

It was time to cut to the business and get out of here. 'When did you last see him?'

'Morticia' was stroking her long grey hair. It made a rasping sound. Wiry and dry. There was something repulsive about the texture. 'See him?' she said. 'I don't *see* him. I *smell* him. I know he is there when I *smell* him.'

Joanna was losing patience with this woman. Her oddness, she had decided, was surely an affectation?

'OK,' she said briskly, thinking, I can play this game. 'When did you last *smell* him?'

'Dead – or alive?'

Joanna and Korpanski exchanged another glance.

'OK, let's start with alive?'

'I don't know.'

Was this purely a tease?

'Dead, then?'

'He died at eleven o'clock on Tuesday the 11th of September. The same date as the twin towers tragedy,' 'Morticia' said, with more than a touch of melodrama.

Joanna fixed her eyes on her. 'How do you know that?'

Teresa Parnell had an asymmetrical face; one eye that slanted while the other lay straight, a mouth that curved on one side and was straight on the other. Joanna found her so odd it was difficult to concentrate on her words. 'I am psychic,' she said solemnly, holding her newly washed hands out.

I'm not buying this, Joanna thought, and met Korpanski's eyes with a sceptical lift of her eyebrows.

'I can close my eyes and I simply know things,' Teresa continued. 'I am sensitive to the sufferings of people. I can *feel* their un-happiness.' She looked straight at Joanna. 'As I can recognise your uncertainty, In-spector. I knew you would be coming. You *had* to.' She turned her head towards Korpanski, wafting her grey hair around her face like a free-floating spider's web. 'I wasn't so clear about you, though.'

Thank goodness for that, Korpanski thought, distinctly uncomfortable at the thought of being in this woman's head.

'It could have been somebody else.'

She stood up and they knew the interview was at an end. Joanna gave it another shot. 'What do you actually *know* about Jakob Grimshaw's murder?'

'Morticia' stared past her. 'He was a long time dying,' she said.

'Just for interest, Mrs Parnell, where were you on Tuesday the 11th of September, around mid-morning?'

'Here.'

'Did you hear anything, see anything?'

Joanna was frustrated, believing that the woman was hiding behind her strangeness. Her temper was getting the better of her. 'We're investigating the savage and cruel murder of an old man. An old man who had worked hard all his life and didn't deserve such a dreadful end. If you really know anything or can help us in our investigation you must tell us.' She fixed the woman with a hard stare. 'Withholding information from the police in a murder investigation is a serious crime. Now then, I'll ask you again: is there anything *concrete* that you can tell us that might help us track down this evil killer and prevent him or her from ever doing anything like this again?'

Teresa Parnell rose to the anger in Joanna's voice. 'You might not have noticed,' she said, 'but I keep my curtains tightly closed.'

'And peep out of the windows.' Joanna was aware that this was turning into a slanging match but she wanted to flush the woman out of her mystic, affected, nebulous comments.

'I saw nothing,' Teresa said, 'except in my mind.'

'We will be asking you to come down the

station to make a formal statement,' Joanna said. 'I suggest you try to document anything that you saw, heard or smelt.'

Annoyingly she was tempted to ask her straight out who had killed old farmer Grimshaw but even though she thought this woman was talking rubbish she was aware that it could still influence the police investigation. She was equally aware that keeping an open mind was a vital ingredient in police work. Lose that and you can make false arrests, have the case rejected by the Crown Prosecution Service or even if they passed it, have it thrown out of court. It had never happened to her yet but she had watched plenty of colleagues fall into this pit. She didn't want the same to happen to this case.

Teresa Parnell shook her head, walked with them to the door, then engaged Joanna once again. 'Just remember, my dear,' she said. 'Pearls are for tears. And black ones – well...'

Joanna couldn't stop herself from touching her ring superstitiously. Ignoring Mike's sudden look of sympathy, she headed for the car.

'I hope you didn't take any notice of that,' he said when they were safely out of earshot.

'She's just a weirdo.'

'I know.' She was still fingering her ring. 'I know that. But the trouble is, Mike, how much of her statement should we ignore on the grounds that she's strange? Possibly deliberately so. It could even be a cover for her own guilt.' She felt like banging her fist down on the dashboard. 'What we need is some good, firm forensic evidence. A clue. A lead. We've got nothing.'

Korpanski touched her arm. 'Steady on, Jo,' he said. 'It's early days yet.'

Joanna turned to look at him, a thought seeping into her mind. 'What if she did hear something on the Tuesday, something that made her wonder? What if she then tucked it away into her subconscious and inter-preted it as a psychic insight?'

Mike, as always, was reassuringly blunt. 'Why not simply come out with it then?'

To that there was no answer, except that this was a woman who hid behind a wall of oddity.

They sat in the car for a while without switching on the engine. It was as though they both needed something to galvanise them back into action. Joanna looked around the estate. It looked so normal, peaceful, so thoroughly twenty-first century. So why did she feel as though it was one of those film villages – little more than a hollow façade, two-dimensional? Never the most patient of people, it was frustrating her. They must make a move.

In the end she took the initiative.

'The last person we know who definitely saw and spoke to Grimshaw appears to be the Mostyn girl. The children will be out of school by now. Let's talk to her father and see if we can arrange an interview.'

They were in luck: Peter Mostyn was at home. He'd been peering frantically into his computer screen when he heard their knock. And Rachel was downstairs, watching television.

Mostyn came out into the hall just as Rachel was opening the door, looking shyly up at the tall policeman.

'Is your daddy in?' Mike was good with children. Much better than his inspector.

Mostyn sidled up behind his daughter. 'Can I help you?'

They introduced themselves and his eyes narrowed. 'So we'd like to ask your daughter a few questions.'

The little girl looked up at her father for guidance.

'OK,' he said. 'If it'll help solve this unpleasant business I don't see any objection.'

'Good.'

They sat in the sitting room. The light was fading and Mostyn flicked a couple of lamps on before settling down beside his daughter.

Joanna opened the questioning, addressing the child. 'You like riding?' The question conjured up an image of the ten-year-old Eloise, neat in jodhpurs and Pony Club sweater, and a pony named Sparky. She brushed the memory away.

The girl nodded enthusiastically. 'Oh yes.'

'And the farmer let you ride his pony?'

The girl looked suddenly distressed. 'Daddy told me he's had an accident, Mr Grimshaw.'

'That's right.'

'Is Brutus all right?'

Brutus, presumably, was the pony. Korpanski stepped in to fill the breach of knowledge. 'He's fine, love. He was safely up in the top field and has looked after himself ever since then.'

Phew, Joanna thought. She wouldn't have liked to have broken the news that the pony was dead too.

She continued. 'You last rode Brutus on the Sunday, a week and a bit ago?'

The girl nodded, happy now. 'We didn't go far,' she said. 'He liked me to trot around the field so he could keep an eye on me.'

Mostyn nodded his agreement.

'He said,' she was laughing now, 'that I reminded him of his daughter when she was little and nice. He said it was a long time ago.' She looked proud of herself for relating this conversation and looked to her father for approval – which she got. Mostyn smiled at her and nodded.

'Was anyone else there?'

The girl shook her head. 'There was never anyone else there.' She paused and said with childish insight, 'He was quite lonely, I think.'

'Did he tell you that?'

The girl nodded. 'Oh yes. He really liked it when I went to see him. He *said*,' her eyes opened very wide, 'that he looked forward to my visits.' She looked very pleased with herself now and with that pride came confidence, which Joanna intended to try and use to her advantage.

'Did he say if anyone had been annoying him or hanging round the farm and making a nuisance of themselves?'

The girl shook her head.

'Did you ever hear him shouting at anyone?' Again this elicited another shake of the head.

'This next one is a difficult question, Rachel, but I can tell you you're helping us very much, so I want you to think carefully about your answer. Do you know if Mr Grimshaw kept any money around the house?'

Her eyes were as round as saucers. She swallowed hard, again looked at her father for a cue. 'He did,' she whispered. 'One day someone came with animal feed. A big lorry. He went upstairs. I don't know where but when he came down his hand was full of twenty-pound notes. Full,' she repeated.

Joanna looked at Mike. This was one avenue they had omitted to explore. But now...

She turned back to the little girl. 'This won't get you into trouble, I promise. You've done nothing wrong. But did you tell anybody about the money?'

The girl's head shot round to look at her father. Peter Mostyn flushed. She might as well have pointed the accusatory finger.

There was an awkward silence, which the child filled with her plaintive voice. 'Will I be able to ride Brutus again?'

'I don't know, love,' Mike said. As a father, he knew better than to make idle promises, to keep it vague. 'I expect so. We'll have to see what happens to him and then ask his new owner.'

Again the child looked at her father and asked the tacit question. This time he shook his head with regret. Rachel didn't protest but lowered her head before looking up again and volunteering new information.

'He didn't like me going near the pigs, though.'

'Oh?'

'He said they were capable of eating me.' She looked at Mike. 'Is that true?' she asked.

'I don't think so,' he said gruffly. 'I've never heard of a man-eating pig, have you?'

By turning the grim question into a joke he'd reassured the child. Though where this little gem of information could possibly lead, Joanna couldn't guess. She kept trying. 'Is there *anything* you can think of that might help us know who hurt Mr Grimshaw?'

Again that doleful shake of the head.

They thanked the Mostyns, father and daughter, and left.

So what had they gained?

They were back at the station, drinking yet another coffee out of a styrofoam cup. The station had recently installed a coffee machine so they were on cappuccino, which wasn't as bad as it might have been.

Joanna leant across the desk and spoke to Korpanski and DC Alan King. 'So far, we've concentrated on the inhabitants of the estate,' she said. 'But Rachel Mostyn's claim that there was money stored at the farm makes me wonder how far that story might have spread. There are plenty of villains hanging around who would kill for a fistful of–'

'Dollars,' King put in.

Korpanski swivelled his chair round to face the computer screen. 'I'll run a few checks.'

'Which leads us to another line of inquiry,' Joanna continued. 'The lorry driver – the supplier of animal feeds. He knew there was money upstairs, too. We need to run a check on him.'

She stood up. 'Well, we have a few leads thanks to the Mostyn girl.' She considered for a moment, recalled the desperate glance the girl had given her father when she had asked who else knew.

'Run a check on Mostyn,' she said. 'I'd be very interested to know his current financial state.'

They spent another hour collating the information they'd gathered and preparing for the following morning's briefing. Korpanski and Alan King decamped to the pub, inviting Joanna along with them, but she shook her head. 'No,' she said. 'I have a fiancé to return home to.'

She owed Matthew that, at least.

She arrived home at nine-thirty to find Matthew sitting on the sofa, lamps on, his blond head bent over a book about Egyptian Mummies. Matthew had eclectic reading habits. Their bookshelves were overflowing with books on varied subjects – from history to modern art, poisons to birds of America, travel and, naturally, forensics, while Joanna preferred her crime novels.

Matthew looked up and grinned as she entered. 'Hello,' he said. 'How about I massage your neck while you drink a glass of wine?'

She kissed him before flinging herself down on the sofa. 'Are you trying for the Man of the Year award?'

'No,' he said. 'Husband of the Year.'

She let the comment ride until he was rubbing her neck and she'd taken a few sips of the wine. 'It's September now,' she said, testing out the ground. 'Are you suggesting we get married before the year is out?'

'Not seriously,' he said, his fingers digging

into tense muscles. 'Unless you want a very low-key Registry Office sort of wedding.'

She turned the ring around on her finger remembering Mrs Parnell's dark warning. She still hadn't got used to the feel of the pearl, smooth, round and bulky. 'Well, there's an idea,' she said without turning around.

'By the way, on the same subject, your mother phoned.'

Joanna swivelled around, making him lose contact with her neck. 'Did you tell her?'

He was smiling down at her. 'Yes, I did. She was very overexcited and started babbling straight away about bridesmaids and churches and things.'

'Oh? Did you disillusion her?'

'No,' he said steadily, his eyes on her, 'because you and I haven't really sat down and talked about the actual wedding.' He paused. 'And what it means to us both.'

She took a long draught of the excellent wine. 'Perhaps we should at least open the subject?'

'OK.' He went into the kitchen, brought back the bottle of wine and a beer for himself and sat in the armchair, opposite her, his green eyes steadily focused on her face.

She inclined her head towards him. 'You start.'

He took a deep breath. 'To be honest,' he said, 'I don't really care much about the actual ceremony – as long as it's legal.'

She was in agreement with this. 'Same here except I *don't* want a church wedding. The thought of slinking up the aisle to the sound of the "Messiah" or something fills me with the heebie-jeebies. Anyway,' she gave him a straight look, 'not all churches will marry you if you're divorced.'

'True.'

'I did wonder...'

'The hotel near the Roaches does weddings,' he said quickly. 'The entire package. It's right on the moors, very wild and very much our sort of place.'

So typical of Matthew to have done the groundwork. 'You've been there?'

'A few months ago,' he admitted. 'One weekend when you were working. I was out that way and saw it and thought it looked great so went in and got a brochure.'

She held her hand out and he fetched it from his desk.

He was right. It was Victorian Gothic, right out on the Roaches, a high and wild place between Buxton and Leek, part of the National Park and popular with climbers. She leafed through the brochure. The rooms looked exquisite and atmospheric, the views stupendous, the food mouth-watering.

Suddenly she was imagining it – a winter wedding, a frosting of snow and a wild wind, holly and scarlet berries, plenty of red and green, mulled wine and the scent of cinnamon. Music, lots of it, from reggae to pop, from Chopin to Scarlatti. Violins, a harp, a church organ.

She looked up and nodded and let her mind scamper away again.

White velvet for her and a white fur cape, her hands buried in a white fur muff. An Anne Boleyn headband sparkling with crystal and a short muslin veil, and her niece, Lara, in scarlet.

She looked across at Matthew and by telepathy realised that they were sharing the same vision.

'I don't think Eloise will want to be a bridesmaid,' he said.

She shook her head. It wouldn't be Eloise's idea of fun at all. 'But I do want her there,' he added.

She nodded. 'Of course. She's your daughter.'

Matthew came and sat by her, very close. She could feel the warmth of his body, the hard muscles of his legs, and inhale the scent of shampoo from his hair. He was right next to her but didn't hold her hand or put his arm around her. She glanced at him. He was biting his lip.

She knew what was coming next and decided to save him the trouble of having to ask her.

'You know I don't want to give up my job,' she said tentatively.

He nodded. His eyes flickered.

'But *I* know you would love another child, preferably a boy.' She hesitated. 'Matthew, no woman can promise that,' she said. 'These things have a habit of sorting themselves out.' She smiled into the fireplace, not at him, recalling her miscarriage. 'But if it happens, I wouldn't mind,' she said. 'Not a troop of offspring,' she warned. 'One – at the absolute, ultimate most two. No more but...' His hand was stealing towards hers. He took the hand wearing the pearl and kissed it.

And for the first time she saw real happiness in his face. It was creased with joy.

Oh my goodness, she thought. This means so much to him and I have withheld it all until now. She felt almost humbled.

She'd driven in again, resenting the denial of her bike ride. Autumn was sliding away. It would soon be too dark to cross the moorland alone on her bike, so she'd be using her car every day. She'd have to try and go out over the weekends or she'd lose her 'form'.

She kept the briefing factual, using wall charts to illustrate her points.

She spoke to Alan King and Dawn Critchlow about Teresa Parnell and they said they'd found her strange.

'Get some medical information on her,' Joanna said.

She detailed Bridget Anderton to look into the animal feeds lorry driver and Hannah Beardmore to run some local villains through the computer. She sensed there was more to this crime than met the eye – something criminal underlying the assault. She couldn't say why she believed this except that it seemed logical. This was no simple murder.

As the officers gave their reports she was sure that the teams had all done their best and interviewed everyone on the estate, but it was equally obvious that no one had actually seen or heard anything.

Joanna knew that she had some issues to deal with. She had to see Jakob Grimshaw's body for herself, run through the attack, speak to the pathologist who had performed the post-mortem.

At the back of her mind was Teresa Parnell's flat statement. 'He died at 11 o'clock on Tuesday the 11th of September.' Why had she been so specific? Joanna didn't believe in mumbo jumbo but as a psychology graduate she did realise there could be an interaction between a physical incident and the subconscious, which could translate into intuition. Something had fed Mrs Parnell that specific time and date and she wanted to know what it was. At the same time, she would be interested to meet Mr Parnell.

Roderick Beeston rang at eleven confirming that Ratchet, the dog, had died of a barbiturates overdose and the cattle and the sow of dehydration. 'Old Spice,' he said jauntily, 'has been rehoused in a neighbouring farm, where he seems most content.' He chuckled. 'Not missing his wife at all.'

Joanna laughed with him. She was fond of pigs herself, and not just as bacon. She thanked the vet for his trouble and asked about the pony, Brutus.

'Well,' Beeston said. 'He's just turned out in the field at the moment. I don't know what's going to happen to him. I suppose like the other animals, he'll be considered part of the estate and sold. When it's all wound up. These things take a heck of a time, don't they?'

Joanna felt a momentary sympathy for Rachel Mostyn, who had formed an attachment to the animal, but she soon forgot about her.

Some of the forensic results were starting to roll in already. The dog's dish had had plenty of fingerprints on it – all of them Jakob Grimshaw's. The contents confirmed the vet's findings. Ratchet's last dinner had been heavily laced with barbiturates. Phenobarbitone.

'Any old can't-sleep-biddy has access to the stuff,' the chemist said. But there weren't any old can't-sleep-biddies on the Prospect Farm Estate. So where had the barbiturates come from? Mrs Parnell? Was she on a sedative?

After the officers had dispersed, Joanna sat with Mike discussing the case. 'We've looked at the people on the estate,' she said. 'Let's look at possible motives.' She sighed. 'They all seem weak. Money being the strongest one. The land? Frankwell wanted to build on it and he was never going to manage that until the farm had been sold but Grimshaw wasn't playing ball. *Over my dead body* was his attitude.' The irony of the words seemed almost cruel.

She carried on, 'Pollution from the farm? They all seemed to complain about the smell and Teresa Addams – sorry, Parnell – is one of those hand-washing people. Did you notice the kitchen, Mike?'

He nodded. 'Yeah.'

'Remind you of an operating theatre?'

Again he nodded.

She shivered. 'Spooky.'

They were both silent until Joanna spoke again.

'Ill treatment of animals? Kathleen Weston is an animal lover, isn't she?'

'Yes, but–'

'Exactly. Would her love for animals have led her to this?'

'It was a vicious, risky and prolonged violent attack. I don't think so.'

'I need to see the body for myself,' she said. 'This isn't working. I just don't have a complete picture. I got back a day too late.

Did Jordan Cray say it had to be a male who carried out the assault?'

'Apparently not. The copestone could have been simply slid off the wall and Grimshaw was a skinny, frail old thing. A woman could have attacked him.' Korpanski qualified it with, 'a reasonably fit woman, anyway.'

They were interrupted by Danny Hesketh-Brown and he looked excited.

'Guess what?' he said. 'We've just spoken to Grimshaw's bank manager. He was worth a bit.'

Joanna looked up. 'How much of a bit?'

'£750,000 worth of a bit,' he said, grinning. 'And that's not including the farm and the land.'

'And the money under the mattress,' Mike said. 'All that slashing and tearing. I wonder how much he was *really* worth.'

She realised Danny was still standing in the doorway. 'Is there anything else?'

'Yes. Some of the money came from the sale of a field earlier on this year. I spoke to Grimshaw's solicitor. Guess who bought it?'

She couldn't deny the detective his moment of fame.

'Catherine Zeta Jones,' she said.

Hesketh-Brown grinned, unfazed by Joanna's sarcasm. 'Peter Mostyn. According to

the solicitor he bought the field off Grimshaw for £8,000 – well over what it would be
worth as farming land but a good investment
if...' He crossed to the board and pointed to
the map. 'This is the field,' he said. 'Beyond
the farm. It has no other access except
through the farmyard. Its far side is bordered
by a stream. The neighbouring fields belong
to another farmer, who has two strong sons
who farm with him. They're not going to sell
up. No, the field was virtually worthless
unless...'

'Grimshaw sold his farm,' Mike chimed
in.

'Interesting,' Joanna mused. 'And it's the
little Mostyn girl who rode the pony. Mmm.'
She looked at the officer. 'What else?'

'Pretty predictable,' he said. 'Grimshaw
died intestate.'

'What?' Joanna was surprised. Farmers, in
general, were very careful how and where
they left their money. This was another
puzzle. 'Well, his daughter will probably inherit.' But even saying it she was dubious.

'Or his wife. Were they divorced?'

Hesketh-Brown shook his head slowly.
'Not that I can see.'

'Well, well,' Joanna said. 'And she's a
nurse?'

'Yes.' Korpanski answered.

'Wouldn't that give her access to barbit-urates?' Both detectives were watching her mind tick away.

'Perhaps I was a little hasty and unsym-pathetic this morning,' she said, 'in my deal-ings with Mrs Wilkinson. Maybe I should get to know her a little better. What do you think, Mike?'

Korpanski wedged his thick thighs between the two desks and made his way to the door. 'Even Judy Grimshaw looks a bit more of an attractive proposition with all that dosh behind her,' he said.

Chapter Seven

WPC Bridget Anderton was a competent police officer. Born and bred in the Stafford-shire Moorlands, she understood the work-ings of the natives' minds, their prejudices and attitudes. She drove out to Cheddleton, passing the Flint Mill and the Caldon Canal. Farrell's Animal Suppliers was a cluster of Dutch barns where the feeds were stored and a small, square office. It was an extensive concern; their lorries were to be found right across Staffordshire, and parts of Derbyshire too, supplying plenty of hungry animals throughout long winters.

She focused on the red-faced director, who was grumbling noisily. 'I can't think what any of this has to do with us,' he said. 'We've nothing to do with poor old Grimshaw's death.'

Bridget was short and dumpy with stubby legs but her beauty was in her smile. Wide, warm and friendly, it usually disarmed people, made them feel welcome and confidant. Her hair was toffee-coloured and naturally shiny, swinging to her shoulders, and her eyes were another good feature. Warm brown, with a direct gaze. WPC Anderton was blessed in another way – with an optimistic nature – which she needed as her husband suffered from chronic depression and had spent time in hospital. He had trouble keeping a job and flittered from one to another between bouts of the sad disease.

WPC Anderton was using all her charm on Robert Flaxon, manager and company director of Farrell's Feeds, but it was having little effect.

'We need to know which driver delivered to Prospect Farm,' she said.

Flaxon tried to stare her out, failed and tightened his lips. 'Bradeley,' he muttered. 'Tim Bradeley covers that area. But he's a sound chap.' Flaxon was scowling at her now. 'There's no way he'd be up to any monkey business.' He raised tired eyes to hers. 'He's a family man. He's worked here since leaving school.'

'I just want to talk to him,' Bridget Anderton said, unruffled. 'We need to ask him some questions.'

'Well, you can't,' Flaxon snapped. 'He's out on his rounds.'

'When will he be back?'

Flaxon gave a quick look at his wristwatch. 'In an hour,' he said, 'or so.'

'Then I'll return in an hour,' Bridget Anderton said sweetly. 'Please tell him we need to talk to him, will you?'

Flaxon gave no answer but stared fixedly into his computer screen while she left the room.

She sat in the car, wondering. Was Flaxon *naturally* rude? Did he consider helping the police with their inquiries wasting company time? Or did he have something to hide? Did he resent the police sniffing around his premises? If so, why?

Interesting.

185

But she didn't want to wait around so she headed back to the station.

Joanna and Mike were holed up in their office. 'I think it would be a mistake to focus solely on the inhabitants of the estate,' Joanna was saying. 'Let's look at that list Hannah Beardmore compiled of other villains in the area.'

Mike tapped a few computer keys on the PNC, gave a grunt and leant back in his chair so that Joanna could see the result of his search.

'Kenny Roster's gang robbed some farms,' he said, 'a couple of years ago. They never resorted to murder, though.' Joanna stared at the screen. 'Well, they've been banged up in Walton jail anyway,' she said, 'since March of last year, so they're out of the picture.'

'There's always the Whalleys,' Mike said. 'Lovely family business of burglary and helping themselves to other people's stuff.'

'Haven't they retired?'

'We haven't heard anything from them for a while,' Mike said. 'I think I picked up a rumour that they'd headed off to Spain. I'll ask around.'

Joanna smiled. She knew who he'd ask. Like most police forces, they had their old lags who would swap a bit of information for twenty fags and/or a bottle of whisky, depending on how valuable the information was. Legitimate expenses that could save pounds on a major investigation. And Melvin Grinstead was theirs – about as seamy a character as it was possible to imagine. Long grey hair, scruffy, always dressed in the same smelly clothes: an ancient tweed coat, saggy brown trousers and grubby trainers. But he was also sharp-eyed and at times unobtrusive to the point of invisibility.

'Anyone else?'

Korpanski shook his head. 'Not unless some minor criminal is maturing.' He swung his chair round, his blunt features screwed up in concern. 'But murder, Jo? Poisoning the dog? Letting animals die of thirst? I don't think so.'

She stood up, suddenly frustrated, and crossed the room to the window. It was her bad luck that the office assigned to her was no more than three feet from a high, brick wall. It was an uninspiring view for a senior investigating officer. All too often it simply reflected the progress of an investigation. She turned around to face Mike. 'So who then? One of the neighbours? His daughter? Or someone else? And why? Why kill a harmless old farmer? Why poison the dog? Was he aggressive? Would he bark? Was it a robbery? Why not wait until Grimshaw was out for the day?'

'He virtually never was,' Korpanski answered.

'Why the sustained attack? Why murder, Mike?'

She wandered back to the computer, practically *willing* the screen to spew something out. Anything that would give their investigation some direction. The early days of an investigation were always bad – worrying that it would join the Unsolved Cases folder.

'Mike,' she said in a low voice, and he knew what was coming next.

'Time I left for the mortuary.'

Korpanski nodded.

'No need for you to come, Mike.'

'OK.'

It was a slow drive into the Potteries, crawling down the A53 Leek road and threading through the city. Traffic was practically stationary in parts and there were the usual road works in Endon. She bit her lip, drove patiently, and finally arrived at the mortuary.

Matthew met her at the door. 'Jo?'

She gave him a warm, intimate smile.

There was something about wearing this ring, that he had chosen and bought for her, that made her feel extraordinarily close to him. It wasn't her way to belong to anyone, to become a man's property. She had always prided herself on her independence, but she knew she was as close to Matthew Levin as she ever could be to any human being. She brushed his cheek with her lips, smelt the spicy tang of his aftershave, felt the bony prominence at the back of his neck under her fingers and wondered how long she would feel like this towards Matthew. Would this passion, this strength, this weakness continue for ever? Even the word 'fiancé' spread warmth throughout her. It was a different status. One she had not known before. No wonder engaged women looked so *smug*. If being affianced brought this, how would she feel when she was married?

'Matt,' she said, as they walked along the corridor. 'Do you know *all* the post-mortem findings? Or do I need to talk to Jordan?'

'I think I know most of it. Everything you need.' He looked at her fondly. 'If you ask me a question that stumps me, I'll get hold of Cray. OK?'

She nodded, already knowing that he would know all the answers she needed.

Matthew took great pride in his thoroughness.

They'd reached his office. The door was ajar and they wandered in to sit at the desk. 'So, Jakob Grimshaw's injuries,' she began. 'Were they the result of a gang attack or was there one assailant?'

Matthew thought for a minute. 'There's no evidence,' he said carefully, 'that it was a gang attack. We're working on it being a single killer. There weren't that many injuries and it's easy to trace what happened. It began with a full frontal assault with a weapon similar to a baseball bat, during which he sustained his defensive injuries – the broken arm, bruising etcetera.'

'And would it have to be a male? Did it require strength?'

Matthew shook his head. 'Grimshaw was frail,' he said, 'almost emaciated. He weighed only eight stone. A relatively fit female could have attacked him. And he finally collapsed against the wall. Jordan found traces of moss on the back of his sweater. It only took our assailant to topple the stone on him. It just happened to be there.'

Joanna fixed her eyes on him knowing that he disliked coincidence as much as she did. 'Just happened?'

Their eyes met. 'I think so.'

'I see,' she said.

Matthew shifted in his seat. 'I suppose you want to view the body?'

She nodded slowly, reluctantly. 'I think I ought to.'

He led Joanna into the room with its tiers of chilled drawers. He selected one then pulled it out.

The old farmer was neatly wrapped in a shroud, a tag looped around his toes. Matthew untied the shroud and pulled it back, allowing her to look, for the first time, at the subject of her murder investigation.

He was skinny almost to the point of emaciation and looked older than his years. His waxen face was, considering, surprisingly peaceful. The damage to his skull was easy to see, also the bruising to his arms, the misshapen right limb.

'Fractured ulna,' Matthew supplied. 'And the radius was dislocated. They used to call it the swordsman's injury.' He held his own arm up in a defensive pose. 'Like this. That appears to be the initial injury. It would have hurt like hell and winded him.'

'Anything else?'

'Head injury, fractures of the cervical spine, extensive bruising on the shoulders, probably from the assault as well as the stone as it dropped, a rose thorn in his hand,' Matthew finished. 'Poor chap.'

He waited a moment, then said gently, 'Have you seen enough?'

'I think so.' She looked at him. 'It hasn't brought me any nearer to the killer though, Matt. I thought it would, but it's done nothing.'

He slid the body back into the fridge. 'So what next?'

She made a face. 'Much as I don't want to, I'm going to have to speak to Grimshaw's daughter again. She's an unpleasant thing but I have a feeling there's something there that I've missed. Something important. But first,' she said cheekily, 'I wouldn't mind being taken for lunch.'

Matthew's eyes sparkled. 'Hospital fare?'

She linked her arm in his. 'Just as long as it isn't tripe and onions.'

He drove her to the restaurant in the City General Hospital and they shared gammon and onion rings. Then they returned to the mortuary, Matthew to complete his afternoon's work and Joanna to pick up her car and drive back to Leek.

She found Mike speaking to Peter Mostyn.

'Great, Jo,' he said. 'Mr Mostyn brought himself in to make a statement.'

'Very thoughtful,' she said.

Now why would Mostyn volunteer information? She looked at the pale, soft man with a permanently worried look on his face. 'Shall we go into the interview room?'

Mostyn was nervous. 'I thought I'd better come in,' he began, 'because I was worried you'd get the wrong end of the stick.'

Joanna raised her eyebrows.

'You see...'

Joanna waited.

Mostyn gulped in a lungful of air. 'I didn't know whether you knew...' his voice trailed away. His eyes darted from Joanna to Korpanski and back to Joanna.

'I own some of the farm land.'

Silence.

'A field,' he said, 'beyond the farm.'

He started to relax and babble. 'It doesn't have planning permission,' he said. 'It's just grazing land.'

Joanna lifted her eyebrows and let him prattle on.

'You see – I'd hoped to buy the pony, Brutus, for my daughter as a Christmas present. As a surprise. Grimshaw said we could keep it in the stable.'

'Very nice,' Joanna commented. 'She's a very lucky girl.'

Mostyn's face changed. 'She would have been. I don't think the farmer's daughter's keen on me having Brutus. I don't know why,' he said peevishly. 'It's far too small for her.'

He looked at Joanna out of the corner of his eye and she felt a tingling in her toes. This might be Mostyn's story but it *was* a story. A plausible one but she didn't believe it for a minute. A man in his straightened circumstances wouldn't have paid over the odds for a piece of land for sentimental reasons. He'd paid double the price for grazing but if it got planning permission it would have worked out a bargain. She gave him a bland smile. No. It was much more likely that he had bought it as an investment.

But she let the matter pass.

'Just out of interest,' she said, 'where were you on Monday and Tuesday?'

'Work all day,' he said quickly. 'I work in Macclesfield. It's an easy commute.'

'And in the evenings?'

Mostyn thought for a minute. 'I was at home on the Monday,' he said. 'I arrive back at about seven-ish. Tuesday I was with a client from Holland. We were out in a restaurant until around eleven.'

'I see,' Joanna said. 'Have you anything more to add?'

Mostyn shook his head, keeping his pale eyes firmly fixed on her.

She let him go after that.

Joanna arranged to speak to Judy Grimshaw and prepared herself to be more patient, more civil this time around. After all, the woman had just lost her father in violent and upsetting circumstances. She had a right to be brusque.

Judy lived in one of the older terraced houses with a front door that opened straight out onto the pavement. Her face appeared at the window in response to Joanna's knock. Moments later she pulled opened the door and led Joanna inside without a greeting.

Inside, it was small but homely, tastefully decorated with magnolia walls, a cream carpet and black leather suite.

She sat down opposite them. 'Are you any nearer to finding out who killed my father?' she demanded.

It had taken Joanna less than a minute to decide that she didn't like Judy Grimshaw any better the second time she met her.

There was something smug about the

woman – something too self-possessed, as though she held the key to all the problems of the world.

Joanna spoke formally. 'Judy, we're trying very hard to find out who killed your father.'

'I should think so,' she said tartly.

It wasn't helpful.

'The trouble is that we don't even know for certain *when* he died. Not only the time but the date, even. He was a very solitary person.'

'You don't have to tell me.'

There was something hostile and calculating in the goggle-eyes behind her glasses. Joanna looked at her and wondered why she was getting the distinct impression that Judy Wilkinson wanted them to fail on this. She didn't *want* them to discover who had killed her father.

Extraordinary, Joanna thought. Quite extraordinary.

'Is there anything you can think of that might point us in the right direction?'

Judy shook her head. She had light brown hair, an indeterminate colour, unflattering to her pale face.

'Had your father had any ... trouble recently?'

'Not apart from half the people on the

Prospect Farm Estate trying to winkle him out of his home.'

'He felt threatened by them?'

Judy gave a short, humourless laugh. 'You didn't know my father, did you, Inspector?'

'Obviously not.' Joanna could match curtness with curtness.

'He was in a world of his own. Threats wouldn't have penetrated his thick, stupid hide.'

Joanna almost started at the dislike in the woman's voice.

'No wonder my mother left him,' she finished.

Ah yes, Joanna thought. The mother.

'When did she leave?'

'Eight years ago.'

'Were you aware that she had plans to go? A hint of someone – somewhere – else?'

A mean, unpleasant look crossed the woman's face.

'Not her,' she said triumphantly. 'Tight wasn't the word. She kept herself to herself, did my mum.' There was a note of pride in Judy's voice. Not affection, Joanna noted. That was missing.

'And after she'd left?'

'Sent postcards.' A pause. 'From all over.'

'Did you see the postcards?'

'No – my father just told me. *Her's in Spain or Portugal. The Algarve. France.*' She affected a gravelly, moorlands voice. *'You know, spreading her wings.'*

This, then, was the discordant note. 'Why didn't your mother keep in touch with *you?*'

A toss of the head and a flash of pure spite. 'She only sent the cards to mock him.'

Joanna practically recoiled at the hatred in the woman's voice. 'What was your mother's name?' she asked.

'Avis.' A touch of sour humour twisted the thin lips. 'Like the rentacar.'

Joanna felt weary. There was something draining about this woman.

'Is there anything,' she appealed, 'anything that could help us?'

But the appeal simply provoked a sneer. 'Are you that stuck? No.' Judy shook her head, picked her handbag off the floor. 'Well, that was a waste of time,' she said nastily.

Yeah, for me too, Joanna thought.

Whatever her personal feelings – she would liked to have told this woman to get on her bike – Joanna responded politely. 'Thank you for speaking to us. It's been most help-ful.' If Grimshaw's daughter picked up the note of sarcasm in Joanna's voice, she ignored it.

During the journey back to the station Joanna was recounting the woman's words. Something wasn't ringing true. She had a bad feeling about this entire case. At the core was something very rotten.

She returned to her office and found Korpanski drinking coffee. 'Mike,' she said. 'Run a check on Avis Grimshaw and ring Mark Fask. Ask him if he's found a box containing some postcards.'

He picked up the phone and connected with the scenes of crime team, spoke for a minute or two, replaced the handset then shook his head. 'No,' he said, 'but they haven't finished their search of the house yet.'

Joanna looked across briefly. 'Did they give you any idea how much longer they'll be?'

'Later today,' Mike said.

'Right.'

Bridget Anderton was facing Tim Bradeley across a pine desk in the main office of Farrell's Animal Feeds, and privately she agreed with his boss. He didn't look a murderer but an honest Staffordshire man, with blunt features and steady grey eyes. Big hands rested still on his lap.

'You know about Mr Grimshaw?'

He nodded.

'I believe that you made deliveries to his farm?'

'Aye.'

Bradeley was patently a man of few words.

'When did you last go there?'

Bradeley was quiet, so quiet Bridget Anderton wondered whether she should repeat the question.

But Bradshaw was thinking. 'Would have been late August,' he said eventually. 'The last Tuesday. We have an offer on summer deliveries and he generally goes for it as late as possible.' The hint of a wry smile. 'I generally drop on a Tuesday in that area.'

Bridget Anderton looked at her diary. 'That would be ... the 28th,' she said.

'Aye.'

'How did things seem?'

Bradeley shrugged. 'Same as ever.'

'Nothing out of place?'

Slowly, almost wonderingly, he shook his head.

'Was Mr Grimshaw on his own?'

Bradeley thought for a minute. 'No,' he said. 'The little girl was with him, sitting on her pony.' He smiled. 'Proper little horse-woman, she is.'

'Did you notice anything else?'

Bradeley shook his head, his brief spurt of

200

vigour gone.

'Mr Bradeley,' Bridget said carefully, 'I have to ask you this: did you know that Mr Grimshaw kept money around the house?'

Bradeley was unfazed by the question. 'Don't most people?'

'I'm talking about a large sum of money.'

Bradeley looked confused. 'No,' he protested. 'How would I?'

'He paid your bill in cash.'

'So do most farmers.'

Anderton waited.

'I never thought about it,' he said. 'If I did, I would have thought he'd been to the bank to get the money out, knowing I was coming, like.'

Bridget nodded. Coming from this area, it made sense to her.

Tim Bradeley went red. 'How do you know that, anyway?'

She started to say, 'I'm not at liberty to tell you that,' but slow as Bradeley's thought processes were he was not dull. 'Oh, I've got it,' he said. 'The little girl. It has to be. No one else has ever been there when I've called. Only old Jakob.'

Bridget Anderton stood up, glanced at Bradeley and wondered. He seemed a little too obvious, his answers slightly too pat.

Everyone has faults, she thought, recalling one of Inspector Piercy's mantras. It's up to you to unearth them. So what was Bradeley's?

She fumbled in the dark. 'Where does the animal feed come from?'

He shrugged. 'India mostly. They export to us via Eastern Europe. Really cheap, it is.'

Bridget Anderton stored the fact away as one does an old toy – in the attic. It might be useful and be aired again. Then again, it might not.

Mike had been fiddling with the computer. 'You know you asked me to look up Grimshaw's wife?' he said slowly. 'I've checked her under her maiden name and her married name. We've looked through deaths and marriages, tried out her National Insurance number and tax details. We can't find any record of her for the last eight years. She appears to have vanished into thin air.'

But people don't just vanish into thin air.

And now Joanna was starting to understand why she had had a horrid feeling about this case. Much as she'd fretted they weren't moving forward fast enough now she was almost dreading moving forward at all. She froze for a moment. Then said briskly, 'Ring

Mark Fask. I want to know about those postcards. Tell him to find them.'

She knew now it was vital that they found Avis Grimshaw, that finding *her* would help understand the murder of her husband.

Chapter Eight

It was six o'clock in the evening when Joanna looked up at Korpanski. 'I've had a thought.'

Korpanski was feeling grumpy. It was his night at the gym and he was missing the physical challenge. That and the frustration this case was causing were playing havoc with his emotions.

Korpanski's dark eyes were fixed on her face. 'Whatever you got to say, Jo, it had better be good.'

She grinned at him. 'Don't be so grouchy, Mike. I'm thinking "Morticia Addams", aka Teresa Parnell, and the noise she heard.'

Korpanski regarded her patiently. 'I'm not trying to be over cynical,' he said, 'but as far as me and the spooks go, I think there's only one way someone can know the exact time of death and it sure as hell isn't intuition.'

She leant forward, her face alive and eager. 'I'm not saying I believe in second sight and all that, but I'm always ready to take ideas on board. I think that she might have heard something and translated it into fact. Either that or she knows something more definite.'

Korpanski dipped his head. It was the closest she was going to get to an agreement.

Mark Fask rang back at 7 o'clock, just as Joanna was arranging the following day's briefing.

'I don't know if you want to come over,' he said slowly. 'We've almost finished the search of the farm. I haven't come across any post-cards, though.'

'Is there *anything* to do with Grimshaw's wife?' Joanna said desperately.

'Well, I have come across something that's obviously to do with the mother. A small box containing a wedding ring and one other piece of jewellery, but no postcards.' He paused. 'None of her clothes are here, nothing except the jewellery box. I haven't emptied it yet.' He paused. 'I thought you'd want to be here.'

'We're on our way,' Joanna said.

It was a dull, damp evening, the only splash of colour provided by some chestnut leaves just beginning to turn yellow at their edges. The Ashbourne road was damp and quiet, with little traffic except for a couple of tractors rumbling along slowly. She overtook, resisting the temptation to switch the blue light on and touch ninety along the straight road. She turned off the main road and passed the entrance to the housing estate.

The farmhouse loomed ahead, a vague, square shape in the gloom. She could see the yellow of the lights, fuzzy in the damp haze, the police cars parked along the sides of the lane. She parked behind one and they climbed out. Once outside she could smell the animals that had, until recently, lived and died there. To her, it was a reassuring farmyard smell. She sniffed it appreciatively as she and Korpanski approached the farmhouse. The nearer she got, the more run-down the place looked. Considering the number of personnel she knew to be there, it was quiet, eerily so, and appeared deserted. It was hard to believe that Fask and his team were inside, beavering away, gleaning every last shred of evidence from the crime scene. As she reached the oak tree she could see the backs of the estate houses, all of them lit bright and clear. Grimshaw must have looked out on this scene often. She could hear the wind whispering through the leaves, pick up on the distant bark of a fox and hear a quiet *whoo whoo* of an owl. Even with the bulk of Korpanski at her side she was relieved to reach the back door. This place had a bad atmosphere.

Just as they arrived at the door a spiteful gust of rain caught her, spattering her jacket. Still acclimatised to southern Spain, she shivered. Korpanski gave her a quick look. She couldn't work out whether he was worried she was going down with something or critical at the effect the place was having on her. He said nothing but plodded heavily at her side.

Fask opened the door to them, a good-looking guy with nice brown hair, thick and prone to curling at the ends, his paunch accentuated by the unflattering forensic suit, which billowed around his middle. In his gloved hand was a wooden box, intricately worked with the picture of a bird inlaid on the top. Joanna slipped on some gloves and held out her hands. It felt heavier than she would have expected. It was a nice piece of work, not particularly old, probably dating from around the 1980s, but out of place here, where everything was utilitarian with no attention to beauty or decoration. Joanna reflected that this applied to the farmer's daughter, too. Judy Grimshaw dressed in plain clothes, wore little make up. There was little attention paid to aesthetics here.

Wondering whether this was equivalent to the release of evil from Pandora's box, she placed the box on the dining-room table, raised the lid and was confronted by a small, plastic ballerina in a white net tutu, pirouetting slowly to the strains of 'The Blue Danube'. Joanna watched her for a while, feeling Korpanski's breath against her cheek. She suppressed a grin. This was about as far from the muscular detective as it was possible to be. She allowed the ballerina to perform a few more turns before switching her off and examining the interior. In the top was a tray containing a narrow, flat gold wedding band.

'Where did you find this?' she asked, curious.

'In the attic,' Fask answered. 'It was covered in dust. It must have been there, untouched, for a while. A year at least. The access hole was quite stuck.'

'So Grimshaw could have put it away when his wife left. But she left behind her wedding ring.' Superstitiously Joanna fingered the black pearl on her own finger, then glanced at the hands of the two men. Neither Mark Fask nor Korpanski wore a wedding band. This symbolism obviously meant more to her than to them.

She lifted the top tray out to search underneath, recalling Judy's mimicry of her father's voice.

'Her's in Spain or Portugal. The Algarve. France. You know, spreading her wings.'

'The postcards should be here somewhere', she mused. 'This was the obvious place to store them.'

There was only one item in the bottom of the box: a brooch, studded with turquoise and seed pearls in the shape of a butterfly, tiny rubies or garnets on the end of its antennae. Joanna picked it up and studied it. She didn't know a great deal about antique jewellery but it looked late Victorian or possibly Edwardian. Not hugely expensive but a lovely keepsake. Perhaps an heirloom? Like the box it was a pretty piece. It crossed her mind that Judy might like to keep these mementos of her mother. She might even know where the two objects came from. But one thing puzzled Joanna. By her surmising, she believed that Avis Grimshaw had had an affair. That much her daughter had told her and it explained Mrs Grimshaw's disappearance: she had left with the man. Joanna furrowed her brow and thought as she felt the sharp edges of the pretty butterfly's wings. It was hard to imagine Jakob buying his wife such trinkets, baubles. Both the box and the brooch smacked of the lover.

So why did she leave them behind?

The wedding ring she could understand. It was a symbol of the past she was abandoning. But the box and the butterfly were different. Still, it possibly meant nothing.

She turned her attention back to the box. It was lined with tissue paper of a rather sickly pink, a soft nest to cradle the butterfly. Joanna removed it. And found her clue.

Under the lining was a blue Basildon Bond envelope with the name *Judy* scribbled untidily on the front in black ink. The envelope was sealed. Joanna slit the top with the blade of Korpanski's proffered Swiss Army knife. She slid the one sheet of paper from inside, unfolded it and began to read it out aloud, feeling a dread sickness well up inside her. Just like the feeling she had had as a child when reading the Gothic horror of Edgar Allan Poe tales: *The Masque of the Red Death* or *The Fall of the House of Usher*.

'Judy I expect your wondering what really happened to your ma why she never wrote or telephoned. I knew what she was up to. I knew she was planning on going and that would have split the farm because I had to give her money. I couldn't have that, Jude. This farm has bin in our family for genera,' this had been crossed out and replaced with *ever*. *'Remember when I bought Old Spice? You thought him funny. Well I kept him hungry for a week and I fed er to him and that's where she is. Recycled you could say into her piglets. Doin her bit fo the farm.'*

She could almost hear a throaty chortle from the old farmer. There was a gasp from the two men as she read the note out loud.

'I suppose you've only found this becos i'm dead. I never would have told you if I was still alive but you need to know she isn't having a fine time at all unless there really is a heaven. She's not livin it up nowhere and you so proud of her doin her own thing and that but I tell you Old Spice and is missus ate er.'

Joanna looked at the two men. *'Her's in Spain or Portugal. The Algarve. France. You know, spreading her wings,'* she quoted.

Only not.

The letter was simply signed, *Dad*. No love; no kisses.

Joanna felt really sick now. She looked at Mark Fask. 'Is it possible?' she asked, shocked.

He shrugged. 'Don't ask me,' he said. 'I don't know about man-eating pigs.'

Korpanski had his mouth open. 'Puts you off bacon, Jo.' She forgave him the brave attempt at black humour. It relieved her nausea.

She locked eyes with Korpanski. He knew as well as she did that this put Judy Grimshaw right back in the hot seat. It gave her a powerful motive for wanting her father dead. Revenge. And unlike all the other reasons for Grimshaw's murder, this was a very credible motive. If she'd known of her mother's fate. It all hinged on this; was it possible that Judy had read the letter and resealed the envelope? Or even, whether she'd seen the letter or not, had she suspected that her father's version of events was a lie?

She turned to Fask. 'Did you say the box was covered in dust?'

He nodded.

'And the attic hadn't been entered in years.'

Mark Fask pondered this one for a while.

'Given the general state of the place,' he said, 'it could have been up there undisturbed for two, maybe three years.'

Joanna gave a satisfied smile. Well after Avis Grimshaw had vanished. Had Judy simply bided her time?

Possibly.

She slipped the box and its contents, together with the letter, into a specimen bag. If they found Judy's fingerprints on it they would know she had read it. Joanna suppressed a triumphant smile. She wanted it to be Judy Wilkinson. There is nothing in the world better than fingering the collar of a nasty suspect. At that moment, for the first time since she had taken over the case, she felt optimistic.

'Well, firstly I need to know whether it's possible that a pig could eat an entire human being without leaving any trace,' she said briskly. 'Anyone got the vet's telephone number?'

Fask produced it from his mobile and Joanna dialled up.

Roderick Beeston listened to her request and she could hear puzzlement in his voice as he responded.

'Yes,' he said. 'It is possible. Pigs have extraordinary–'

She interrupted him. 'I take it they would eat a *corpse*, not kill a live person?'

'No. No records of a pig actually *killing* anyone. Leastways, not like that.' Even Beeston sounded vaguely shocked at the thought. 'But they've got a fearful bite, which *might* get infected. I suppose they could kill you like that but no other way. They wouldn't actually *slay* someone. Surely you're not suggesting that Posh and Old Spice...?' His voice trailed away as though he couldn't bear to voice the thought.

'Is there any chance I can see this animal?' Joanna knew it was an impulse but in the past, impulses had served her well.

'Why on earth do you want to *see* the pig? Do you think *he* can tell you who did it?' Beeston had a little too much black humour for her liking.

'Possibly,' Joanna answered. 'You know what I'm like. I have to *see* things for myself.'

'OK. I can meet you in fifteen minutes at Apple Tree Farm, if you like.' He gave her directions with a chuckle. 'The farmer will enjoy showing off his new acquisition, I'm sure. Old Spice is a *fabulous-looking* animal.'

She was reflecting on the odd association between vets and beasts as she drove. She couldn't imagine ever describing a pig as *fabulous*.

The weather was even more dingy by the time she met Roderick Beeston at Apple Tree Farm, a further mile out of Leek on the Ashbourne road. She'd always liked the vet with his dark hair, bright blue eyes and irrepressible, if sometimes over-developed sense of fun. They had worked together on a few cases in this largely rural community and he had played his part in helping her solve each case where an animal was involved; a fierce dog, neglected farm animals, cases of cruelty. He took a torch from the back of his Land Rover and together they approached the farmhouse – cautiously. Most farms have dogs, dogs that are meant to protect their territory, and farm dogs invariably have sharp teeth and nasty tempers, a little like the deceased Ratchet.

The farmer met them at the door, a young man in his early thirties with a mop of blond hair. His face was bright with curiosity as Beeston introduced Joanna.

The farmer smothered his smile. 'And you think the pig can 'elp you?' His voice was good-natured, his face pleasant. 'Fine old Tamworth,' he threw over his shoulder as they crunched across the yard. 'Known Old

Spice for a number of years, I have. Had a few of the little piglets to fatten up myself. Made *lovely* bacon.'

Joanna felt nauseous again. How would this decent and hard-working farmer feel if he knew what had produced the '*lovely* bacon?'

He wagged his finger at her. 'That is, if you hang it for a month or two,' he added. 'Old Jakob always promised I would have Old Spice if anything happened to him.' He shook his head, looking grieved.

Joanna felt even more nauseous at the thought of the meat 'hanging'.

Patently at home with the vet and enjoying Joanna's audience, the farmer continued prattling. 'But I still never thought the old boar'd end up in *my* backyard. Jakob was *devoted* to the animal. Sit there for hours, he would, just leanin' over the sty door, lookin' at him, admiring him, like. I imagined Jakob would easily outlive the pig. I'd watch 'em and think what a pair they made.'

Indeed, Joanna thought. What a pair. Murderer and evidence-eater. But the real question, hiding behind this musing, was, what bearing did this new development have on the murder of Jakob Grimshaw? If any?

But surely, she argued to herself, it *must*

have a bearing. It *had* to have one. Serious crime begets serious crime. The farmer died because he had killed his wife and disposed of her body in a barbaric way.

Tussling with her thoughts, Joanna peered over the sty and met a pair of piggy little eyes fringed with ginger eyelashes. The pig looked back at her and blinked, snorted once, twice, kept his gaze on her face. She stared back and was reminded of the sharp and devious intelligence of Napoleon in *Animal Farm*. She asked Beeston the question again, in a slightly different form. 'Could a pig *really* devour an entire human body?'

'Every last bit of it,' he said cheerfully, while the farmer eavesdropped, confused. 'Even the femur,' Beeston continued. 'They've got *fantastic* jaws.' There was a note of admiration in his voice before he too looked unsure. 'But surely old Grimshaw's body was found, wasn't it?'

'I can't tell you any more,' she said stiffly, depressed at the sight of Old Spice snuffling in the dirt, snorting like the man-eater she now knew him to be.

She left the farm but didn't go home straight away. The day's developments had unsettled her. Instead, she drove back to Prospect Farm, sealed off now by Fask's team, who had gone home for the night leaving only a lonely PC on solitary watch. It was chilly; autumn had arrived. The evenings were dingy and dull making a fireside – particularly with Matthew – an attractive proposition. She leant against the gate and stood peering over. What a dreadfully barbaric and sinister place it was, the scene of two murders. At her side, she could just see the backs of the estate houses, hear the sounds of modern urban living, strains of music, the ceaseless chatter of a television, doors opening and closing, laughter, the tinny electronic tune of a mobile phone ringing. The contrast between the two civilisations had never been more apparent.

Chapter Nine

Friday, 21st September. 8 a.m.

Mike met her with some welcome news. 'We've had a call from a Mrs Barnes,' he said. 'Hilary Barnes. Number 9. She says she thinks she heard something.'

She sank down on her seat. 'What? When?'

'On Tuesday,' he said, 'the 11th, mid-morning. Around eleven.'

'The same day and time that our friend Mrs Parnell mentioned.'

He nodded.

'So what exactly *did* Mrs Barnes hear?'

'Sounds of a struggle.'

She frowned. 'Why didn't she tell us before, Mike? It's almost two weeks ago.'

'She says she's only just put two and two together, realised what it was.' His eyes, like hers, were full of doubt.

'OK. We'll go round and see her after the briefing.'

Half an hour later she was facing the eager faces of her investigating team and filling them in on the latest developments.

'You understand this puts Grimshaw's daughter right into the centre of the picture,' she said, 'but there is also the man her mother is *alleged* to have had an affair with. We don't know whether it's true or not. Or who he is. We only have Mrs Wilkinson's word for it. She says her father told her, but obviously he would have a clear motive for wanting a rational explanation for his wife's disappearance if anyone asked. However, if what Grimshaw claimed was true and there is such a man, if he had his suspicions that

218

Jakob had murdered his wife he could be a suspect for Grimshaw's murder.'

She frowned and everyone in the room could see the obvious flaw in this latest theory. There had been too much of a time lapse between the two crimes for them to rely on this. Grimshaw's wife had disappeared eight years ago. 'I suppose it's possible that Mr X only found out recently,' she mused. 'Or perhaps he only gained proof recently. We don't know.'

It struck her that they didn't *know* anything apart from the fact that Grimshaw was dead along with his wife. Both murdered. Had one crime born the other? It seemed a logical conclusion.

She returned to the area plan. 'And we must still consider the inhabitants of the Prospect Farm Estate as well as anyone else who might have a connection. Steve and Kathleen Weston.' She looked at Korpanski and opened her mouth. 'I've remembered,' she said, clapping her hand to her forehead.

Korpanski frowned at her. 'Remembered what?'

'Why Kathleen Weston looked familiar.'

Korpanski waited.

'I was driving down St Edward's Street last summer some time. It was a boiling hot day and the traffic had stopped. It was piling up a bit. I wondered what was going on so I pulled over. And it was her. Mrs Weston. Standing in the middle of the road. She'd stopped her car, put her hazards on. A cat had been run over – a ginger thing – and she was retrieving the body.' She recalled the woman cradling the dead cat, lying it gently on the back seat of her car while around her the motorists watched, confused and un-characteristically obedient at the strange tableau being played out in front of their eyes. 'Blow me, Mike,' she said, 'if I didn't see flowers at the site a day or two later. Can you believe it? I actually read the message on the cellophane. "You poor thing," it said.

'And it was her?'

'Yes,' she said. 'I'm sure. The name on the flowers was Kathleen.'

She turned back to the assembled officers, who were well used to asides between the inspector and her sergeant.

'Mrs Weston is a fanatical animal lover who objected to the state Jakob Grimshaw kept his animals in. So...' she wanted them to realise this, 'the inhabitants of the estate begin to look a little more involved in the farm and the farmer. Charlotte Frankwell, divorced wife of our property developer...'

She paused for a minute. 'I can't see why she would want the farmer dead unless it was, perhaps, hoping for an increase in the value of her property. Peter Mostyn, who bought the field beyond the farm without planning permission for a knockdown price, and is in financial trouble since his divorce. Mr Gabriel Frankwell, who stood to gain a huge amount of money if he could disrupt the farm and buy the land. He was probably pretty furious with Grimshaw for sneakily selling off a field to one of his neighbours and is anxious – no desperate,' she corrected, 'to leave the country.' She narrowed her eyes. 'And he doesn't have much time to be messed around, which might have made him flip.' She stopped for a moment, pondering. She could well imagine Gabriel Frankwell to be a man with a temper who would not appreciate being thwarted. She could picture him being a killer. Cold-hearted and pitiless. So how could she reconcile that image with a man who wanted to be present at his child's birth? All killers have their Achilles' heels, their soft spots, their little tendernesses.

She resumed her talk. 'We have Hilary Barnes, who apparently heard some suspicious noises that might have been the sound of the crime being committed, but she took a few days to come forward. Why? Why the delay? Teresa Parnell, who is trying to convince us through her supernatural powers that she knows *exactly* when the crime was committed and it does appear to tally with what Hilary Barnes said.' She eyed the rim of sceptical faces. 'So if you believe in the supernatural or collusion or they both really did hear something – which is quite feasible given the sustained attack on Mr Grimshaw – we have the time and date of the murder. Just bear in mind,' she warned, 'that if we go down this path *anyone* who has an alibi for midmorning on Tuesday the 11th of September is innocent.' She let the words sink in before adding unnecessarily, 'It's a big assumption to take and takes out our chief suspect, the woman with a dual motive – revenge and inheritance.' She eyed the officers. 'Let's look at the rest of the inhabitants of the estate. In number 8 we have the Watkins family: Mum, Dad, three children. Dawn?' She looked across at Dawn Critchlow.

'Nothing there, Joanna,' she responded. 'Very much an average family.'

'OK, so we'll discount them for the time being. And in number 6 we have the Chappells, whom I understand are on an extended cruise of the Mediterranean and have been away since the beginning of September. So we can discount them too. What about number 2?'

DS Hannah Beardmore spoke up. 'I interviewed Mrs Probert,' she said. 'Faria. She's a belly dancer.' A couple of the junior officers sniggered and Joanna caught the comment, *Wish I'd interviewed her* and so on. She let it pass. Police work needed a touch of humour.

'She's what you'd expect,' Hannah continued in her soft voice, her hair shining around her face almost like a halo. 'Flirty, a bit of a sexpot, I suppose, with a very quiet husband who barely said a word all the time I was there. He seemed to agree with everything she said.' She wrinkled her brow as though trying to find the right words. 'I think Faria is a bit of a firecracker. No more Turkish,' she continued, 'than I am. I caught a distinctly Brummie accent when she was off her guard. She could cause trouble in a marriage, I would think, leading someone on.' Her pause and flush were barely perceptible, the stillness in the room even less so. Hannah's husband, Roger, had had an ill advised affair with a woman at his work.

Hannah had become unhappy, quiet and pale. But recently they had had a holiday together and she was almost back to her old self. Almost. The scars were obviously still there.

Hannah resumed her briefing. 'But Grimshaw was surely beyond that sort of temptation? So I can't see the fact that Faria was a flirt would have any bearing on our investigation.' She screwed up her face. 'I mean, this isn't a sex crime, is it?'

Most heads shook a negative.

'She looked *completely* disinterested when I asked her about the farmer. I got the impression that she hardly knew him. And the same goes for her husband.'

'Right.' Joanna flashed her a smile. 'Thanks. This helps to clarify things. Narrow the field. So far,' she continued, 'we have little to go on. We don't even know the *day* let alone the *time* of Jakob's death.' She frowned. 'Not for certain. As it was obviously days if not a week before the body was found and Jakob basically led a quiet, isolated life, neither pathological evidence nor neighbour sightings have been very helpful. I'm going to make the usual plea to you – that we keep our investigations going in every corner...' She stared at the upturned faces, Timmis and McBrine, Hesketh-Brown, Bridget Anderton, Dawn Critchlow, Hannah Beardmore and the rest, and resumed her lecture. '...Every stone lifted up and peered beneath. We intend inviting Judy Wilkinson to come down to be finger-printed.' She gave one of her bland smiles, 'to exclude her dabs. We found no finger-prints at all on the box, which is strange. Mrs Grimshaw's should have been there, Jakob's and possibly his daughter's, so a couple of years ago it was wiped clean and placed in the attic.'

To accumulate dust.

'What about Farrell's Animal Feeds?' She addressed Bridget Anderton.

PC Bridget Anderton took her time before replying. 'The boss, Robert Flaxon, seemed annoyed by my presence. He was quite angry.'

'And the driver?'

'Tim Bradeley,' Bridget said, thoughtfully. 'He appeared above board.' She recalled Bradeley's blunt features and steady grey eyes. 'I didn't get the feeling there was any-thing there. He knew the money was there, though whether he realised how much I couldn't say. But...'

Joanna waited but PC Anderton would

not be hurried.

'I found out,' she said, 'that the feeds are imported from Eastern Europe, sourced from India. Sorry,' she said apologetically. 'It's probably got nothing to do with anything.'

Joanna was inclined to agree with her.

'I was just surprised, that's all,' Anderton mused to herself. Having to import animal food seemed strange to her.

And now it was time for action. Joanna charged the officers with specific duties, and as they filed out, she turned to face Korpanski.

He was leaning forwards, staring into space and running his hands through his hair, a well-known precursor to bad news.

'If she did find the box,' he said gloomily, 'why leave it there, in the farmhouse? Even Judy would have known it would lead us straight back to her.'

So this was what he had been brooding about. She shrugged. 'No idea.' She sensed what was wrong. 'Look, Mike.' She was finding this awkward. 'If you don't want to be there when your old school friend is questioned, it's OK.'

His face was tough and a blank. 'I've got no objections.'

'She wasn't a sort of...?'

'No,' he said, 'nothing.' His dark eyes held a plea. 'I just find it difficult,' he burst out. 'She was simply a hanger-on. But I feel...'

'Spit it out, Mike.'

'I don't know,' he said, 'sort of responsible.'

'Oh.' She decided then that he would be no use at her side. 'I'll interview her with one of the others.'

But Judy Wilkinson was playing hard to get.

Joanna tried her mobile number and got an answering service.

She realised she felt an antipathy towards this woman, recognised that it was irrational and certainly not professional, and did her best to leave a neutral message.

'Mrs Wilkinson, it's Detective Inspector Joanna Piercy here. We need to talk to you...' She paused, 'again, as new evidence has turned up.' She left her direct number plus her mobile number and rang off. At the moment there was no evidence to charge her on. They could keep it informal for now. Stick to fingerprinting her 'for purposes of exclusion'. If Judy Wilkinson was innocent, she had just lost her father. If the police were too heavy-handed, the Press would be down on them like the proverbial ton of bricks, quoting police harassment. No she had to play this one right by the book.

Korpanski wafted the piece of paper containing Hilary Barnes's message in front of her.

'OK,' she said wearily. 'I'd better go round.'

Hilary Barnes proved to be an energetic-looking woman in her fifties with a business-like air. She led them into a palely carpeted living room and motioned for them to sit down on a brown leather sofa before sitting down herself, her eyes round with nosiness.

'I'm so sorry,' she apologised. 'When I heard the noises I didn't realise what it was. I thought it was just the farmer and the animals shuffling around.'

'Let's start at the beginning,' Joanna suggested. 'What date are we talking about?'

'Tuesday,' Hilary Barnes said. 'It was Tuesday the 11th. I know because my husband went away on the 9th for a few days – he works for Wedgwood – so I was alone in the house. I normally put the radio on but that morning I was going to visit my daughter in Leigh-on-Sea for a couple of days and wanted to concentrate on what clothes I was taking, so the house was quiet. I was in the bedroom, packing.'

'And?' prompted Joanna.

'At around eleven I fancied a cup of coffee so was boiling up the kettle in the kitchen when I heard a shout from the farmyard.'

Behind the glasses there was apology mixed with guilt. 'It wasn't unusual,' she protested, 'to hear noises. The farmer, Jakob, he was *always* shouting at the cattle. And they'd moo away back.' Her lips twitched. 'Or baa or whatever. The farm made a lot of noise, always a dog barking and things.' She gave a vague smile.

'I did look out of the window but I saw nothing.'

'Do you mind?' Joanna stood up.

Hilary Barnes led her into the kitchen, which was at the back of the house. It was incredibly neat. Cream units, glazed cabinets, terracotta floor. Bang up to the minute. Joanna crossed to the large window that overlooked an equally tidy garden; patio furniture, decking, an immaculate lawn bordered by a row of apple trees almost bent double under the fruit – the wet summer had resulted in a bumper harvest – and beyond that stood the dry stone wall, the epicentre of the murder investigation. Through the leaves of the trees she could just make out the corner of the cow shed and the muddied concrete path at its side. To the left, the sheep were grazing in the field, unconscious survivors of the tragedy. But Hilary Barnes's house was at the top of the estate. The farmhouse was invisible from here, as was the actual spot where Grimshaw's body had been found. Unless she had looked out of her kitchen window at the precise moment Grimshaw had come round the corner of the cowshed, she couldn't have seen him. Joanna felt a sharp stab of disappointment. Hilary Barnes struck her as a reliable witness. She trusted her much more than Mrs Parnell. And it would have been good to learn the time and date of the murder. It would narrow the field and move their investigations forward like nothing else.

Hilary moved to her side, agitated. 'I was standing right here,' she said, 'when I heard the cry.' Her face was stricken. She believed she had heard her neighbour's cry for help and done nothing.

Joanna was piecing together Matthew's version of the forensic sequence, trying to picture the skinny shape of the man, old and bowed well before his time, pursued by...?

That cry would surely have been the result of the initial blow, the one that broke one bone and displaced another. *The blow that*

230

winded him.

'Then what?'

Hilary Barnes was frowning, struggling to recall everything. 'Nothing for a while,' she said, 'just some banging and clattering. I thought I heard the barn doors open. Honestly,' she was appealing to Joanna not to blame her for failing to interpret the significance of what she had heard, 'there was nothing out of the ordinary apart from the shout.' She moved away from the window, looking shaken.

'I boiled the kettle,' she said, 'and went back upstairs to my bedroom.'

'Would you mind?' Joanna asked politely.

'No, no, not at all. Follow me.'

Mrs Barnes led her into a large master bedroom with an en suite bathroom beyond. Joanna realised at once that the room was at the front of the house; the window overlooked the road. Not over the farmyard.

'Did you hear anything more?'

'Just grunts and scrabbling.'

'Barking? Did you hear the dog, Ratchet, barking?'

For the first time Hilary Barnes looked confused, as though she didn't know the answer. 'I can't remember,' she said slowly. 'It would have been natural to have heard him. He was a very *noisy* dog,' she said.

'So when did he *stop* being noisy?'

'I don't know.' Ms Barnes was frowning. She didn't have an answer to this one. 'It's easier to remember a noise than the *lack* of it.'

It was true. Korpanski was looking even gloomier.

Joanna resumed the questioning. 'Did you look across to the farm later?'

Mrs Barnes shook her head. 'I didn't,' she said. 'Now I wish I had. I might have saved the poor man's life.'

'Who knows,' Joanna said. 'You might have put yourself in danger.'

Hilary Barnes looked appalled. 'You don't think the killer will come back?'

Joanna shook her head. 'No. No, I don't think he will. Anyway, there is a police guard on the farm so,' she smiled, 'for the moment you're safer than ever.'

Hilary Barnes looked mollified.

'Did you go out into the garden later on that day?'

Hilary Barnes shook her head. 'No. I set off for my daughter's early afternoon.'

'Did you see or hear anything else?'

Again Mrs Barnes shook her head regretfully.

'Did you notice a car or hear one at any time that morning?'

Again Mrs Barnes shook her head. 'No. Not particularly.'

'Do you know Mrs Parnell?' Joanna asked abruptly.

Unexpectedly, Hilary Barnes looked embarrassed. 'You mean from number 4?'

'Yes.'

'Not well.' She spoke stiffly.

Behind Joanna, Korpanski cleared his throat and shifted his feet. She got the message. They were both thinking the same thing. 'Interested in the occult, Mrs Barnes?'

'A little.'

So was this a clumsy plot the two women had hatched to divert attention away from the real time of the murder?

Could be. Why? As they'd obviously been there at the time. Had Mrs Barnes confided in Mrs Parnell and the medium used the information?

'Did you mention hearing this disturbance to Mrs Parnell?'

'I don't think so. Why?'

Joanna decided to keep this rogue card up her sleeve. 'It doesn't matter. Thank you for getting in touch.'

'Do you think I did hear the murder?'

Joanna met the pale eyes. 'It's possible,'

she said. 'Quite possible. You may have given us the breakthrough we needed.'

Outside, she addressed Korpanski. 'Don't tell me,' she warned. 'If eleven o'clock on Tuesday the 11th of September *was* the time of the assault, our chief suspect has an alibi.'

'Unbreakable. Judy Wilkinson works at a doctor's surgery. She was seeing patients all that morning. I've seen the patient printout. She had half an hour for lunch from twelve thirty to one. There wouldn't have been time for her to drive out here, take fifteen minutes to murder her dad and then get back for her afternoon's work. It simply isn't possible. If our two witnesses are correct and that's the time of the murder, Judy Wilkinson's in the clear.'

'Bollocks,' Joanna said.

She finally got hold of a snappy-sounding Judy Wilkinson at precisely ten thirty.

'What is it?' she asked. 'I'm in the middle of my morning surgery.'

'We need to interview you again,' Joanna responded calmly, 'and fingerprint you to exclude your prints from the crime scene.'

No need to mention the box – not at this point, anyway. 'When is it convenient for you to call in here?'

'I finish at five. I can be with you for five thirty, if that's all right, Detective Inspector Piercy.'

Joanna felt her face and voicebox tighten. 'Fine,' she said. 'See you then,' and put the phone down with a crash.

Most people believe that police work is impersonal. Little do they realise it can get very personal indeed.

With a sigh she picked up the next message on her desk. Colclough.

Chief Superintendent Arthur Colclough. He of the bulldog jowls, all-seeing eyes, scary intuition and ultimately benevolent, paternalistic character. He was like a terrifying but fair headmaster and whenever Joanna was summoned to see him she felt like a fourteen-year-old schoolgirl caught smoking behind the bike sheds. Teetering on the very edge of retirement and bliss in the sun, Colclough had a holiday home in Cyprus, at which he entertained all the family including his adored granddaughter, Catherine, for increasing periods of time.

Joanna faced him warily.

He began nicely enough. 'How are your investigations progressing?'

'Slowly, sir.'

'Any sign of a breakthrough?' She knew he hated the tabloid talk as much as she did but she smothered a grin. 'Nothing confirmed and certain, sir, but we do have a few lines of inquiry we're exploring.'

'Ah.' Colclough eyebrows could have been sold on the Internet as a wig they were so long and thick, curling and black. It made him look a formidable character – which he was.

He cleared his throat noisily. 'I understand congratulations are in order, Piercy.'

It felt puerile to blush but blush she did. 'Yes, sir.'

'And when is the wedding to be?'

'December – January – not sure yet. We haven't booked.'

'I see,' Colclough said. 'And what effect will this have on your career aspirations, Piercy?'

'None, sir.'

'You know that there's been talk of promoting you to chief inspector?' He smiled. 'Chief Inspector Levin.'

'I shan't change my name, sir. I intend to remain Piercy.'

Colclough looked faintly disapproving. 'I see,' he said. 'One of these...' he paused, 'feminist types.'

She was bound to protest. 'No ... sir.'

The pale eyes twinkled. 'It's OK, Piercy. I was only pulling your leg – knowing you'd rise to the bait.'

She took a risk then. 'And if it's all the same with you – sir – I like being out in the field. A desk job would depress and bore me.'

Colclough gave her a real smile then. Warm and kindly. He stood up, threaded round his desk and patted her shoulder awkwardly, like a shy grandfather. 'Good for you, Piercy,' he said warmly. 'We need more people like you.'

Judy Wilkinson was at least prompt. Bang on five thirty Joanna's desk phone rang and Judy's presence was announced.

She looked sly, Joanna thought, and prepared herself for trouble.

'Why do you want to fingerprint me?' she demanded. 'Should I be getting a lawyer? Am *I* a suspect?'

'A lawyer won't be necessary. We simply need to exclude your prints from our crime scene,' Joanna explained smoothly.

'And then will they be destroyed?'

Great, Joanna thought, Human Rights as well.

'Naturally.'

Mrs Wilkinson looked sceptical.

'Tell me, Judy,' she said, conspiratorially, as though they were the best of friends, 'what do you *really* think happened to your mother?'

Grimshaw's daughter looked taken aback but not before Joanna had read a spark of something in her pale eyes. Deceit?

'You know about my mother,' the woman snapped.

'Do we?'

This time Joanna was *certain* there was a level of duplicity in the woman's eyes.

'What are you saying?'

Joanna could *sense* the unease – almost *smell* it.

'You've no evidence as to what happened to your mother,' Joanna pointed out, 'apart from your father's word.'

For the first time, Joanna saw Mrs Wilkinson lose her control. She was struggling to hold back her tears.

'Why don't you sit down,' she said gently. 'I'll get you a cup of tea.'

It was like peeling back layer after layer of an onion. Tears and a strong smell.

When she returned with some tea one of

the Specials had brewed, Judy was openly sobbing. 'I couldn't understand,' she said, 'why Mum never ever contacted me. Why did she leave without a word?'

It was the old chestnut of abandonment.

'So?' Joanna prompted gently.

The woman's eyes filled with tears again. 'I found a letter,' she whispered. 'I read what he'd done to her. I knew he'd killed her and...' The look of horror on her face could not have been affected by even the best actress. It was all there, the round whites of the eyes, the open mouth, the sharp intake of breath. Straight out of a Hammer House horror movie.

Joanna waited for the woman to continue.

It took all of five seconds. 'I didn't kill him,' she said in a low voice. 'I didn't murder my father.'

Joanna was silent.

'I didn't do it,' she said again.

'When did you find this out?'

'Summer before last,' the woman whispered. 'Dad was out in the fields. I'd come over to visit him but was waiting a while.' She gulped. 'I thought I'd look for the postcards. I found the box and – well, you know the rest.'

'Did you confront him?'

Judy shook her head. 'No. I stuck the envelope back up and put it in the jewellery box. I didn't want him to know I'd found it. I just watched him and wondered how he could have done such a thing. I found it difficult to visit him after that.'

'Did you tell anyone?'

She looked up. 'No.'

'You're sure about that?'

'Yes, absolutely.'

It seemed the truth.

'Why didn't you tell the police?'

For the first time the woman looked uncertain. 'I don't know,' she said. 'I don't know. I wasn't sure if I wanted my dad to... I couldn't bear the thought of him going to prison. But ... my mum...' She looked stricken.

'I think you should get yourself a solicitor, Judy,' she said gently, 'before we go any further. But I think it would be a good idea for you to write down your movements between, say, Sunday the 9th of September and Thursday the 13th.'

Judy gulped and nodded.

'You're free to go now.'

When she stood up for a moment Joanna thought the woman's legs would not hold her. She staggered then made her way towards the door, paused for a moment, then bolted.

Joanna listened to her footsteps tapping swiftly along the corridor. Fleeing. Then she sat and thought.

It was nearly ten o'clock when she finally arrived home. Matthew was dozing over a medical journal, slumped across the couch. He murmured something as she walked in and kissed the top of his head. He struggled to sit up. 'Hi, Jo.'

She felt a surge of warmth towards him. 'Hello, you,' she said, slipping her shoes off and sitting down next to him.

He studied her face. 'You're looking pleased with yourself. Are you cracking the case, Inspector Piercy?'

'Maybe,' she said. But all the while she was warning herself, just because you *want* someone to be guilty does not necessarily mean they are. Moderation, Piercy, she exhorted herself. Moderation.

Matthew cleared his throat. 'Do you want the bad news or the good news first?'

'The good,' she said, 'of course.'

'There's a bottle of Chablis chilling in the fridge.'

She sank down beside him. 'That *is* good

news,' she agreed. 'And the bad?'

'You mother wants you to ring her,' he said, 'whatever time you get in.'

'About the wedding?' she asked warily.

He nodded.

'Did you tell her we'd more or less sorted it?'

'I did. To be honest, Jo...' He disappeared into the kitchen, returning with a small silver tray bearing two wineglasses and the promised bottle of wine, 'I think she approves. But there is one sticking point.'

She already knew what it would be. 'Don't tell me,' she said. 'She wants Lara to be bridesmaid.' She sipped the wine slowly, eyeing him over the rim of the wineglass. 'Well, I've been thinking about it. My sister's daughter is nine years old and a law unto herself. I'm going to ask her direct. If she wants to be a bridesmaid she can be. If not, I won't have one.' She took a sip of the wine. 'I take it Eloise wouldn't be seen dead in a puffy pink dress carrying my flowers?'

Matthew suppressed a smile. 'I think that's correct.'

'So whatever my beloved mother says that's what I'm sticking to. She must leave it to us.'

She took a long draught of the wine, braced herself and picked up the telephone.

Chapter Ten

Saturday, 22nd September

She was in early, Korpanski too. No briefing today, just the two of them, working doggedly through the statements, trying to piece together what was fact and what was carefully contrived fiction.

Korpanski spoke first. 'So Judy admitted she knew what had happened to her mother?'

'Yes.'

'When? I wonder.'

'Sorry?' She spoke lazily. Last night had turned into a later night than she had planned and she felt distinctly sleep-deprived.

Korpanski, it seemed, did not.

'Two summers ago.'

'Mmm.' Korpanski absorbed the fact. 'Let's try another angle,' he suggested energetically. 'Let's look at the man Mrs Grimshaw was supposed to have had an affair with.'

'Except she didn't have an affair, did she?

That was obviously a fantasy Grimshaw dreamt up to explain Judy's mother's disappearance.'

'OK, OK.' He held his hands up. 'Maybe.' His eyes were on her. 'So why did her husband kill her then?'

'I don't know.' Joanna was exasperated. 'Maybe she didn't feed the cows right or knocked the milk churn over. Or maybe he needed the pigs fed. Maybe he was just fed up with her. There's all sorts of reasons why a man might kill his wife. Anyway, Mike,' she continued, 'you're getting side-tracked. We're not investigating the murder of Judy's mother. We *know* who killed *her*.'

Mike stood up, agitated. 'Do we?'

'We have a written confession from old Jakob himself,' Joanna pointed out. Then she was silent. Korpanski had a point.

'Handwriting?' He didn't need to say anything more.

It was worth checking.

In all cases there is a moment when you start hearing answers to questions. There is no warning. It often comes quite out of the blue. A small statement that seems to unlock a door. A door that leads to a room in which there is a window that overlooks a completely new vista. Perhaps it is a chance encounter. Putting the right question at the right time in the right way to the right person. Perhaps not. Dogged determination, checking, checking, believing no one, taking no one at face value, waiting and moving in the right direction at the right time.

These are what solve cases. All of that plus the *little bit of luck* so frequently sung about in musicals.

They drove out towards the Ashbourne road, both pondering the issues.

Mike turned into the now familiar Prospect Farm Estate.

Their first call of the day was Teresa Parnell.

The apparent collusion between her and her neighbour was not a coincidence. In fact, police take an awful lot of convincing to believe in coincidence at all.

She met them at the door in a faded pink towelling dressing gown and grubby beige fur slippers. Without make-up, she looked less like a mystic medium and more a tired, middle-aged woman.

But she was slippery to deal with. The straighter the questions put to her the more devious she became.

Joanna opened the questioning. 'You seem to believe that Mr Grimshaw was murdered on the Tuesday, at around eleven. But all you actually heard was some noise.' She met Teresa's eyes, tried to read what deviousness was behind them. 'What made you hone in on that particular date and that time?'

Mrs Parnell looked positively sly. 'The forces.'

'What forces?' Mike burst out, scepticism making his voice sound harsh, which only made Teresa look smug. 'If *you* don't understand,' she said in a mocking voice, 'there's no point me explaining.' She folded her hands across her lap.

'Try me.' Joanna's voice was low and controlled. Anyone who knew her even superficially would have recognised the danger signs. Like a cobra, she was at her most still in the seconds before she struck.

'It was an auspicious time,' Teresa said strangely.

Don't give me 'the stars were in Jupiter,' Joanna thought. Per-lease.

'I was in the front room, in a trance,' Teresa Parnell continued, wrapping the dressing gown tightly around her, 'when I was aware of an evil, violent presence.'

Both Joanna and Korpanski were well aware that Teresa Parnell's sitting room faced the road, across and beyond which was the farm.

'Were you sitting or standing?'

'Sitting,' Teresa said. 'One can't enter into a trance-like state–'

'Did you actually *hear* anything?' Joanna interrupted impatiently.

'A rush of wind as though a presence was moving within my soul.'

Joanna hoped that only she had heard Korpanski's muttered, *'Garbage.'*

She could have thought of a few interesting alternative interpretations to this rush of wind but resisted the temptation to smirk.

'Carry on,' she said.

'Later on in the week I was talking to my friend, Mrs Barnes,' Teresa said. 'And I realised that she had experienced a similar feeling.' She gave a slightly proud smile. 'We're in tune, you know.'

'Harrumph.' Joanna cleared her throat and squirreled the fact away. So Hilary Barnes and Teresa Parnell had swapped their experiences, which made coincidence fly straight out of the window.

'Anyway,' Teresa resumed, 'it was more than a week later that we could translate these feelings into what had probably been the very moment of the poor man's murder. God rest his soul.'

Joanna eyed her curiously. Surely the last thing a medium wanted was for a soul to rest? Didn't the entire practice *rely* on souls wandering around communicating, restless and searching?

'Can you remember any other sounds – a car, the dog barking, the animals?'

Teresa Parnell shook her head. 'No. Only that, sounds of someone shouting, a scuffle and that dreadful, icy wind.'

To emphasise her words she wrapped the pink dressing gown around her and gave a theatrical shudder.

'Is there anything else you can add to your statement, Mrs Parnell?'

Teresa shook her head sadly. 'I wish I could help,' she said. She put her large, bony hands in front of her, wringing them in a gesture of distress.

'So – genuine or not?' Joanna asked Korpanski when they were safely outside.

He shrugged. 'I haven't a clue,' he said.

Joanna stood still for a moment. 'If she did really hear something,' she said, 'it leaves Judy in the clear. She has an unshakeable alibi for the entire Tuesday morning. If, on the other hand, Teresa Parnell is leading us astray, deliberately or not, we can keep Judy Grimshaw as our chief suspect.' She turned to face Mike. 'My instinct is that we should keep a very open mind.'

He grinned at her. 'Suits me,' he said.

They crossed the road. 'We're missing something, Mike,' she said suddenly, half-way across, 'some connection.' She looked up and down the peaceful estate. 'Some underbelly of this little bit of suburbia. It all looks so peaceful, so innocent, so...'

He was watching her. 'I know what you mean,' he said.

'Someone,' she said softly, 'is playing a game with us. The question is, who?'

Korpanski said nothing. He gave a little snort.

As it was a Saturday, most of the inhabitants of the Prospect Farm Estate were at home, catching up with house-chores, cleaning the car, polishing windows, pruning bushes.

Gabriel Frankwell, in jeans and a navy polo shirt, was polishing his Porsche Boxster with a vigour that made him look a much younger man. Though Joanna knew he'd seen them, he ignored them until they were right behind him.

'Inspector,' he said. 'You made me jump.'

Was nothing real about this man? She studied the suave face, white-toothed smile and smooth tan, and decided probably not.

Except it seemed that he did feel some devotion for Lucia. She looked closer at the man. He was older than she had first thought and around his eyes there were sharp lines of tiredness. She had a sudden insight. He was sick of all this. He simply wanted Elysium, his mistress and their child, in the bright sunshine of Brazil.

She glanced at the car. 'You've had the scratch resprayed,' she commented.

Frankwell's fingers instinctively stroked the paintwork. 'I wouldn't have been able to sell it otherwise,' he said regretfully.

So the Porsche was to go as well. He really was scampering away from the UK as fast and as completely as he could.

'Quite,' she said and followed him indoors.

'Explain to me,' she asked when they were sitting on his leather sofa, cups of coffee in their hands, 'just how this land deal works?'

Frankwell's eyes flickered. 'It's complicated,' he said.

Joanna leant forward, placing her coffee mug on the glass coaster provided. 'Try me.'

'OK.' Frankwell seemed resigned. 'Initially, I bought the acreage on which this estate is built without planning permission. It's a chance you take and I was able to buy it substantially cheaper than if I had waited for the planning applications to be granted.' He gave her a smile that had a tinge of sadness about it. 'I obtained planning permission and built the houses. To be honest, it was all a bit speculative. The estate...' he smiled, 'or development, as I called it, is four miles out of Leek. I wasn't sure how that might impact on the price. Also, I was aware that at the time Mr Grimshaw defined himself as a farmer and was unlikely to sell the farm in his lifetime. Even beyond that there was a daughter who *might* have wanted to farm. Naturally, all this would also make a difference. People who've paid a lot for a smart, modern house, don't, in general, want to overlook a fairly scruffy farm.' He gave a wry smile and Joanna realised that the purchasers of the properties had possibly made Gabriel Frankwell's life difficult – to say the least.

'All this,' Frankwell continued, 'might have made the houses difficult to sell.'

'And were they?'

Frankwell gave her a guarded look. 'They didn't exactly fly out,' he admitted.

It was Korpanski's turn now to put the

thumbscrews on. 'So why try to buy the extra land?'

'Because I was offered it for an advantageous price.' He gave another engaging grin. 'I'm a property speculator. It would have been against my nature to have turned it down. The houses on Prospect Farm sold eventually, which isn't bad considering this has not been a good year for the housing market. Even in Leek, which has become quite the place to live. I got a good price for them and lately Mr Grimshaw had told me, in confidence, that he was ready to retire from farming. Naturally, the farm would have come up for sale. I could buy that too, and then the land, with planning permission, of course, would have been worth many times what I paid for it.'

'Really?'

Frankwell nodded. 'I was fairly sure I'd eventually get planning permission for the whole lot,' he admitted. 'The farm had been the main stumbling block and the access from the far side of the farm, as there's a small stream there. The cost of living in Brazil is a fraction of what it is here and I could have managed the project easily with a few business trips a year. I could, I suppose,' he said disdainfully, 'have continued with my building interests over there but the law is very different and the property market not quite as...' he hesitated, choosing the word carefully, 'stable as it is over here. I think it perfectly possible I would have retired and simply spent time with my new wife and child.' There was something both sad and cynical in his voice as he spoke the next few sentences. 'I was very busy when my own daughter, Phoebe, was young. I missed out on her early years. She's growing up fast.' Another twisted smile. 'I don't want to make that mistake again.'

And now Joanna found herself wondering about him. Was he a big-hearted daddy or a conniving and greedy businessperson capable of murder for gain?

She stared at him, searching his face for clues, caught none and tried another tack.

'Were you aware that Mr Grimshaw had sold another plot of land to a private buyer?'

Frankwell look astonished. 'What?' he said. 'Where?'

'The field immediately to the right of the farmhouse.'

Frankwell was silent for a while, chewing this new fact over. Then he said, 'The double-crossing...'

Joanna felt sure the expletive would have

been insulting.

'Would that have that altered your purchase of the land?'

Frankwell spluttered. 'Yes it bloody well would. It would have scuppered my plans completely.' He looked furious.

A different person, eyes bulging, face distorted. Not Mr Charming any more.

How easily the mask had slipped.

If he had known about the land deal he could have... What? Committed murder? Out of fury?

'Who bought it?' he asked.

'I'm not at liberty to tell you but it's in the public domain.'

She stood up. It was time to go.

The Westons were out, the house locked up and dark, but they were in luck with Peter Mostyn. He opened the door to them, looking strangely pleased to see them.

'Inspector Piercy, Sergeant Korpanski,' he said. 'What can I do for you now?'

They caught sight of Rachel descending the stairs very slowly, her eyes wide and curious, fixed on Joanna's.

'Daddy?'

Her next query was to Joanna. 'Is there any news of Brutus?'

254

'He's being well looked after by another farmer,' Joanna said. 'I suggest you contact him and ask if you can ride him.' She dredged up the tiny bit she knew about ponies. 'He'll be missing the exercise.'

'Yes, he will.' The little girl looked over-joyed and not for the first time Joanna mused that children could be heartless. The farmer's death had not touched Rachel, but the loss of her pony rides had.

She wondered whether to Eloise, Sparky had made up for Matthew's defection. The thought tacked miserably on to the fact that in a few short days Eloise would be at Waterfall Cottage. And if she gained her place at the medical school in the future...? A frequent guest, no doubt. At the very least.

'Mr Mostyn,' Joanna said, 'I'd like to ask you a couple of things about the field you bought.'

Mostyn looked instantly alert. And in that very moment Joanna decided that she didn't like him. There was something creepy about the man, those plump, sausage fingers, that nervousness whenever money was men-tioned. She'd always had a suspicion of accountants – particularly ones who had not made it beyond junior partner of the firm.

She looked into his pale but unfathomable eyes and wondered whether he could read her thoughts. A swift glance at Korpanski told her that he, at least, did. He gave her the ghost of a smile.

They sat in the kitchen, Joanna deliberately facing Mostyn so his face was lit up by the sunshine. It was as good as a Gestapo interrogation light.

'When did you buy it?'

'Just over a year ago.' Mostyn looked shifty but Joanna didn't take too much notice of this. She tended to have this effect on anyone even remotely connected with a case.

'That must have been not long after your divorce.'

Mostyn's mouth tightened, making it look as sour as though he had just sucked a lemon. After a pause he nodded, his eyes flickering around the room.

'I would have thought money would have been tight then,' Joanna said conversationally.

'It was,' Mostyn said through clenched teeth, 'but I had to think about my future.'

'Quite, quite.'

Korpanski continued the line of questioning. 'So did Mr Grimshaw offer it to you or did you approach him?'

'He asked me.' Mostyn looked thoughtfully at both of them in turn, patently wondering where this was leading.

'Go on,' Joanna prompted.

'He saw me over the wall one day.' Mostyn smiled and stroked his chin. 'I was telling him about the divorce and how angry and powerless I felt. I knew his wife had walked out.' He gave a twisted smile. 'It sort of bonded us, you could say.'

Korpanski's eyes flickered across the table and Joanna tightened her mouth. The story would leak out eventually.

Mostyn continued. 'He seemed to want to do something to help and asked me if I would be interested in buying the field beyond the farmhouse.'

'Yes?'

Mostyn seemed unsure how to continue. 'He didn't seem to like the fact that that slimy devil Frankwell was mopping up the whole farm.'

'You must have commented that the field would be no good while the farm blocked access. I understand there's a stream on the far side.'

'He said it would be an investment.'

'Did he also say that he was thinking of retiring from farming?'

257

Mostyn shook his head then sucked in a deep breath.

'But I could tell his days in farming were numbered.' The words came out in a rush. 'He was always complaining about his arthritis.' There was an unexpected twinkle in his eye and Joanna smiled. She suddenly had a vision of the old farmer, bent double, complaining. It was a nicer image than the 'stiff' she had viewed at the mortuary.

She and Korpanski ate sandwiches in the car, watching the peaceful-looking, select estate. Violent crime was usually a foreigner to these middle-class havens. Not for the first time, she reflected on the oil and water mix of the twenty-first century rubbing shoulders with eighteenth-century rural England – a more law-abiding time?

Not if you search through the history books.

She took a final swig from her bottle of Ashbourne water and opened the car door.

The smell of a rich, meaty meal wafted down the drive as they called in to see Hilary and Richard Barnes. Hilary, it seemed, was a good cook.

She looked flustered as she opened the

door and Joanna sensed she was anxious for the food not to spoil. 'We won't be long,' she said. 'I realise that you're preparing a meal.'

This seemed to put Mrs Barnes at her ease. She relaxed and gave Joanna a warm smile.

'Are you any nearer to finding out who did this horrible thing?'

'Unfortunately and truthfully, no, we're not,' Joanna said.

No point hiding behind fiction.

'I just want to go over your statement, Mrs Barnes. What exactly did you hear?'

Hilary Barnes did not answer straight away but looked thoughtful. 'The trouble is, Inspector Piercy,' she said frankly, 'that now I wonder what I *actually* heard and what I've added later. I *thought* I heard a cry, sounds of a scuffle. I don't remember when I last heard the dog barking. Oh, yes, I do,' she said suddenly. 'He woke me early on Sunday morning.' Her eyes were unfocused, as though she was remembering that morning. 'He was making an absolute racket and I wondered what on earth was happening. Then he went quiet. I don't remember hearing him bark again,' she mused. 'I think he was quiet on the Tuesday. Even though the garage had come out to mend the tractor,' she rolled her eyes, 'again.'

Joanna's mind was busy thinking. 'You didn't mention this before, Mrs Barnes.'

'No? Well, the tractor was always breaking down.'

She didn't seem to realise the significance of what she was saying.

'I saw the van, didn't see the farmer but heard the tractor spluttering away a few minutes later.'

As they came out of the Barnes' house they caught sight of a racing green Range Rover. The Westons were back, rowing noisily as they climbed out of the car.

'You've been–'

'No. I promise you...' There was an air of desperation in his voice.

Joanna gave Mike a swift glance. Perhaps all marital arguments are essentially the same? Accusations, denials. No resolution. A relentless hammering.

They waited a few minutes before banging on the door. Kathleen Weston opened it to them.

She looked in despair, hopeless, and it was easy to see why. Her husband was standing behind her with the guilty air of a boy who has been stealing sweets ... or a man who has been found out courting a mistress. Both would deny and both were patently guilty as hell.

'Yes?' Even Kathleen's voice was hopeless, colourless and flat. She looked a woman at the end of her tether.

'We're just checking all the inhabitants of the estate,' Joanna said, 'hoping to find out a little more about Mr Grimshaw. Tell me, what did you think of him?'

Kathleen Weston's face lit up with a passion.

'He was a dreadful man,' she said. 'Very, very cruel to his animals. The way he left the poor dog barking on the end of a chain all day was positively barbaric. He shouldn't have been allowed to keep any animals, let alone a farmyard full.'

But, Joanna thought, farmers do not neglect their animals. Sure – they don't treat them as Poochy Pets but cows that are not cared for don't thrive or yield milk. Sheep that are neglected contract diseases. Farm animals have to be cared for. Still, she listened.

'He should have been shot,' Kathleen ranted on without realising what she was saying.

Her husband, standing behind her, did

261

though. 'Steady on, Kath,' he said mildly.

She turned on him then and vented her venom. 'Steady on? What do you care, Steven? What do you care about anything except...?'

He mumbled something in reply but she simply sniffed.

Joanna fingered the smooth pearl on her finger. When, she wondered, does a loving couple turn to this? When does the marital bed become such a battlefield? When a man takes a mistress – as Matthew had. Had it been that which had soured his marriage or had it already been cold?

She tried again. 'Is there anything else?' she asked again.

'No,' said Kathleen, and her husband nodded his agreement.

She and Korpanski donned their wellies and walked right round the boundary of the farm. The weather remained dry – they were even treated to the odd patch of blue sky – but the ground was waterlogged and full of thistles and rushes. Still, it did them good to be out of doors for a while. Returning to their desks was an anti-climax. They managed a few hours' work before calling it a day.

Sunday, 23rd September

'Bugger.' Joanna was zipping up her new jeans. Perhaps, optimistically, she had opted for the very snug fit of the size eight. Breathing in, in the shop, and without the benefit of a healthy breakfast, they had seemed relatively comfortable. But this morning Matthew had tempted her with the scent of frying bacon and shouts of 'Breakfast, Jo.'

And although it was a Sunday morning and they were meeting Caro and Tom for lunch at one of the moorland pubs, she had succumbed. But now, struggling with her zip, she was already regretting it.

Matthew was lying on the bed, watching her, smiling at her struggle. 'You don't think you should have opted for the size ten?'

She turned to look at him. 'Absolutely not – well, maybe,' she admitted before picking up a pillow and aiming it at him. 'Matthew Levin,' she said with mock severity, 'are you accusing me of putting on weight?'

'Certainly not,' he answered, still grinning at her.

She finally won over the zip. 'There,' she said, 'ready.'

'Ah, but can you breathe?'

'Who needs to breathe?' She laughed, twirled around and extended her hand to pull him off the bed. 'Come on, Matt,' she said, 'we don't want to be late.'

'We've plenty of time. It won't take longer than ten minutes to get out to Grindon.'

'And the temporary traffic lights on the Ashbourne road?'

'Will be green.' He stood up, put his arm around her and planted a kiss on her mouth. 'Plenty of time,' he said again and pulled her down on the bed on top of him, hungry for her.

Later, she struggled for a second time with the fastener, zipped her ankle boots up – without any of the fight she had had with her jeans – whisked a brush through her hair and left the bedroom. Matthew was waiting. But at the top of the stairs she paused and peeped into the second bedroom. Waterfall Cottage was small and when Eloise came to stay, it seemed smaller still. She sighed and skipped down the stairs to see Matthew standing at the bottom. He grinned at her and she knew from the gleam in the green eyes that he was about to make another comment about the skinny jeans. She gave him a severe frown, which he ignored, simply smiling.

Matthew had a beautiful smile. She had loved it from the very first, catching sight of it in the mirror over the sink in which she was vomiting. It had been her very first post-mortem and she hadn't expected that the cadaver's face would be pulled down like a rubber mask. She had met his eyes and read the humour there. He was laughing at her squeamishness. Later, she reflected that she couldn't have been the first detective he had seen bent double over the sink and wondered, what had they seen in each other that had made them both catch their breath, stare and find themselves unable to return to their equilibrium?

She had never really found the answer except that they hadn't. Weeks later he had bought her some sandwiches. A month down the line they had been sharing dinner and when Jane had burst in on them at a restaurant, they had made an effort to forget each other.

Except they hadn't been able to. Something had happened. A chain of emotions.

The stuff of Mills & Boon – that much derided romantic fiction which can mean so much. Yet most romances are similarly clichéd.

Knowing he was married, she had avoided

attending post-mortems when he was to be there, but even then she had constantly wondered about the tall, blond pathologist. Now, looking at his face again, so familiar, she couldn't resist him. She gave him a light kiss, giggled and stepped back.

'Jo,' he said. 'You look...' He paused, choosing his word carefully. 'Sexy,' he came up with.

She raised her eyebrows. 'Thank you,' she said archly. 'I shall remember that. Later.'

Matthew said nothing; the light in his eyes said it all.

In spite of the delay they made The Cavalier in Grindon at precisely two minutes past one.

It didn't take them long to locate Caro. They could hear her voice the moment they stepped inside. High-pitched, loud and definitely not a native of the moorlands. She was busily chatting up the barman, who was staring at her as though she'd just stepped in from another planet – which, in a way, she had. Caro was Joanna's journalist friend. She had cut her teeth on the *Leek Post and Times* before taking up a post in London. A few years ago she married another friend, a local solicitor named Tom.

Caro was always on the lookout for another story.

She rested her chin on her hand and eyed the barman up. 'So how *do* you make the Chicken Cavalier?'

'Well, you see,' the barman was scratching his head, 'we takes a breast of chicken and hammers it out flat. Then we fills it with breadcrumbs and stuffing and skewers it and then we cook it in the oven.'

'Hmm.' Caro sounded impressed. 'What's in the stuffing?'

The barman looked confused. 'I don't rightly know. I'll ask the missus to write it down for you, if you likes.'

'I would likes,' Caro said innocently. 'I might even give it a try. And can you also find out how hot the oven should be and how long I should cook it for?'

She turned around and caught sight of them, shrieked and threw her arms round them both. 'Ah,' she said, 'my very best friends in the world looking simply wonderful. Jo – how do you do it? Those skinny jeans. You look fantastic. Have you lost weight?'

Joanna smirked until Matthew supplied the answer. 'She's just poured herself into a smaller size.'

'Hope you can breathe. You look good too, Matt. The States must have agreed with you.'

'In a way,' he said uncomfortably.

They'd hardly noticed Tom, already sitting at a table in the corner. If Caro, with her ash-blonde hair and pencil-thin figure, was someone you always noticed, Tom was the exact opposite. Quiet, soberly dressed, with thinning brown hair and large, horn-rimmed glasses, he always blended with the background – wherever he was. He blinked at them, grinning broadly, and stood up. 'It seems ages,' he said. 'We haven't been together since the wanderer returned.'

Matthew shook his hand warmly while Joanna gave him a hug. 'Good to see you, Tom,' she said. 'I've missed you.'

Caro returned from the bar with a menu and a tray of drinks. 'Though,' she said airily, dropping the menus on the table, 'I don't think you need to look at these. The special of the day is Chicken Cavalier and it sounds very edible. Shall I just order four?'

'Yes. May as well.' They were all in agreement.

As Joanna had expected, it didn't take Caro long to spot the black pearl. She looked at it, then at Joanna and Matthew, who both felt incredibly smug. Matthew's arms stole around Joanna's shoulders.

'Congratulations!' Caro said. 'When's the great day to be?'

They explained that they hadn't fixed an exact date yet but that it would be soon.

'Some time over the winter,' was Matthew's contribution.

'Having decided,' Joanna said, 'we can't see the point of a long engagement.'

Matthew nodded vigorously.

Then Caro dropped her bombshell, patting her stomach. 'And I have something to tell you,' she said.

They could guess.

'Well,' she said defensively, 'I'm not getting any younger, you know, and Tom really wants this child.' She patted her perfectly flat stomach indulgently.

'But your career...' Joanna protested.

'I can go freelance,' Caro said airily. 'Lots of people do.'

Tom tried to look bland but his eyes, behind their thick glasses, already looked every inch a proud father.

But what Joanna couldn't stomach was the look of undisguised, pure envy in Matthew's eyes.

They ate their food, the Chicken Cavalier

living up to its promise, but for Joanna the day was losing its shine. Matthew wanted more than just the wedding and she couldn't ignore it. Each time she looked at him she knew that he was guiding her towards something he wanted very much. And once they were married she couldn't fend off this lust for ever – to be a father again. Provide a half-brother or sister for Eloise. And if Joanna couldn't ignore Matthew's desire, neither could she ignore the sick feeling in the pit of her stomach that she was walking up a road in the wrong direction.

They arrived back at Waterfall Cottage a little after six. The evening had turned damp and drab, which reflected Joanna's feeling of apprehension perfectly. She was glad when Matthew switched the TV on. It avoided the need to talk.

But if she was quiet throughout the evening she was also aware that Matthew needed the silence too.

Chapter Eleven

Monday morning, 24th September

They should have been feeling energetic, full of power and optimism. But as Joanna faced the assembled force, they knew that all they had were a motley collection of statements and no real facts. Nothing to connect them. There was a link missing, because this was a fractured case. For a start, they still didn't know for certain the time or even the date of death. Knowing the time of death would lead in turn to establishing alibis ... or not. The key to unlocking the door. Mark Fask had been as thorough as only he knew how but the fact was he had gleaned little forensic evidence from the crime scene. It was frustrating for the entire team. They were not short of motives. In fact, one thing this case had for sure was an abundance of motives. It was all here: love, hate, land, money, revenge. A barbaric murder. These were all the traditional motives. Solid, believable. Plenty of murders had been committed for each one of these reasons, and yet something told Joanna that they had not uncovered the epicentre, the heart of this seemingly simple murder – that of an aged farmer.

But, of course, Jakob Grimshaw had not been the simple man he had appeared. He had murdered his wife before disposing of her body in a way only he could have thought of, taunted his daughter with this fact, teased and deceived his neighbours.

No, this was no simple murder. It was more subtle than that. It was a crime of layers.

And now Joanna had gone full circle. It all came back to the time of death.

True, both Teresa Parnell and Hilary Barnes had suggested that Jakob Grimshaw had been killed on the Tuesday. It was tempting to accept their beliefs, but they were based on thin evidence: supposition without any real support. Unfortunately, it was the nature of these housing estates to be virtually deserted during the day.

Joanna couldn't understand why she felt that the time of death was the key to unlock the door. She'd gone to great lengths to try and find out the truth. They'd put boards up on the Ashbourne road but these had born no fruit. Apart from these two oddly connected women, no one else had come forward, which led Joanna to start considering alternative times of death. Maybe Teresa Parnell and Hilary Barnes had colluded. Maybe not. Or maybe the noises they had heard had been something else. What? Maybe she and Mike should take another look around Prospect Farm and see if they could gain something.

The officers were getting restless. Inactivity suited none of them and they were too intelligent to keep busy and distracted by endless house to house inquiries.

She stepped forward.

'OK,' she said briskly. 'We still don't know time of death.' She felt Korpanski's steady eyes on her but kept her gaze right out into the room; she needed to reach all of them. 'So instead, let's look at motive. Obviously the person with the strongest motive is Jakob's daughter, who will, presumably, inherit the farm.'

They all knew that as Grimshaw had died intestate it would take much longer for his daughter to be able to take control of her father's estate and probably sell it.

'How much was his estate worth?'

It was Korpanski who'd asked the question, in a lazy, half-interested voice, which fooled no one.

Dawn Critchlow turned to focus on him. 'A million and a half,' she said, 'when everything's taken into account.'

There was a Mexican wave of nods around the room. A million and a half was easily enough to justify a murder.

Joanna turned to the whiteboard. 'So,' she said slowly, 'let's consider the inhabitants of the Prospect Farm Estate again. Try and give me a flavour of what they're like. We'll start with the families whose gardens back on to the farm. Number 1, the Westons – Steve and Kathleen. What do we know about the couple and what can we surmise?'

Alan King moved forward. 'No children. Just the two of them. Kathleen is a fanatical animal lover. Mrs Weston resented the way Grimshaw ran his farm, seeing it as cruel.'

The faces around the room were all dubious.

Joanna frowned. 'Has Mrs Weston ever been in trouble with the law over her animal rights sympathies?'

King answered with a slow, reluctant shake of the head. 'Her husband, Steven, appears to be very much under his wife's thumb. However...' he was leering, 'Mrs Weston strongly implied that there was a relationship between Mr Weston and Faria Probert, the "Turkish" lady who teaches belly-dancing.'

'Did you get a chance to speak to Mr Weston on his own?'

King shook his head regretfully. 'His wife always seemed to be in the way. I got the impression that she didn't want me to speak to her husband alone.'

'Hmm.'

'And who interviewed Mrs Probert?'

Hannah Beardmore's finger was raised. 'She sort of implied that everyone gossiped about her on the estate. But she's got five kids. Five kids *and* an affair? *And* teaches belly-dancing? That's some energy output.'

Most of the officers nodded – in admiration.

'What's she like?'

She hesitated. 'A bit of a flirt – likes to think she's really sexy. But...' Everyone in the room could have finished the sentence.

'How many nights a week does she teach?'

'Two. Mondays and Thursdays. Monday in Leek and on the Thursday she travels to Rudyard. Apparently she's quite good.'

'Really?' Joanna couldn't resist pulling her leg a little. 'A potential pupil, are you?'

Hannah blushed. She had a very healthy appetite, which was reflected in her spreading waistline.

'And her husband?'

'George. He seems a quiet, inoffensive sort of chap. Pleasant but not exactly sparky.'

Joanna smothered a smile. 'Right. And the person who lives in number 3?'

Korpanski supplied the answer. 'Charlotte Frankwell. Divorced from the lovesick Gabriel, and her daughter, Phoebe, ten years old going on twenty.'

'We'll get to him later,' Joanna said. 'I have met him.'

'She runs a dress shop on St Edward's Street,' Danny Hesketh-Brown supplied. 'Quite a successful business, I understand. She's a smart-looking woman with quite a dress-sense.' He recalled the tight jeans and low-cut T-shirt with a smirk of appreciation mainly for the benefit of his male, testosterone-fuelled colleagues.

'And she did quite well out of the divorce,' he added. 'She's a survivor, that one.'

Joanna nodded. That was the impression she had derived from Frankwell's ex-wife: a hard-headed business woman. The divorce had suited her.

But try as she might she could not seem to force Charlotte Frankwell into the frame. Having sorted her life out so comfortably, why on earth would she want to rock her boat by murdering the old farmer? Like the Westons, there was no motive. Not clear or strong. It bothered Joanne, and privately tempted her to discount them as suspects.

It was one thing not knowing the time of death but quite another sorting out which motive was the correct one. Motiveless murder was bad news for the police force. Motives provided clues.

'Number 5?' she asked, almost gloomily.

'Peter Mostyn?'

McBrine shot to his feet. 'Well, at least here we have a hint of a motive. He bought the land beyond the farm for a couple of grand. He's up to his ears in debt since the divorce. It's cost him hard. His ex-wife drove a tight bargain in spite of leaving him for a wealthy man. For an accountant to slide into debt is bad news. What with that and looking after his kids, he's a very bitter man. He could only realise a good profit from his purchase if the farm was also sold for building land. The money would have made a great deal of difference. Quite apart from the money stashed away in the mattress.'

'Ah yes,' Joanna said. 'The money. The phantom money. Or not. Quite apart from the balance in Grimshaw's bank account.'

Dawn Critchlow nodded. 'Well,' she said, 'Grimshaw might have kept some money around the house to pay bills but certainly he had more than eighty thousand in Barclays bank.'

Joanna nodded. 'So no money in the mattress.' One by one the apparent motives for the crime were dissolving away, like sugar in hot tea.

So which was the real motive? She looked back at PC McBrine. 'Carry on,' she said.

'It's become obvious,' he began, 'that Grimshaw was stringing Frankwell along, pretending he still owned it, tying it in to the field directly behind Frankwell's property, the sheep field.'

Which gave Frankwell a motive: wanting revenge on the farmer. Frankwell had struck Joanna as a man who would resent being double-crossed – particularly by someone he would consider an unworthy opponent. Joanna felt a twinge of familiarity. Now this seemed more plausible as a motive. She could imagine Frankwell as a killer more easily than Peter Mostyn.

She tucked the facts away. 'So what was the plot worth as farming land and what potentially as building land?'

'Farming land is worth roughly three

thousand an acre.' McBrine hesitated. 'If you can find a buyer. And that's the sticking problem. Realistically, the market is limited to neighbouring farmers. Naturally, farmers want land that adjoins theirs so they can easily move animals and machinery. Otherwise there can be a lot of travelling along main roads, quite apart from cattle stealing, which has gone on in the moorlands for the last few centuries.' He leant forward. 'Building land, on the other hand, can be worth twenty or thirty thousand – and upwards – an acre, depending on how many houses the developer can squash in and what price-range the properties are in. But of course, as it was, the access to Mostyn's few acres was hopeless, right through the middle of the farmyard. Added to that, there's a brook bordering the far side of the field, which could make access almost impossible except right *through* the middle of the farmyard, and that would mean demolishing the farmhouse. Otherwise he wouldn't have a hope in hell of getting planning permission for anything other than farmland, which would have meant spending money he could ill afford for absolutely no profit.'

Joanna sat up. 'So Mostyn stood to gain quite considerably by the farmer's death.'

The next question was obvious. 'Did he need the money so much?'

'Oh yes. He's been sliding into debt over the last year. There's another thing. He's desperate to keep solvent and stay in the house. He'd like the children to be with him, particularly Rachel. He seems very close to her so he encouraged her to pop across to the farm and ride Grimshaw's pony. It meant she was always very keen to be with her daddy.'

Joanna had to ask it. 'Was there anything sinister in the friendship between little Rachel and Grimshaw?'

'No – I don't think so,' McBrine said quickly. 'I think she reminded him of happier days. Grimshaw was obviously lonely. He and his daughter seemed to do nothing but argue. I think he liked little Rachel to ride the pony. She was like a granddaughter to him.'

'And Mostyn's other two,' Joanna glanced at the board of names. 'Sam and Morag?'

'Sam is virtually addicted to computer games and doesn't much care where he plays them, and Morag's only four. She doesn't really qualify for anything much.' McBrine gave an indulgent, father's smile. 'She's just a little tot.'

'One more question,' Joanna said softly. 'Just out of interest, if Grimshaw had sold, who is the neighbouring farmer?'

'A guy called Dudson. Early sixties. Been there for years.'

Joanna nodded. 'OK. Let's move on to Hilary Barnes, one of our witnesses.' She paused. 'One of our *key* witnesses. Her husband's name?'

Hesketh-Brown supplied it. 'Richard. Both in their fifties. They've three children, none of whom live with them. They're all grown up, married and moved away. She's quite a pillar of society charity fundraiser for anything from Saving Maer Hills to supporting the Douglas Macmillan Home and the Donna Louise Trust. She was packing, ready to visit her daughter, Alexandra-Rose, who lives in Leigh-on-Sea with her husband, Mark, when she heard the noise, which she describes as a clatter.'

Joanna squirreled the word away. *A clatter.* A clatter, to her sounded like something metallic falling. Not an assault on a frail old man.

A clatter.

Hesky continued. 'She left later on that Tuesday, sometime in the mid-afternoon. Her car was seen at various places down the motorway. In a way, you could say she has the best alibi of all. She was well away from it all.'

But Joanna wasn't falling for that one. 'If the noise,' she said pleasantly, 'was the sound of Grimshaw being murdered, you couldn't be more wrong. She was there. And she admits it. It could be a clever move, Sergeant.' It was practically a reproval. 'Is there any reason that you unearthed why Mrs Barnes – or Mr Barnes, for that matter – might want their neighbour dead?'

Hesketh-Brown looked sheepish. 'No. Nothing that I picked up on.'

'And have you any comment to make on the relationship between Mrs Barnes and Teresa Parnell?'

'No, ma'am...'

Joanna's lips tightened at the 'ma'am'. She hated being addressed as such. It made her sound such an old bag.

Hesketh-Brown looked up. 'Nothing apart from being neighbourly.' He frowned. 'But I wouldn't have thought they were the same type. I'd be surprised if they were good friends.'

'Apart from a mutual interest in the occult?'

'Even that doesn't seem likely, Mrs Barnes

seems too level-headed to be taken in by that.'

'You'd be surprised at the people who pin their hopes on horoscopes and such like,' Joanna said lightly. 'Did she, for instance, consult Mrs Parnell on astrological matters?'

'Not as far as I know.'

Joanna glanced at Mike and resisted the instinct to give a really deep sigh. They were going to have to sort this one out themselves.

She wished the assembled officers didn't look quite so despondent at this obvious failure. It was necessary to move them on.

'So – let's come down the other side.' She glanced down at her notes. 'The Watkins family in number 8 saw and heard nothing and the Chappells have been away on a cruise since early September. Then we come down to number 4 and Teresa Parnell, who is either in touch with the spirit world, plain barmy or else very clever.'

She could see that all the waiting officers felt the same as she did. So was it a giant con? A trick so clumsy it was clever? Or did Teresa Parnell genuinely believe she was connected somehow with the spirit world? She searched the faces in front of her but found no answer. And *she* certainly didn't have one. 'Apart from the inhabitants of the estate, who else is in the picture?' She answered her own question. 'Two people. Flaxon from the animal feeds company and, of course, our farmer's daughter.'

It always seemed to come back to Judy.

'Or is there a third?' she mused slowly. 'Or even a fourth? We have Mr Dudson, the neighbouring farmer, who might have had an interest in the land but only if it was sold as agricultural. And then there is Mr X – the man with whom, it has been suggested, Mrs Grimshaw was having an affair.' She gazed, out of focus, at the back of the room. 'Someone who may or may not even exist. And that's where we are.'

She looked around the room. 'Keep digging,' she said.

She knew as well as the others that once they had a suspect forensics could move in, search the car, look for mud right up in the wheel arches. Something would be there. Locard's Principle said so. Each contact leaves a trace. A visitor to a crime scene takes something from it and leaves something behind. She had solved more frustrating and puzzling cases than this. The darkest hour, as they say, is just before dawn. Her face twisted into a smile. And this certainly was a dark hour.

The officers filed out, their feelings displayed by a dropping of shoulders, a heaviness in their walk. She badly wanted to inspire them but could not find the way to punch through.

Korpanski, too, was quiet, his eyes resting on her face. He was waiting for her to take the lead.

She looked across at him and couldn't resist a smile. Korpanski was a large, powerful man who spent hours at the gym keeping fit and muscular. But right now he looked almost vulnerable. She felt an urge to pat his shoulder. 'Let me sit here quietly for a moment, Mike,' she said. 'Something significant has been said in the briefing. I just need to think for a while.'

She sat without speaking, going over all that had been said. Returning to the beginning was always a good start. The old farmer had been murdered. *That* was the crime they were investigating. In doing so they had unearthed a second murder. Why? Why would Grimshaw kill his wife if not because she had been unfaithful? So how did the two murders interlock? What bearing did the first crime have on the second?

What connection could there be? Cause? Effect?

The answer was obvious. Mr X.

She picked up the phone and was connected with an irritated Judy Grimshaw on her mobile. She didn't bother with any preamble. 'Your mother,' she began. 'Tell me about her affair.'

There was an irritated snort from the other end of the phone.

'This isn't a good time, Inspector,' she began, a tight band of sarcasm making her voice harsh.

'I don't really care,' Joanna replied equally rudely. 'Your father has been murdered, your mother too, it appears.'

'It isn't my fault the police don't have a clue.'

Joanna felt her dislike for the farmer's daughter grow to huge and almost unmanageable proportions. She swallowed the bile that was rising in her mouth and decided on a subtle attack. 'You don't want to cooperate with us, Judy? You do surprise me, under the circumstances.'

'I didn't say that.'

By the defensive tone in the woman's voice, Joanna knew that she'd managed to crawl under her skin.

She smiled and waited. Sometimes silence asks more questions than the most articulate interrogator.

But Judy was silent too.

'Come on, Judy,' she coaxed. 'Stop obstructing us.'

'I'm not.'

Joanna permitted herself a smirk. *At last.* At last Judy Grimshaw was beginning to crack. She could sense the vulnerability in her voice, hear the tremor, the hesitation, the sheer fright. She knew what had rattled her. It had been the term obstruction. A nice legal term, which Judy Grimshaw was wise enough to recognise as such.

'The next door farmer,' she said slowly and reluctantly, 'is a widower. His wife died of breast cancer years and years ago. I was just a kid. She was ill for ages before that. My mother used to cook meals and take them round. I always wondered. He's a nice man. Cultured and different...' there was wonderment in her voice, 'from my dad.'

'His name?' *Joanna already knew it.*

'Mark Dudson. He's vaguely connected with the Dudson pottery family. I think he's still living next door. He has a prize herd of Charolais. I haven't seen him for a long time but I believe he's still there.'

'Thank you,' Joanna said coldly and put the phone down.

She turned to Mike with a wide smile. 'Come on, Korpanski,' she said teasingly. 'Wake up, put your coffee down. We've got work to do.'

Mark Dudson's farm was approached from a track two miles beyond Prospect Farm. It looked prosperous and well-cared for, with a board painted with a creamy-white bull announcing the prize herd of cows.

As they drove through the farm gate a man stumped towards them. He looked to be in his sixties, strong with a broad pair of shoulders.

Joanna got out of the car. 'Mr Dudson?' She displayed her ID card.

'Aah,' he said with satisfaction, taking it in. 'I wondered if you'd get around to me. I've been half expecting you. Come in,' he said. 'My housekeeper, Mandy, will make us a brew.'

Inside, the farmhouse kitchen was all that it should be. Quarry tiles, a huge Aga, a comfortable clutter of papers and magazines – *Farmers' Weekly*, mainly – and the housekeeper, complete with flowered apron. She was young and thin, in her forties, wearing no makeup and a careworn expression. Dudson addressed her with careless goading, 'Get on with it, girl. Put kettle on, will you, the inspector and her sergeant will want a cup of tea.'

Without a word, Mandy moved the kettle over to the hotplate, went through the motions and brewed up. Her shoulders remained bent. She looked humourless – a victim herself.

Dudson removed his wellies, plonked himself down on a chair and stretched his feet out, displaying thick, blue, woollen socks with a neat darn over his right big toe. 'Let me guess,' he said, fixing Joanna with a piercing stare of very pale blue eyes. 'You're curious about my neighbour's murder, aren't you?' Surprisingly, there was a touch of humour in his face. Without waiting for an answer he continued, leaning suddenly forward. 'How much do you know, Inspector? How much do you *really* know?'

She met his gaze without flinching and wondered why she felt a certain warmth towards this man who had to be, after all, a suspect in a murder case. 'We believe you were once – friendly – with Mrs Grimshaw, years ago.'

Dudson stared at the Aga. 'Aye,' he said.

Joanna waited.

'Do you know what happened to her?'

With an effort, Dudson lifted his head. 'Put it like this, Inspector,' he said, 'I had my suspicions.' He stared at her.

'Elaborate.'

'He told me she'd gone away. I couldn't believe that she would have gone without a word to me. It wouldn't have been like her.'

'Were you having an affair with her?'

Again that touch of humour lightened Dudson's eyes. 'That's between me and–' he began, but Joanna forestalled him.

'Jakob Grimshaw left a confession that he'd killed his wife and fed her to his pigs,' she said brutally. 'Anything you can say that might shed light on this crime might point the way to the murder we are currently investigating.'

Dudson was quiet, his face suddenly white and grave. 'So that's what happened to her,' he said. 'Poor thing.' He looked up, his eyes flaming. 'Then I'm not sorry Grimshaw met with the end he did.'

Joanna watched him. 'And after Mrs Grimshaw disappeared, how did it affect your relationship with Mr Grimshaw?'

Again that touch of humour softened his face. 'Strained,' he said.

Again Joanna waited. Dudson was not a

stupid man. He must know what was in her mind.

But stubbornly he dropped his head to stare at the floor and smiled. It was a sentimental smile, as though he saw there some pretty memory. Of lambs in fields and a woman in a sprigged dress?

He kept smiling. Then shook his head and answered the question she had not even asked. 'No,' he said. 'No, I did not kill him.'

Korpanski spoke up. 'When did you last see him?'

Dudson shrugged. 'No idea,' he said. 'Absolutely no idea.'

'Think, Mr Dudson.'

Obediently, he did think for a moment. 'A couple of weeks ago, I suppose.'

Mike spoke up. 'You can't be more specific than that?'

'Sorry, Sergeant, no.' Dudson said firmly.

'The land he had for sale...' Joanna was picking her way delicately through the questions.

Dudson's answering gaze was shrewd. 'He was playing a dangerous game,' he said. 'A very dangerous game. Playin' people off against each other.' There was a flash in the blue eyes. 'He didn't understand city people, Inspector,' he looked up with a smile, 'and

Sergeant. He simply didn't understand the way their minds work. He didn't realise how greedy they could be. Greedy, vindictive and proud. I warned him. I told him he was teasing a crazy bull but he thought he was smart. I knew he wasn't.' A pause. 'And it seems I was right.'

'So you think Mr Grimshaw was killed by one of his neighbours because of the land deal.'

There was a flash of spirit in the farmer's face. 'Yes,' he said, 'I do.'

They left soon afterwards, having drunk Mandy's excellent tea. Made, Joanna noticed with approval, in a teapot, strained and served in china cups with saucers. Impressive for a farmer. She began to see what Judy Wilkinson had meant.

'So what do you make of him, Mike?' Joanna asked when they were safely outside, striding back towards their car.

'I think,' Korpanski said slowly, 'that Mr Dudson would have been perfectly capable of murdering Jakob Grimshaw if he had found out what Grimshaw had done with his wife.'

Joanna looked at him. 'I agree,' she said. 'Under the cultured veneer there was a certain steeliness about him, wasn't there?'

Korpanski nodded and they opened the car doors.

As they drove past the entrance to the Prospect Farm Estate they saw Faria Probert turn into her drive in a People Carrier. On impulse, Joanna turned the car in and followed the belly dancer.

They watched her coax the children out of the car.

She was an exotic-looking woman with fine, huge, heavy breasts and ample hips. Even as she walked up towards her door, seeming not to notice the police car sliding in behind her, her gait was rhythmic, swaying and, even to Joanna's critically female eye, sexy. She was wearing loose olive green cargo pants slung around her hips and a pink shirt unbuttoned to reveal a deep, fleshy cleavage.

They had followed her to the door before she suddenly swung round and addressed Korpanski. 'Can I help you?'

Joanna loved it when Korpanski was caught on the hop. 'Umm.' He looked at Joanna for a cue.

She produced her ID card. 'Detective Inspector Joanna Piercy, Leek Police, Mrs Probert.'

Faria's thickly lipsticked mouth dropped open. She raised large dark eyes to Joanna.

'It's about your neighbour, Mr Jakob Grimshaw.'

Faria nodded. Her eyes, heavily made-up with black lines and treacly mascara, were very expressive. She looked both lugubrious and apprehensive.

Skilfully, she ushered the children into the house. 'Won't you come in?'

They followed her into a neat house. No sign here of her Bohemian hobby. It was plain, a few children's toys scattered in the conservatory beyond the sitting room, the pictures, rather disappointingly, of spring flowers and sheep grazing in the snow. 'Can we just go over the events of Monday the 10th of September?'

Faria settled down on the sofa opposite and fixed her eyes on Korpanski, who, Joanna noted, was thoroughly enjoying the attention. She'd worried about Mike lately. He'd lost some of his vigour. He'd always been a bit of a flirt, particularly with the female junior officers. Korpanski was hugely susceptible to the charms of women. But since her return he'd been subdued. It was good to see the sweat break out on the back of his neck as Faria Probert dropped her heavy eyelashes at him. Joanna smothered a grin. Faria was an expert at flirting. She pulled herself into line, cleared her throat.

'Mrs Probert,' she began, 'I want to know exactly what you heard on that morning. You were home and the estate was quiet. Hardly anyone else was here.'

With difficulty, Faria peeled her eyes from the burly detective sergeant and switched her gaze to Joanna.

'I don't know how many times I have to repeat myself,' she said. 'It was a quiet morning.'

Joanna interrupted. 'Don't you normally work on a Monday?'

'Not until the evening,' Faria said severely. 'You don't get many takers for a belly-dancing lesson on a Monday morning. Anyway,' she resumed, 'it was really quiet round here that morning.'

'Because the dog wasn't barking?' Joanna hated to put words into the woman's mouth but these tiny details were important.

Faria was halted in her tracks. 'Possibly,' she said slowly. 'I only really noticed how quiet it was. I didn't think why it was so quiet. Maybe you're right. The dog wasn't making a noise.' She smiled, showing an impressive set of large, white teeth.

'About eleven,' she said. 'I can't be absolutely precise about the time,' she said with annoyance. 'I've got five kids, you know. And I have my keep fit regime. I don't spend all day staring at the clock.'

Joanna simply nodded. She couldn't be bothered to get into a discussion about clock-watching with this woman. She simply wanted facts. Pure, clear facts. 'Go on,' she prompted tersely, adding a 'please' as encouragement.

'Well, that was it,' Faria said. 'Nothing more. I heard an almighty clatter and then nothing. I didn't think anything of it. There are often noises coming from the direction of the farm. Tractors, animals, machinery. I only really recalled it when your police officers told us what had happened and started asking questions. But Mrs Barnes heard it too, so I can't have imagined it.'

She was definitely on the defensive, Joanna mused, and decided to step over the line a bit.

'How well do you know your neighbours?'

Faria's eyes narrowed. 'Fairly well.'

'Steven Weston, for instance?'

To her surprise, Faria coloured. Her eyes, dark muddy pools, fixed on Joanna's face. She was debating whether to speak.

Joanna waited.

'Steven Weston,' Faria began slowly, 'was a very lonely man.'

'A lonely married man?' Joanna queried.

'It does happen, you know. His wife was so busy defending animal rights and feeding cats that she had no time left over for her husband. Ask her,' she said defiantly. 'Ask her if her husband would like children. She doesn't even know – or care. Talk about taking someone for granted. Such women,' she said haughtily, 'don't deserve husbands.'

'Maybe,' Joanna said cautiously, 'but they were still married.'

Faria nodded, in her dark eyes a gleam of mischief. 'Do you know what the attraction was here?'

Both Joanna and Mike shook their heads.

'Not me. Not rampant sex on the settee. It was children. Toys. Clutter. Life. Young life,' Faria said. She threw back her head and laughed, allowing Joanna to admire her dentition. 'That's what he wanted. He loved being here, on the floor, surrounded by children, Lego, Fisher Price. Some men are essentially paternal.' Her eyes were on Joanna and she flushed. It was as though Faria could see right inside Matthew Levin's soul. Superstitiously, Joanna touched the black pearl on her finger.

Feeling a bit sheepish, the two officers left soon after.

They tried the Barnes's house but there was no answer. There were no cars in the drive and number 9 held the look of an empty house.

Chapter Twelve

Tuesday, 25th September

It was a sunny morning. Joanna sensed it even before she opened her eyes. There was a brightness in the bedroom that danced along the wall. She watched it for a moment then flung back the duvet, touching Matthew's shoulder. 'I'll make the coffee,' she murmured into his ear. 'It's a heavenly morning.'

Matthew grunted but when she returned with the two mugs of strong Nescafé he sat up and reached out for it. 'So what makes you so full of beans this morning, Jo?'

She ruffled his hair then pressed her lips to it. She loved its colour, damp sand, particularly when it was early-morning-tousled. 'Optimism,' she said, relishing the shot of caffeine pumping energy into her. 'I feel I'm about to make a breakthrough. That and the sunshine,' she mused, 'and the thought of cycling across the moorland into work.'

'I only hope you're right,' he said, grinning at her. 'For a simple murder you seem to be taking your time arresting anyone.'

She gave him a mock punch. 'Cheeky,' she said.

They sat companionably together, drinking their coffee, then with a light kiss Joanna disappeared into the bathroom, showered and put on her cycling shorts and top, slipping on the engagement ring last of all. Then, carefully, she folded a skirt and blouse into a rucksack together with some shoes. Downstairs for apple and mango juice and a bowl of Special K, then she wheeled her bike around to the front.

Matthew was still munching his toast, watching her critically through the open window. 'Be careful,' he mouthed.

She waved at him. 'I'll see you tonight.' She forced herself to smile. 'When did you say Eloise is coming?' Try as she might she couldn't erase the tightness from her voice.

He lent right out through the window to

answer. 'Not until tomorrow afternoon.' He paused while he eyed her shrewdly. 'I thought I'd cook,' he said. 'Maybe some pasta. A lasagne or something.'

'Whatever,' she said, buckled her helmet on and sped off.

Waterfall was a pretty village, still with its own pub – smoke-free now but the beams testified to years of nicotine exposure. The government might be able to bring in new legislation but the scent of nicotine would probably remain for ever. She cycled along the flat road, taking the ridge in her stride, feeling the sudden drop in temperature as she climbed, then descending into the valley and the town of Leek, recognisable by the spire of St Edwards and the green dome of the Nicholson Institute piercing the early morning mist.

She showered, changed into the neat black skirt and scarlet blouse, slipped her feet into the black leather court shoes, ran a comb through her hair to bring it back to life, slicked some lip-gloss along her mouth and was at her desk by the time Korpanski wandered in. 'Morning, Mike,' she said.

He grinned at her and she knew he, too, was in buoyant mood. 'You didn't ride in, did you, Jo?'

'Certainly did. It woke my brain up. Mike,' she said tentatively, 'I have a feeling that the noise that Hilary Barnes, Faria Probert and possibly Teresa Parnell heard was not the sound of Jakob Grimshaw struggling with his killer but something else.'

He looked up. 'I wondered that myself,' he said. 'Any idea what?'

'Not yet but we should visit Hilary Barnes again and then comb through the farmyard to take a better look. We've missed something.' She frowned. 'Maybe because we didn't know what we were looking for. But we do now.' She stood up. 'Come on, Mike,' she said. 'Time to get a move on.'

He started grumbling but really she knew he enjoyed the way she goaded him, teased him, pulled him along. It was one of the many reasons they worked so well together.

Ten minutes later they were speeding along the Ashbourne road towards the Prospect Farm Estate. As they turned in, Joanna reflected that they were certainly attractive houses, architect designed, each one slightly different from the rest. Some had integral garages, others pillared porticos. They all had individually designed windows, bow-fronted, sash or casement. A testament to modern, imaginative architecture. They pulled up outside number 9 and were gratified when Hilary Barnes opened the door, looking concerned. Joanna reassured her with a quick smile. 'It's OK, Mrs Barnes,' she said. 'I just want to revise your statement about the noise you heard.'

As before, Joanna was conscious of the woman's intelligence and force of character.

'Come in,' she said. 'I'll make some coffee. I was ready for a cup myself.'

They followed her into the kitchen – clean, white tiled – and watched her boil the kettle and fill a cafetière. As she poured three mugs of coffee and produced a jug of milk, she turned, frowning. 'I've thought a lot about that,' she said. 'There were all sorts of sounds. But in the background I heard something metallic, sharp and very loud. A clatter. I have wondered what exactly it was. But I can't think of anything that would make...' Her eyes wandered around her kitchen. 'The only thing I can liken it to is if you dropped a load of saucepan lids.' Her gaze landed on the shelf of pans over her cooker. 'Do you see what I mean?' she asked dubiously.

Joanna nodded, eyed Korpanski and smiled. She was beginning to see a picture. One of a clever and devious mind. Practised at deceiving.

It had all been set up – a diversion to provide someone with an alibi. When the two women had heard the noise, Jakob Grimshaw had already been dead – possibly for nearly two days.

Joanna was beginning to feel pleased with herself. She wasn't falling for *that* one.

She eyed the woman across the table. 'Mrs Barnes,' she said slowly, 'I want you to think about the Sunday. Probably the afternoon. Did you notice any comings and goings at the farm?'

The woman was silent for a minute or two, her face screwed up in concentration. She pressed her fingers to her forehead. 'I did hear a car,' she said. 'Some time in the evening. It was a dull day,' she said. 'I'd been watching television. I think it was around seven or eight o'clock. Maybe even later.' She raised her index finger in a gesture of excitement. 'I remember now. It skidded away. I remember hearing the gravel spit and thinking someone was in a tearing hurry.' She smiled, pleased with herself. 'I wonder if this will help you, Inspector,' she commented curiously.

Joanna felt smug. It fitted in with the theory she was forming. 'I rather think it will,' she said.

Today, in the dingy weather, there was something desolate about Prospect Farm. Deserted of its animals and its farmer, it looked even more bleak and uncared for than when they had first visited. The neglect was plain to see: the peeling paintwork, cracked windows, weeds growing through cracks in the concrete. Even the tree in the centre looked droopy and dejected. It looked like a place of brooding and years of sadness, filled with foreboding. As indeed it was.

Joanna slipped on her wellies and she and Korpanski climbed out of the car. The stillness was so thick and heavy they could have sliced it through with a knife. It felt as though the entire place was whispering about its years of secrets and neglect, playing the telltale on Jakob. Joanna stepped forward gingerly.

'We won't bother with the farmhouse itself,' she said. 'I don't think we'll find anything in there. I want to concentrate on the outside.'

Korpanski nodded. 'Call me a wimp, Jo,' he said, looking around him, 'but I have a distinctly uncomfortable feeling here, as though someone is watching us.'

As though in response, a crow, perched on the telegraph pole nearby, gave a loud croak and flapped away. It seemed a bird of ill omen.

Joanna looked around her. 'Maybe the best thing will be if this place is pulled down and built over. I don't believe in houses having a bad vibe but this one is giving me the heebie-jeebies.' She stepped towards the barn. 'Come on, Mike,' she said, 'let's get on with it and get back to the station.'

They rounded the corner of the building and faced the two huge doors where the dead cattle had been discovered. Korpanski heaved one open with his meaty shoulder and they stepped inside.

The interior was dingy with an odd, stale-hay smell. There was the reek of death mingled in with the scent of manure. It was a disturbing smell. Pungent and strong.

Joanna touched Korpanski's arm. 'Leave the door open, Mike,' she said, 'we need the light.'

He wheeled around and she knew he wasn't fooled. There was something claustro-phobic about the shed where the animals had suffered and died, and Joanna, sensitive to atmosphere, was spooked.

For once Korpanski had the upper hand.

'Hey, Jo,' he said.

She made a face back at him then looked up towards the hay loft. 'What's that?'

It was a piece of rope, suspended from the high ceiling, moving ever so slightly in the draught from the open door. It looked like a hangman's noose.

The hayloft was reached by a ladder. Joanna ascended a couple of steps to peer at the bales of hay recently stacked by a farmer preparing for a winter he would not now see. There was something poignant about the sight – all that harvesting for nothing and no one to enjoy it. Even the animals who would have eaten it were dead. Joanna wondered what would happen to the sheep that had survived the slaughter and its aftermath, whether the neighbour, Dudson, would get lucky. Or would the hardnosed Judy drive a tough bargain once the settlement of her father's estate was complete and the keys handed to her? Joanna glanced again at the old-fashioned, oblong bales of hay, fastened with orange, nylon twine. Would they simply rot and wait for the building contractors to get rid of them? By burning or dumping?

She had reflected this way before. After a murder there was always the unforeseen, untidy aftermath – the children left fatherless or motherless, the empty home, the bedroom shut off, the belongings treasured and never quite disposed of, the car that sat for years on the drive or in a garage.

The thought invariably depressed her as much as the crime itself.

She peered over the edge of the hayloft into the cattle stalls below. And then she saw it, something she had possibly noticed before but had not realised its significance. A stack of old-fashioned farm implements randomly scattered behind the barn doors.

From the stiffening of Korpanski's shoulders, she knew he had seen it too. 'They would have made one hell of a bang, Jo,' he said.

She was shaking her head. 'A clatter,' she mused. 'So that's what they both heard. But,' she said meaningfully, 'maybe the noise the three women heard was not Grimshaw's murder but these implements being knocked over as someone entered the barn, which created a noise that would then be interpreted as a struggle. These things would not have been left there when Grimshaw was alive.' She allowed herself a moment's reflection before descending the ladder. Joanna went first; in a skirt, it was not advisable for Korpanski to be below her. 'Animals can create all sorts of noises,' she mused. 'I've heard them myself. They can moan and scream, create the same sounds as a human in distress. Bump against a pile of farm implements. What they heard was the sound of the animals crashing around. Not Grimshaw. They probably didn't mean to mislead us. They simply reported what they had heard. But the pile of stuff was set up to be pushed over by desperate animals, make a loud noise and divert us from the true time of death. Which is interesting.' She leant against the door to the shippons and stared into nothing, slotting this new fragment of information into the whole.

Finally she turned to Korpanski, who had been watching her silently. 'I think Grim-shaw died on the Sunday night,' she said. 'Roderick Beeston told me the cattle wouldn't have lasted more than a day or two without water. *They* were in their death throes on Tuesday the 11th, not their master. He watered and fed them last on Sunday the 9th. Actually, Mike, what were the animals doing indoors in September anyway? Most farmers want to leave them outside as long as they can.'

'I did ask about that,' Mike said. 'They were fairly new beef cattle. He hadn't had them long. He was getting them tested by the vet before letting them out to graze.'

'Oh. I see.' She was quiet for a while. Korpanski could be a very conventional police sergeant. 'I've got an idea, Mike,' she said. 'Give me a day or two to think about it and I'll discuss it with you.' She hesitated. 'I want to flush our killer out.'

'You know who it is?'

'I don't *know*,' she said, 'but I *think* I know. That isn't the problem, Mike. It's proving it. We've not exactly had a lot of help from forensics. I doubt we're going to get much more. The killer's clothes would be nice. They make a lovely court case but our villain's had enough time to dispose of those. Everyone who watches *CSI* knows about blood splashes etc. Our problem is going to be making a case stick.' She glanced around the barn. 'We're still missing something,' she said. 'Something important but I don't know what it is.'

They walked outside, into a rare glimpse of sunshine before the sun scurried back behind a cloud, and Joanna knew she was going to have to convince Korpanski about this one. She eyed him slyly. 'There is nothing worse than knowing your killer, by instinct and circumstance, and watching them wriggle through the net in court or, even worse, watching the CPS do the wriggling for them, is there, Mike?'

Korpanski closed the barn door with a bang before turning and studying Joanna's face. He was very sensitive to her moods and knew by the sparkle of mischief in her eyes that made them shine sapphire-blue and the curve of her wide mouth that she was doing what she loved most – plotting. 'You're up to something, ma'am,' he said, using the title simply to rile her and let her know that he knew. She wasn't fooling him.

She waited until they were back in the car before she spoke again. 'The nice thing about the new time of death is that it returns Judy back to the top of the list. Not only that but she fits the bill because she had an unbreakable alibi for the Tuesday morning, whereas I bet she has none for the Sunday evening. So it would have been well worth her setting up the diversionary tactic. We'll start with her then comb through the other suspects' alibis with our team. Concentrating now on the Sunday night. Refresh memories. Start again with a new time of death. Hah.' She slammed the car door shut with a sharp sense of satisfaction, which in turn let Korpanski know they would have a restless few days ahead.

When she called the briefing for six p.m. sharp, and he watched her striding to and fro in front of the whiteboard, fingers pointing to names, times, places, he could feel the entire team whipped into energy. Her old dynamism had returned, which left Korpanski with a worry. Who would inspire them if she vanished for months into maternity leave?

Chapter Thirteen

Wednesday, 26th September

Joanna awoke with the feeling that something unpleasant was going to happen today. Matthew lay still beside her but she knew he was awake. It's hard to fake sleep successfully. There is something about the breathing that gives the masquerader away; it is a little less laboured, slightly faster and less regular than the respirations of someone who is truly, deeply asleep. She worried for a couple of minutes over the emotion of impending trouble.

Then she remembered. Of course. Today Eloise would be arriving. When she returned from work, Matthew would be wearing the fixed, strained smile of a man who is only too well aware of the problem between his daughter and his partner. No. She almost sat up to protest. Fiancée. Next to the half-finished book, the pearl ring gazed back at her from her bedside cabinet, a faultless, beautiful witness to her altered state.

Matthew decided to stir. He reached out for her and found her, pulled her to him, and she thought how very lucky she was, how much she loved him and how glad she was that in a couple of short months they would be man and wife. She snuggled in close to whisper in his ear. 'Want a coffee?'

He opened his eyes. 'Mmm.' Surely, surely, she thought, Eloise could not wreck this happiness, this contentment?

Oh yes she could and frequently did, deliberately. Joanna slipped out of bed, wrestled her way into her thick white towelling dressing gown and padded downstairs, returning minutes later with a cafetière steaming with a rich, beautiful aroma, a jug of milk and two large mugs. Carefully she poured out their coffee and they sat up in bed, awakening to the day with the help of caffeine.

She broached the subject first. 'What time is Eloise coming?'

She could never quite get rid of the frostiness in her voice the second she spoke the name. And Matthew noticed it too. He frowned over the cup of coffee.

'Her interview's at two so she'll drive straight there,' he said stiffly. 'Then she has a written paper. She should be finished by five-ish. We'll be back here by six-ish, depending on the traffic.'

He arched his eyebrows at her. 'I suppose you'll be late home?'

If she struggled to keep hostile tones out of her voice, Matthew struggled to keep irony out of his.

Perhaps now that she was to be his wife, things would improve? Briefly, she had thought they had while Matthew had been in the States and she had suffered a miscarriage; Eloise had sent her some flowers. But later, when she had been healthy enough to think about it more rationally, she had realised that the thought behind the flowers had been Matthew's. Not Eloise's. How could she ever have thought otherwise?

But she must try and build bridges. 'I will try and finish early, Matt,' she promised before springing out of bed and making her way to the shower. She put on her cycling shorts and top and folded work clothes into her rucksack before going downstairs for some Special K and a large tumblerful of apple juice. She heard Matthew upstairs, showering briskly, humming. He was happy to be seeing his daughter, she reflected. She shouldn't spoil it. But it wasn't just her fault. If she was guarded, Eloise was at least equally so – if not more so. In the beginning, Joanna had excused the child. After all, her perception would be that it had been Joanna who had broken up her mother and father, split apart the family home. But as Eloise had grown up, Joanna had become increasingly impatient with the sharp-featured, razor-tongued teenager, seeing in her more than simply a physical resemblance to Jane, Matthew's ex-wife.

She finished her breakfast and went upstairs to clean her teeth just as Matthew was descending. He gave her a slightly wary look.

'See you tonight then, Jo.'

She set off to work, glad to escape the coolness that threatened whenever Eloise's presence was felt.

It did her good to be cycling across the

moorland through a warm and misty fog, which blanketed the peaks and gave the area a mystical feel. She descended the hill from Waterfall and joined the Ashbourne road, conscious of the threat of the traffic that raced past.

She arrived at the station thirty-five minutes later, exhilarated and clear-minded. Full of determination. It had been this characteristic that had finally solved so many of their cases. A tenacious and stubborn optimism, a conviction that they would solve the case eventually. Joanna disliked failure. She had been brought up to *despise* failure by a father who thought of her as the son he had never had. As she locked her bike to the railings, her mouth had a firm set to it and her eyes smouldered.

She had a second quick shower before changing into her work clothes – a black skirt and scarlet T-shirt, low-heeled shoes. Now she was ready for work.

Surprisingly, Korpanski had beaten her to it. He grinned up at her, turning his gaze from the computer screen for no more than an instant before motioning towards two coffee cups already filled. 'Just going through the statements, Jo,' he said, 'ready for the briefing.'

She felt appreciative that he, too, was putting extra energy into the case.

They drank companionably until nine fifteen, peering at the screen, searching for something that might lead them to a conclusion. But they found nothing they had not seen before, nothing that led them any nearer to Grimshaw's murderer.

And yet as Joanna and Mike made their way to the briefing room their tread was quick and light.

The assembled officers seemed to have caught their optimism and looked alert and ready for action. Joanna and Mike exchanged glances. If only they could point them in the right direction. The only new information was that the handwriting on the note had been confirmed, surprisingly, by Gabriel Frankwell as being Grimshaw's.

She directed their energies into analysing the existing statements, checking and rechecking people's whereabouts for the Sunday evening – early.

They were almost through the briefing when a door opened at the back of the room. The desk sergeant, Alderley, stood in the doorway, hesitating. Korpanski walked the length of the room towards him. Listened to some whispered words. Joanna caught a look of complete consternation on her sergeant's face. He looked at her, his mouth open, shoulders up in confusion. What on earth, she wondered, was Alderley telling him that had so imprinted on his face?

Then she saw that someone was standing behind Alderley. A smart woman, late fifties, maybe early sixties, dressed in a dark grey trouser suit, looking so like her daughter it was not possible to mistake her identity. Tall, slim, with nondescript features but a tight, hard, determined mouth and sandy coloured hair. Joanna felt a rushing in her head. This was not possible – surely? A grim voice answered her silent question. In life and death *anything* is possible. But this would turn the entire case on its head, remove every motive, every assumption. She fixed her gaze on the woman, as though worried she would disappear, walked up the room and waited for Alderley to introduce them, yet knowing already.

'Th-this woman,' Alderley was stammering, 'says she's Mrs Grimshaw.'

Joanna gaped at the woman, absorbing everything about her, from the thin, almost gaunt frame, to the hard stare of the hazel eyes, so like her daughter's, the thin mouth, the defiant attitude.

'We-ell.' It was all she could manage.

She dismissed the briefing. It was pointless trying to proceed with the case until they had assimilated this new information, threaded this hitherto unknown and significant fact into the investigation. It would alter everything. Change the entire balance. At the back of Joanna's mind, the policewoman in her had already added the new suspect to the list and begun to analyse motives. Grimshaw had died intestate. Avis was still his legal wife, therefore his main beneficiary. Had Grimshaw's wife hated him? How would Judy respond to the resurrection of her mother? Had she realised that her father's story was nothing but a cruel trick? Joanna met the woman's eyes, held her hand out and received a limp shake. 'Shall we go into an interview room?'

The woman's gaze slid into hers. Joanna was again reminded of Avis's daughter, stroppy, sneaky and unpleasant. There was something equally and overtly hostile about her mother's stare.

The battle was about to begin.

She and Korpanski sat opposite Mrs Grimshaw, but Joanna found it hard to begin the questioning. Where do you start? *We believed you dead, fed to the pigs?*

318

Where have you been for the last eight years?

Have you kept in touch with your daughter? Is she in *on this?*

What part did your neighbour, Dudson, play in this?

Was he your lover? If not he, whom?

Suddenly helpless, she looked at Korpanski, whose eyes were resting on her, warmed to the colour of toffee with humour. He well knew that for once she was at a loss for words and was enjoying every moment of it. He was laughing at her, hardly bothering to conceal it.

She put her hands on the desk. 'Mrs Grimshaw,' she began. 'You are aware that your husband has been–'

She got no further.

'Yes, yes,' the woman replied impatiently. 'I know Jakob met with a violent end.'

'You left Prospect Farm.'

'Years ago.' The same impatient, irritated, rather rude tone. 'Being a farmer's wife didn't suit me.'

Joanna replaced the words impatient and rude with condescending.

'Where have you been?'

'Is it anything to do with the investigation?' Her voice was razor sharp.

Korpanski cut in, frostily. 'We don't know

319

yet, Mrs Grimshaw. We're just collecting facts at the moment. We had heard–'

Without warning, Mrs Grimshaw burst into peals of laughter. 'Oh, the pig story,' she said, then leaning in, added, 'I never thought Jakob had such a vivid imagination.'

'Can you think of any reason why your husband would confess to such a crime when it obviously isn't true?' Korpanski asked.

Mrs Grimshaw smiled. 'Jakob had a mischievous sense of humour,' she said. 'He knew what a nosey little thing young Judy was. He knew she'd go prying, looking for things.'

Sense of humour? Joanna almost shuddered. She wasn't exactly close to her own mother, but to plant this cruelly false evidence in the mind of a daughter didn't seem like humour, exactly.

But an explanation of sorts.

'Have you had anything to do with your daughter in the years of your absence?'

'No.' Said flatly, almost confrontationally. 'I thought it best.'

'Where have you been?'

'Abroad.' Almost a smirk crossed the woman's face. 'I ran a bar in Spain. Then a few years ago I moved to Eastern Europe.

Poland, the Czech Republic, and so on. I've travelled around.'

'Did you leave with anyone?'

Mrs Grimshaw shook her head. Her pale eyes met Joanna's. 'He travels fastest who travels alone,' she quoted.

'Kipling,' Joanna muttered under her breath.

Mrs Grimshaw continued. 'Once I'd decided to go,' she said, 'I knew I must leave Judy behind.'

'Why didn't you just file for divorce?' Korpanski asked, prosaic as ever.

She looked at him, then at Joanna. 'I don't expect either of you to believe this,' she said haughtily, 'but Jakob's farm was his life – and his inheritance. If I had divorced him the farm would have been split up. It was hardly viable, anyway. Half would have been impossible.'

Joanna nodded. This, at least, made sense. Even if none of the rest did.

She decided to proceed on a different tack. 'When did you return from your travels?'

'A little over two weeks ago.' There was a direct challenge in the woman's statement. She must have known when her husband died.

'Why?' Korpanski asked bluntly.

'I got bored with travelling.'

She hesitated. 'And,' her shoulders dropped, 'to be honest, someone from Leek came into the bar where I was working in Bratislava. He recognised me and told me how things were at the farm. I realised that Jakob was probably about to sell up. He told me about the land deal and I realised I could use the money.' She gave a smile that was really a sneer. 'Bar work doesn't exactly pay well, you know.'

Joanna nodded in mock sympathy, all the while thinking that this certainly complicated things for Judy Grimshaw. No longer her father's next of kin, she was about to be supplanted. Interesting.

'Have you seen your daughter since you've been back?'

'No. Not yet.' For the first time since the beginning of the interview some doubt crept into the woman's voice. And this time her smile appeared genuine. 'To be honest, I didn't how to approach her. After the story Jakob had spun she might faint if I showed up at her house. She might be angry.' Her eyes challenged. 'But a telephone call seems a little cold, don't you think? After all this time,' she tacked on almost casually.

Joanna and Mike stared back woodenly.

I would love to be a fly on the wall at the reunion, Joanna thought.

'How did you learn about the pig story?'

Avis Grimshaw licked her lips. 'Judy told the friends I was staying with a couple of months ago.' She smiled. 'They never believed it and tried to tell Judy it couldn't be the truth but she swallowed it.' A wry smile twisted her face. 'If you see what I mean.'

'Didn't that make you want to see her?'

'Yes and no,' Avis said. 'More yes than no.'

Joanna leant across the table. 'Did you see your husband on your return?'

Avis Grimshaw hesitated, so Joanna pressed on.

'Do you know anything that might have a bearing on your husband's death, Mrs Grimshaw?'

She shrugged. 'Not a thing,' she answered. 'I'm well out of touch, Inspector.'

'And where have you been in the time since you've been home?'

Again Mrs Grimshaw's face changed. She stared at the wall. 'I suppose,' she said, 'I'd had a great idea of walking back into people's lives.'

'Anyone in particular?' Korpanski asked with meaning.

But the spark had left Grimshaw's widow.

'I ... tried to look up a few old friends.'

'Where?'

'I have – had – a brother in Somerset. He apparently died three years ago. I didn't even know. And his widow is – with someone else now.'

She hesitated. 'I contacted a few more friends.' She crossed her legs. 'Life has changed,' she said, 'in the years since I've been away. I expected to be the wanderer returned. The lost sheep. The prodigal son. In fact I am a stranger to everyone – even, probably, to my daughter.'

Joanna was tempted to blurt out, 'What do you expect?' but uncharacteristically she held the words back because Mrs Grimshaw looked truly and sincerely upset.

'And the farm?'

She was holding something back. Joanna knew it and when she looked at Korpanski she could see he did too. The gaze from his dark eyes was unblinkingly on Avis Grimshaw, as though if he blinked he might miss some swift but vital sign.

'The farm,' Joanna repeated. 'Did you go there?'

Mrs Grimshaw looked from one to the other, her eyes almost frightened. 'I did call in,' she said finally, 'on the Monday.'

Korpanski interrupted. 'Do you mean the 10th or the 17th?'

'The 10th. I had rung him early in September just to warn him. He was furious. Absolutely furious.' She was pale. 'Angry with me for leaving him, the farm, our daughter.' She gulped in some air. 'I told him I wanted a divorce and that would mean I would be entitled to half the farm. It would finally have to be sold.' Another of the twisted smiles. 'So when I called in I didn't exactly expect much of a welcome.'

Joanna gave a sharp glance at Korpanski. 'How was he?'

Avis didn't realise how significant the question was. She shook her head.

'I can't tell you,' she said simply. 'I didn't see him. He wasn't there.'

Joanna couldn't resist giving Korpanski another swift glance.

He asked the next question. 'And the dog,' he asked, 'Ratchet?'

'Fast asleep,' Avis said. 'Not much of a bloody watchdog, if you ask me.'

'Did you walk round the farm?' Joanna asked.

Avis shook her head. 'No,' she said. 'I didn't. I knocked on the door, stuck my head round it, shouted for a bit, stood in the yard and yelled for a bit longer but the place...' she turned innocent eyes on Joanna, 'was completely deserted.'

'Any animal noise?'

'Not that I remember,' she said. 'Possibly from the barns. I can't be sure. I stayed less than ten minutes and then went to an old friend's house.' She managed a watery smile. 'One of the few I'd managed to track down who could stomach being with me.' Her smile widened. 'There's something about being regurgitated from a pig that makes you less than an ideal dinner companion.'

For the first time since the beginning of the interview, Joanna was tempted to smile too. 'Carry on,' she said.

'I stayed with her for a couple of days, went to London on the Thursday. She rang me and told me what had happened, including the fact that his body had lain undiscovered for around a week. I was frightened then. I knew it was unlikely that you would know *exactly* when Jakob had died, which would make it probable that I would become a suspect. I thought the best thing would be for me to come here and make a statement rather than have my story unravelled bit by bit during your investigations.'

Joanna could not help but feel some respect for the woman's intelligence. Grimshaw's widow had got it all worked out. And now she had got it all off her chest she seemed to relax. 'That,' she said quietly, 'is the truth. I swear it.'

'You may have to in court.' Joanna let the words sink in. 'Where will you be staying?'

'You mean "don't leave town".' The ghost of a smile accompanied her answer. 'I won't. I'll be staying in Derby Street. I have a friend there.'

'One more thing.'

It provoked an instantly wary look.

'It was mentioned that you had been friendly with Mr Dudson, the neighbouring farmer.'

Mrs Grimshaw composed her features into a neutral stare. 'I was friendly with his wife. There was nothing else between us. His wife was dying. In fact, it was one of the reasons why I stayed for so long at Prospect Farm.' A swift spasm of emotion crossed her face. 'I was really fond of her. She was a lovely woman and appreciated the food I prepared and a few little things only a woman would do around the house. In an odd sort of way, her death paved the path for me to go.'

'Oh?'

Mrs Grimshaw smiled. 'I'm sure this is an

indictable offence. I applied for a passport in her name,' she said simply. 'In one of our many conversations, she mentioned that she'd never been abroad so I knew she'd never had one before. It meant I really could disappear. But it wasn't just that. I didn't want to live my life like hers. She – and I – had done so little, married young, never travelled, had children, been a mother and a farmer's wife. She died in that role. I wanted more from my life. As I watched her getting weaker, I strengthened my own resolve. It is not a decision I regret,' she said with dignity.

'I see.' Again Joanna was at a loss for words. But she must ask one more thing.

'Did you kill your husband, Mrs Grimshaw?'

Again, the woman's answer was puzzling. 'There would have been no point, Inspector,' she said. 'At least not for money.'

But that wasn't strictly true. Jakob had died intestate. He and his wife had never divorced so she would be the beneficiary.

When the woman had gone, leaving behind traces of lemony perfume and sadness, Joanna turned to Mike and spread her hands out in a gesture of utter puzzlement. 'So where does this leave us, Korpanski?'

He folded his arms. 'With another suspect

to add to the list,' he said with satisfaction. 'And an interesting story.'

She almost cuffed him.

'Maybe we should have another talk to Mr Dudson,' she said, pushing her chair back. 'Was he in on this or not?'

They found the farmer sitting in a tractor, about to take a large and smelly machine across one of his fields. He looked less than pleased to see them but he was, at least, polite.

'Inspector,' he said, climbing down from the cab. 'What can I do for you?'

She waited until he was on the ground, facing her. 'It seems,' she said, 'that Mrs Grimshaw is alive.'

Nothing passed across his face. No surprise, puzzlement. His blunt features remained a perfect blank. 'Well,' he said finally. 'So–'

'You didn't know?'

He shook his head. 'No,' he said finally. 'I did not. I believed what she told me.'

'Who, Mr Dudson?'

He looked faintly irritated with himself for having blurted that out. 'Judy,' he muttered.

'And when did she tell you?'

Dudson looked furtive. 'Can't remember exactly.'

Korpanski climbed into the tractor and switched the ignition off. 'I think it would be a good idea if you came down to the station. Maybe that'll jog your memory.'

For a minute, Joanna thought the farmer would refuse. Then he bent his head. 'Give me a minute,' he mumbled. 'I'll change out of these work clothes.'

He reappeared less than five minutes later in a clean pair of green corduroys and a Barbour coat.

Joanna knew that the answers Dudson gave would be significant. And that he knew this. So she took her time, skirted round the issue.

'Your wife was a local girl?'

Dudson blinked then narrowed his eyes. 'What the devil's that got to do with any-thing?'

'Just answer the question.'

'She was,' he said, leaning forward. 'Local born and bred.'

A twist of cynicism crossed his face. 'You wouldn't find anyone else to put up with the conditions round here.'

'It's a tough life,' Joanna mused.

Dudson nodded in agreement.

'And you haven't married again?'

Dudson shook his head. 'Didn't really have the heart for it,' he said gruffly.

'You were friendly, though, with Mrs Grimshaw.'

Dudson smiled. 'Friendly, yes. Anything more, no.'

'Think back, Mr Dudson, to when you last saw Mrs Grimshaw.'

'It were the day after the funeral,' he said. 'She came round with a shepherd's pie. She looked sort of...' he fumbled for the word, 'distracted. Bothered about something. She put her arm round my shoulders and said we would both be mourning together.' He smiled. 'She looked smart. As though she were going somewhere. So when Jakob told me afterwards that she'd gone with another man it all made sense. I believed it.'

'But then Judy told you otherwise.' Joanna said softly.

Dudson nodded, glanced furtively around the room. 'She's a nasty girl, that one,' he said. 'Used to beat that poor little pony of hers something rotten. She had a cruel, un-forgiving streak in her. Something like her dad. Jakob was like that,' he mused. 'He found things funny that weren't. She took after him.'

'So tell me about the day that Judy told

331

you what her father said had been her mother's fate.'

'It were a Sunday,' he said. 'She appeared in the doorway holding a piece of paper. It were a letter. She read it out to me.' Dudson was quietly chewing his lip. 'At first I couldn't believe it. I thought it were Jakob pulling the wool over my eyes. I couldn't understand why he'd written it down. He'd know that she would find the letter one day.'

Korpanski leant in. 'How did she seem? Angry?'

Dudson swivelled round to look at him, and then turned back to look Joanna straight in the eyes. 'There's two sorts of angry,' he said. 'There's hot angry and there's cold angry. She was cold angry. Every muscle in that woman's body was full of hate.'

Joanna couldn't ignore the look of triumph Mike gave her.

The noose was tightening around Judy's neck. They let Dudson go.

Joanna glanced at her watch. Six thirty. She'd promised Matthew she would sit down to dinner at seven thirty. More than anything, she wanted to haul Judy Grimshaw in and question her through half the night. But Matthew would not forgive her. Whatever the

332

reason, he would think of it as an excuse. Korpanski was eyeing her expectantly. They'd worked together on enough cases for him to be able to anticipate her next move. With a sigh, she stood up. So this was what it meant to have conflicting loyalties: always to feel wrong-footed.

Avoiding Korpanski's eyes, she spoke. 'We'll talk to Madam Wilkinson in the morning.'

Korpanski watched her, incredulous. 'You're kidding?'

He knew her methods. Knew she really wanted to grill the woman until she told them something. She felt the struggle inside her, and then picked up the phone, almost seeing Matthew's lips curl in disbelief as he answered. 'I'm really sorry, Matthew,' she said. 'Something's come up. I'm sorry,' she said again.

He spoke the words for her.

'Don't wait up,' he supplied. 'Funny,' he said angrily, 'that it should "come up" now, at this time, just when Eloise is here. Well, I'm sorry too, Jo. Sometimes, you know, you simply have to make an effort.' And he put the phone down.

Joanna fingered the pearl on her finger. It hadn't made things any easier, had it? More difficult, if anything. She was more than ever conscious of the grit that was at the centre of this lovely gem.

Judy was defiant, her pale eyes staring at them when she opened the door of her terraced house. 'I don't know why you keep bothering me,' she said grumpily. 'Typical of the police. Grab the next of kin and you're halfway there.' She gave a heavy sigh. 'So what is it this time?'

'We simply want some clarification,' Joanna said steadily. Initially, she'd felt dislike for this woman. Now it was turning into something much stronger. Not a good idea to feel such prejudice against a suspect; she was well aware that it could cloud her judgement.

Judy's eyes became wary. 'Clarification,' she demanded, 'on what?'

'You knew about the letter your father wrote,' Joanna said. 'When did you realise it wasn't true?'

Judy's face changed. Still wary but tense now. 'Sorry?'

'Your mother is not dead, is she?'

'I don't understand.'

'I think you do.'

Judy took a long time to speak again. Her

chest moved, her face moved but she said nothing. Finally, she did speak. Differently. She had lost some of her bounce, her aggression, and simply looked a skinny, sad woman. 'Can I get this straight, Inspector?' she said. 'Are you telling me that my mother is still alive?'

Oddly enough there was anger underlying her voice. That and a terrible uncertainty. Joanna watched the emotions cross her face, wondering, what's going on?

She nodded. 'Yes. Your mother is alive.'

Judy sank back in her chair. 'Bitch,' she spat. 'So where's she been?'

'She's been working in Spain and other countries.'

'And she never once got in touch with me. What a mother,' she exploded. 'What a fucking mother!'

Joanna had to agree with her.

Quite unexpectedly her own feelings towards Judy Grimshaw changed. She felt sorry for her. 'I think,' she said, 'that your mother wanted to escape the stifling atmosphere of farm life rather than you. You were the price she paid.'

And just as unexpectedly Judy looked furious rather than mollified by the words. 'I don't want your opinion on my mother and her dirty behaviour, Inspector,' she said viciously. 'Just find out who killed my father. And I suggest you do concentrate on his next of kin.'

Behind Joanna, Korpanski cleared his throat noisily.

They left soon afterwards and drove back to the station. 'I'm toying with the idea that maybe we should consider getting a warrant to search Judy Grimshaw's house,' Joanna said. 'And I would love to be a fly on the wall when mother and daughter are reunited.'

Korpanski nodded in agreement, his mouth pursed up.

It was nine o'clock when she crept in, feeling utterly guilty. Mike had given her a lift home, which seemed to rub in the conflict between work and home life. She had almost been tempted to stay the night in the police station but that would solve nothing. She could not stay there for ever taking evasive action.

They were talking as she entered the room. The two of them in earnest conversation, blonde heads close together, Eloise's pale hair making a contrast with Matthew's straw-coloured locks.

'Hello.'

336

Matthew managed a smile. Eloise simply regarded her steadily, dislike sharpening her small features so she looked even more like her mother. It didn't help. 'Hello, Joanna.' Eloise spoke finally. 'Looks like you'll be seeing even more of me in the future.'

Joanna couldn't dream up a suitable response.

Matthew stood up. 'Shall I pop some lasagne in the microwave?' he said awkwardly.

She answered without turning her head. 'That'd be nice. Thanks.'

He disappeared into the kitchen and Joanna settled into the armchair opposite. 'So,' she said to Eloise, 'how did your interview go?'

'They've offered me a place.'

Joanna's heart sank. 'Will you take it?'

Eloise was watching her. Too much perception in the green eyes. Her father's eyes. Her father's beautiful eyes.

She nodded. 'I haven't had the formal offer yet,' she said. 'There are the tiny fences of A levels. They're bound to want high grades for entry, but I would like to go there. I was impressed with the university campus and the quality of teaching. It's one of the best for practical medicine. Besides...' Her eyes were still resting on Joanna, challenging her. 'I'd like to be near Dad. He can help me with my studies and things.' She smiled. 'I'm going to struggle with chemistry and they'll insist on that to gain entry.' She hesitated before her next sentence. 'Don't worry, Joanna, I'm not about to try and intrude on your little Arcadia but he is my dad and I've missed him in the time since he left. I'd like to stay close to him.'

Right on cue, Matthew walked in with a tray of food and three tall glasses.

'So,' he said, with hearty jollity. 'Shall we toast?'

'It could be a bit premature, Dad.'

'No,' Joanna said softly. 'Let's toast. To you, Eloise, to the grades that you need and to having your father near you.' She felt happy, relieved. It would work out – surely?

Matthew popped the cork from some sparkling wine and the three of them drank, more companionable than they had ever been before.

Eloise sipped from her glass. 'And to you, Joanna,' she said. 'Congratulations.'

The green eyes looked perceptively deep into hers and Joanna flushed then drank the toast.

It was later when Matthew asked her about the events of the day.

'Extraordinary,' she said. 'I don't want any of this coming out.' She gave a warning glance at father and daughter. 'But Grimshaw's wife turned up, right out of the blue.'

Matthew threw his head back and laughed, and she knew he wasn't laughing because of what she'd said but because he was happy. Genuinely happy. After a second or two she and Eloise joined in.

'Is nothing safe, nothing predictable?'

Joanna took a thoughtful sip of the wine. 'To be honest,' she said, 'this has been the last straw. For a simple homicide it is proving to be the most frustrating of cases. Every time I think I know something it turns out to be false. It's pissing me off, quite honestly.'

'How does this affect the daughter's inheritance?' Eloise asked the question slowly.

'We-ell,' Joanna pondered the point. 'Mrs Grimshaw will be the next of kin. Grimshaw died intestate. It might go to court for an expensive argument. Judy doesn't strike me as the forgiving sort and there's patently very bad blood between mother and daughter. Unless she and her mother have more to tell me and they *have* been in touch, this has been nothing more than a pointless charade. I'd say that they'd be well advised to come to a private agreement and keep it out of the courts. Of course, there's no predicting what will actually happen.'

'Hmm,' Matthew said, grinning. 'A three-pipe problem?'

She was tempted to aim a cushion at him.

But sitting, drinking quietly as father and daughter chattered, she rolled a few possibilities around in her mind. Was it possible that Judy had shown Dudson the letter to provoke him? To murder? Had Mrs Grimshaw returned out of the blue coincidentally or to claim her inheritance?

Was her reappearance cause or effect? Had she killed her husband?

They were questions she badly needed the answers to.

Chapter Fourteen

Thursday, 27th September. 8 a.m.

Breakfast was a stilted affair with Eloise appearing, yawning, pushing the blonde hair out of her eyes, wrapping herself tightly in a dressing gown over a pair of pink pyjamas. She looked very young, much younger than her eighteen years, almost the small girl Joanna had first met when she had visited Matthew's farm once to question him about the murder of a nurse. Eloise accepted some cereal and fruit juice and swigged away at an enormous mug of coffee Matthew had brewed.

'Well,' Joanna said awkwardly, standing up and clearing her dishes into the dishwasher. 'I have to go now. Good luck,' she said to Eloise. 'I hope you get your place.' She gave a sly peek at Matthew. 'Your father will love to see more of you.'

Eloise's green eyes gave her a look so transparent Joanna could read their message: *Not you, though.*

The two women smiled at each other and Matthew looked happy, taken in by the charade.

Joanna kissed his cheek, then, feeling a wave of affection at the scratchy bristles, his mouth. 'Bye, darling,' she said. 'See you later.'

He nodded. She ran upstairs to clean her teeth and minutes later was on her bike, which Mike had managed to stow in the back of his Volvo last night.

As she cycled across the moors her mind was as furiously busy as her legs. Question after question presented itself. Who was the friend who had recognised Mrs Grimshaw? she wondered. Because this supposedly chance encounter had set in motion a train of events. If Mrs Grimshaw was telling the truth, her discovery, living under an assumed identity, had been the key that had led to her return home. What bearing might this have had on her husband's murder? There was one way to find out.

Even though Joanna shared one character-istic with most other police officers – a mistrust of anyone's statement – the answer was inescapable. Ask her.

Mike almost groaned when she put her suggestion to him. His dark eyes rested on her with a look of impatience. 'I don't see where that's going to lead us, Jo,' he said grumpily. 'The murder was committed here, not abroad. It's a local thing. A squabble about land, resentment about the intrusion of a farm on a posh housing estate, a false claim of murder of our victim's wife, a daughter who stands to benefit from her father's death. It all happened in Leek. So it's here that we need to look for motive and method. Not some bar in Eastern Europe. Grimshaw had never even been out of the country. So why would there be a foreign connection?'

She was surprised at Korpanski's outburst. Whatever her line of inquiry, he generally went along with it. Not opposing. He tended to trust both her judgement and her decisions. Unbidden, a vision of the inside of the barn at Prospect Farm swam in front of her eyes. Plastic sacks of animal feed, the rope, dangling free, the oblong bales of hay, neatly stacked. 'There is a foreign connection,' she said stubbornly, 'but we won't know what it is unless we probe a bit more.' She attempted to retrieve Korpanski's missing good humour. 'You know how I hate loose ends, Mike.' She picked up the phone.

Mrs Grimshaw was in an equally negative

mood when Joanna put her question to her. 'What's that got to do with anything?' she snapped.

'Mrs Grimshaw,' Joanna said. She was getting fed up with all this. 'Just give me the name and let me decide what, if any, bearing this has on your husband's death.'

There was a long pause, so long that Joanna was on the point of asking the question again, but Mrs Grimshaw finally grunted and provided the name. Reluctantly. Joanna had the impression that she had caught Grimshaw's widow on the hop. Whatever questions she had expected, this had not been one of them. Ergo, she did not have an answer prepared.

'Brian Young,' she said, the name being dragged out of her. 'He was an old school friend of mine, years and years ago. He wandered into the bar where I was employed and – well – he recognised me. I knew then that the game was up, that he would soon spread the gospel.' The bitterness in her voice was a puzzle to Joanna. Avis Grimshaw could easily have moved on to another city, another country, even, and vanished again even if her cover *had* been blown. It would have taken the police years to catch up with her; she would have been a low priority on the long list of criminals.

Avis continued. 'He never could resist being the centre of attention and seeing me there, going under the name of a neighbour he knew to be dead – well – I didn't have a chance, did I?'

'His address?' Joanna repeated, unwilling to be deflected. Sulkily, Mrs Grimshaw gave it to her. 'I don't know the actual address,' she said, 'but he owns a garage on the Ashbourne road. He lives above it – on his own – in a flat. He and his wife split up years ago. I don't know who his current partner is. When he was in Bratislava, he came alone.'

Joanna thanked her and put the phone down. 'Brian Young,' she said thoughtfully to Mike. 'Now why does that name ring a bell?'

Korpanski supplied the answer. 'He came out of prison eight months ago.'

'What was he in for?'

'Drugs. Quite the little baron. He had a ring that extended down to the south of Spain, using the back door of Morocco, smuggling in marijuana. Made a nice packet out of it right up until he got busted by the Drugs Squad.' Korpanski nibbled the top of his pen. 'Now, I wonder what he was doing in the Czech Republic.'

'Right.' Joanna was thoughtful. 'What did we discover about this end of the operation?'

'Not a lot,' Korpanski said, then added, 'not enough really. We tracked down some of his accomplices but never felt we had the full story. And he wasn't telling. In the end they banged him up for eight years. He was out after three.' He gave a long, heartfelt, regretful sigh. Had it been up to Sergeant Mike Korpanski, the entire parole system would have been scrapped.

Joanna stood up. 'Well, Korpanski, let's go and visit this Mr Young.'

They tracked Young down to the workshop at the side of a very busy and prosperous-looking site. Queues of cars were waiting to fill up with fuel. There was a rumour of yet another price hike in the oil industry so customers were taking no chances. Young was standing with his head under the bonnet of a blue Honda Jazz and looked up warily at the two police, recognising them instantly. It's a talent most ex-cons have – the ability to recognise police personnel at forty paces – even if they've never met before. It's a useful instinct in the criminal fraternity.

He didn't even question their identity or

wait for them to flash their ID cards before speaking. 'I've done my time,' he said. 'You've nothing on me now.'

Joanna decided to play him along.

'Your visit to Bratislava,' she began.

Young looked instantly even more wary. 'So, what of it? I'm allowed a legitimate holiday, aren't I?'

'Of course,' Joanna said soothingly. 'I'm only really interested in someone you met over there. An old school friend?'

Young looked bemused.

'A Mrs Grimshaw.'

'Oh.' His brow cleared. 'Her. What of it?'

'You didn't know she was there?'

Young wiped his hands on an oily rag. 'Not only did I not know she was *there*,' he said. 'I understood she'd vanished. You could have knocked me down with a feather when I walked into the bar and there she was, serving at tables. She'd walked out on her husband years ago. No one knew what had happened to her. Like most people round here, if I thought about it at all I just assumed she'd gone off with a man. She always was a feisty sort of woman. Not your typical farmer's wife. It gave me a shock to see her. And I don't think she was too pleased to see me either. She started off asking me not to say anything to anyone at home.' His eyes were pale blue and surprisingly shrewd with tiny, sharp pupils. He smiled with his teeth without it even grazing his eyes and Joanna guessed that he had not reassured Mrs Grimshaw that he would keep quiet. He was more likely to have tried to blackmail her. She returned the smile, noticing that he had omitted to mention that his old school friend was living in a foreign country under an assumed name. 'Next thing I knew,' Young finished, 'I heard she was back. And then–'

'Her husband gets bumped off,' Korpanski supplied.

'Exactly.'

And that, Joanna thought, was that.

She decided to rattle Young. 'And how did you enjoy your...' her pause was deliberate, 'holiday, Mr Young?'

Young scowled.

She tried one more tack. A blind leap. 'What was the name of the bar? Where exactly was it? Who owned it?'

'It's called Posh.'

Joanna couldn't resist a smirk at Korpanski.

'It's in the Old Town just behind the main square. Fantastic place, it is. Must be worth

348

a fortune. It was packed every night I was there. Heaving.'

Now Joanna was curious. 'What sort of a place is it?'

Young shrugged. 'Bit of everything. Music, cabaret, food, drinks. And round the back is a sort of motel extension. Must be twenty or thirty rooms. And the grounds. Well...' He narrowed his eyes.

'Who owns it?'

Young looked surprised. 'Didn't I tell you? Avis does,' he said.

This was food for thought. Joanna and Mike exchanged startled glances. It wasn't exactly how Avis had portrayed her missing years. 'Really?'

They left Young to his mechanics then and returned to the station.

As soon as they were safely back in their office, Joanna began to speak. 'Not quite the penniless barmaid then, was she?'

Korpanski shook his head.

She continued. 'What bearing this'll have on our investigation I don't know, Mike. But it is significant.' She met his eyes. 'Where did she get the money from, Mike? How did she make so much?' She hesitated for a moment before adding a question. 'Do you smell a rat, Mike?'

'Property's probably done well over there since the mid-nineties. She could have done it legitimately.'

Joanna said nothing.

He tried again. 'She's obviously a good businesswoman. She could have borrowed the money and made the whole thing work.'

'Under a false name. Open to blackmail,' she continued. 'But if her business over there was legitimate except for her assumed name, she could still have continued. She'd have to have come back here, assumed her own identity, had her wrists slapped. But if on the other hand she was up to something more...' She narrowed her eyes. 'There's something else, Mike. Something we've missed out on.'

For no apparent reason the image of the barn was still in front of her eyes, nagging for her attention. The neat bales of hay, the plastic sacks of animal feed, the rope swinging, almost beckoning her to follow.

She knew the clue was there. Right in front of her eyes.

When she looked up, Korpanski was watching her with a strange, almost worried expression in his eyes.

'There's something in this that intrigues me, Mike,' she said.

He perched on the corner of the desk, swinging his muscular legs to and fro. 'What exactly?'

She met his eyes with a hard, confident stare. 'I'm not sure,' she said slowly, 'except coincidence. Mrs Grimshaw remains hidden for years, a fellow from Leek finds her. She returns and the next thing her husband's dead. She openly tells us she was on his premises on one of the days that he could have died. This knowing she would be chief suspect. Why? Why? All along I've felt time of death was significant. A false trail was laid deliberately to lead us to believe that Jakob Grimshaw died on the Tuesday, in which case Avis could have spoken to him. But we've surmised that the Tuesday was a false trail.' She frowned. 'Why? To give Judy an alibi? One we could never break – a list of patients waiting to see her. Did mother and daughter have contact in the intervening years? Is their apparent hostility nothing but a clever device to make us believe they could not have worked together, covered for each other? How did Avis Grimshaw make all that money? A lot of evidence leads us towards Jakob's wife and daughter but it isn't the entire story. The farm is encircled by a ring of hostile neighbours who all have their own reason for wishing the place off the map. The Westons, for animal rights reasons; Mrs Frankwell, to get a good price for her property; Mostyn, who stands to gain if his land beyond the farm is granted planning permission; Frankwell, who is desperate to sell his house and has been deceived by the old farmer.' She couldn't resist a smirk, remembering the deep scratch that had scored the side of the Porsche. 'I can't see Gabriel Frankwell being too pleased at being made a fool of by Grimshaw, can you? Then there is the wild card, that after years, generations, of clinging on to the farm, Grimshaw may have been about to sell up. And we have more. A daughter who has believed her mother dead for eight years, that her father murdered her and disposed of the body in a most barbaric way. If her story is true, Judy Grimshaw held this story to her heart for more than a year before she divulged it to Dudson, the neighbouring farmer, the man she'd believed her mother might have had an affair with but who fairly obviously had not eloped with her.' Her eyes met Korpanski's. 'I don't have to tell you; these are all powerful ingredients for catastrophe. But did one event cause the next, were they a sequence of events, a pack of cards, and if so, which circumstance is the most significant?'

She reached for the phone again. 'Mrs Grimshaw.' The snappy tone of the returning voice made Korpanski wince.

'I just wondered whether you'd met up with your daughter yet?'

'I don't see that it's any business of yours, Inspector,' Avis replied acidly. 'It has no bearing on the murder of my husband.'

'I simply wondered what her response to you might have been.'

Avis's response was swift and unmistakable. 'Mind your own bloody business.'

Joanna replaced the phone and gave a wry smile at Korpanski. 'Friendly as ever,' she said. 'Nice family.'

Korpanski simply grinned. 'Flea in the ear, Jo?'

'If I wasn't such a lady,' she said, 'you'd be getting the two-fingered salute, Sergeant. Now concentrate.'

She frowned. 'We're still missing something, aren't we?'

Korpanski nodded glumly. 'The whole bloody lot if you ask me.'

She smiled. 'Optimistic as ever,' she mocked. 'Have faith. It's like peeling an onion,' she said. 'Strip one bit away; it might sting your eyes but underneath you find something further, more complex. This looked like the most parochial, the simplest of cases but search underneath and there is another dimension. We started with neighbours and local motives. And look what happens?' She raised her eyebrows. 'We end up with a European case, a drugs connection. What next, Mike?'

'It is like peeling an onion,' he repeated. 'It makes your eyes sting and water so much you can't see a damned thing.'

She was silent, waiting for Korpanski to turn the corner as she knew he would – eventually.

'I've been wondering, Jo,' he said slowly, 'why did she go off like that in the first place? Why not just leave, get a job somewhere, write to her daughter and explain? That would be more normal. Why leave the whole thing open so Grimshaw could tell that horrible lie about where her mother had gone, plant the letter in a place he knew his daughter would one day find?' Korpanski was scowling and scratching the back of his neck – a well known gesture when he was both irritated and confused. 'Why are we concentrating so hard on the wider part of the story? After all, we don't think Jakob Grimshaw had anything to do with foreign climes – or drugs, do we? He was never off the farm, Jo.' Korpanski's voice was tight and raised. He was almost shouting at her.

Joanna ignored his aggression and continued calmly. 'So was it a coincidence that his wife heads abroad, makes a lot of money and just *happens* to bump into and be recognised by one of our local drug dealers just out of clink? Come on, Mike,' she said. 'Leek is a tiny place. Avis had never lived anywhere else until she left. The coincidence of her bumping into a fellow native, a criminal at that, is not high. Think,' she appealed.

They worked in silence for a few minutes, then Joanna looked across at Korpanski. 'Mike,' she said slowly, her face worried, 'what if...?' She didn't complete the sentence but realised her mind was working furiously now. Grimshaw had stumbled on something – or someone. It had been that that had caused his death. And why was the image of the barn where the animals had died persistently snagging at her consciousness? She stood up, knocking a file onto the floor. Korpanski picked it up. 'Hey,' he said. 'Don't get overexcited now, Jo.'

But she was feeling impatient, every cell in her body straining. 'When Avis called at the farm on Monday the 10th, we assumed that

Jakob was already dead? Correct?'

Korpanski paused before adding. 'The only problem with that is, what about the dog?'

'Alive? Asleep? Or dead?' she said. 'Stretched out was what she said. All she said was that it didn't bark. And that is if she was telling the truth.'

They looked at each other for further minutes before Joanna spoke.

'She's playing us on the end of a string,' she said softly, stretched out her hand and picked up the telephone, tucking it under her chin. 'Feeding us...' she couldn't resist it, 'little porkies.'

Even Korpanski was surprised at the question she asked when she was connected.

'Tell me, does your garage service tractors?'

She met Korpanski's eyes. 'The ones at Prospect Farm?'

He strained to hear the answer.

'Did you get a call out to there on Tuesday the 11th of September?'

Korpanski guessed the reply was in the affirmative because Joanna's next question was, 'Can you tell me who you sent...? Ah. I see.'

She looked pleased with herself as she replaced the handset.

'Guess who paid a little visit to Prospect Farm on that Tuesday morning, Mike?'

Without waiting she said softly, 'Young.' Then, 'We have to go back to the farm,' she said reluctantly. 'Now.'

He studied her for a moment, knowing there was more she was not telling him, knowing he'd always mocked her *instincts*. When she remained silent he tried to prompt her. 'Any explanations? Am I going to be in on this?'

'No,' she said flatly, 'because I may be wrong, but tell Fran you might be late to-night. I'll leave a similar message for Matthew.'

'Are we telling anyone where we're going?'

She shook her head.

'Not even the duty sergeant?'

'No.'

He picked up his jacket from the back of the chair. 'You expect a lot of me, Joanna Piercy,' he said, a smile lifting the corner of his lips.

For some reason she flushed and touched her ring. 'I know,' she said, frowning to cover her discomfort. 'Believe me, Mike, I know.'

'OK,' he said steadily. 'I'll drive.'

It was dusk by the time they drew up to the gate that led to the farmyard. In some ways it was a perfect time and place for a stakeout. Misty, rainy, dull, mysterious. Colourless. Uninspiring, in a way. Abandoned now that the scenes of crime team had left. Instinctively, Joanna knew that at last she was walking along the right track. It was like the game of hot and cold. Each step towards the property felt a degree or two warmer.

'Put the car round the back,' she instructed Korpanski. 'Out of sight.'

He did little but raise his eyebrows at her but did as she'd asked, hiding the car round the side of the farmhouse, out of sight from the approach. To all intents and purposes, the farm appeared deserted.

'The barn,' Joanna said next.

The creak of the huge doors was as eerie as the sound effect in a Hammer House of Horrors movie.

The place was equally gloomy inside, the scent of the dead cattle fading behind the fusty but not unpleasant scent of hay.

A fresh wind blew in through the cracks in the barn door and up through the opening in the hayloft. Without a word Joanna started climbing the ladder, Korpanski close behind her. They had worked together enough times to make verbal communication hardly necessary.

Mike spoke softly in her ear. 'How long do you think we'll have to stay?'

'All night if we must,' Joanna said, equally quietly. 'We watch. The police guard only left this morning. There's been no opportunity till now.'

'For what?'

In the gloom, Joanna faced Mike. 'Can I ask you a question?'

He stared at her, his nod hardly more than a twitch of his head.

'Do we really believe Judy Grimshaw didn't know her mother was still alive?'

Korpanski shrugged. 'They're a weird family,' he said. 'It's possible.' Then, 'Well, if I'm staying I'd better make myself comfortble. Take a hay bale, Joanna.'

It was minutes later before he spoke again. 'Is this a stake out?'

'Possibly not. I might be wrong, Mike.'

'Ah,' Korpanski said. 'So that's why the secrecy.' He paused. 'That's why no back-up.'

'Exactly.'

'Was that wise?'

In the growing darkness Joanna smiled to herself. 'Can you imagine a dozen clumsy-footed coppers hiding around this place?'

Korpanski said nothing.

More minutes passed in silence. 'Your phone's on silent, Mike?' she whispered.

'Yes.'

'Good. Mine too.'

The silence was now icily penetrating, chill and fresh and heavy. The wait was growing longer. 'It's getting bloody cold in here,' Mike grumbled.

'Sit against me,' she suggested. 'I'm freezing too.'

More silence.

'And if they don't come tonight?'

'My guess,' Joanna said softly, 'is that they'll be in a huge hurry to get their stuff and get the hell out of here.'

'What stuff?'

It was at that point that she realised her eyes and mouth had worked together. 'The animal feed sacks, Mike,' she said. 'Look where it comes from.'

'The Czech Republic,' he said. 'So what?'

'My guess is fake cigarettes,' Joanna answered.

'Where do you get that from?'

'More money than drugs these days with the high taxes, an Eastern European connection, a sudden return when the safe storage place looks like being threatened.'

'Is that what this is all about then?'

'Not quite,' Joanna said softly. 'But nearer to the truth than we've been so far.'

'If you're talking about Judy,' Korpanski said, almost to himself, 'she's no dope. She'll know something's going on.'

'I *know* she'll know what's going on. That's the trick!'

They heard a car leave the Ashbourne road and pull up a few hundred yards away. The engine was switched off. They heard no voices, no footsteps, yet they knew their quarry was near. Alone?

A figure skulked around the barn.

There was a soft mutter as someone realised the barn door was ajar. Joanna cursed herself. They should have shut it tight after them. The worst thing was that she knew *why* she hadn't insisted they close it and shut out the last of the light: a terrible claustrophobia in this place of death. This dreadful atmosphere.

She almost *felt* the stiffening of hairs on their quarry's neck.

'Is anyone there?'

He or she, like them, was spooked by the interior of the barn. 'Is anyone there?'

It was a frightened whisper.

They heard rasping, irregular breaths, in, out, in, out. Heard the sound of feet stepping across the crisp, dry hay, a waft of damp when the floor was moist. Slowly. Slowly, getting nearer. Joanna felt Mike stiffen against her. There was a loud clatter as whoever it was bumped into one of the farm implements, followed by a soft curse.

Neither Joanna nor Mike moved a single muscle. Their quarry must have reached the bottom of the ladder because they heard the slap of shoes against the rungs, the gentle creak of the wooden tread.

Then came the unmistakable click of a shotgun being adjusted.

Chapter Fifteen

'Don't move,' Joanna mouthed. 'Stay still.'

Korpanski was breathing hard. Behind the panic they were both aware that they had broken all the rules. Who knew they were here? No one. They had staked out a crime scene without sharing their knowledge at all. Joanna was cursing herself for the way she had followed her own instincts, broken a cardinal police rule: you don't work alone. And now she had put herself and, worse, her

362

sergeant's safety at risk. She tugged her mobile phone out of her pocket and fingered it, pressed triple nine and let it run as a head appeared over the top of the ladder, silhouetted against the dim lights outside. She saw him raise the gun and steady it on the top rung. 'Police,' Joanna managed in the same instant Korpanski moved in front of her and they heard the blast of a shotgun. She felt the hot wind against her face as Mike slumped across her. Then she felt the warm stickiness of his blood on her hands.

Literally and metaphorically.

She heard the gun click again and moved, shoving Mike's body off her. She grabbed the rope and swung, heard a shout, and their assailant toppled off the ladder. She braced herself but nothing more happened. She heard soft moaning on the floor beneath them and felt a moment of grim satisfaction, swiftly followed by a feeling of blind panic. Korpanski was silent.

She felt sick with guilt. What had she done?

She spoke into her mobile. 'Ten-nine,' she said. 'Ten-nine. Officer shot. Prospect Farm in the barn.' She repeated the phrases over and over again, feeling for a carotid pulse and, thank God, finding one. Better, a strong, steady pulse hammering away in Korpanski's thick neck.

She didn't move again until she heard the welcome scream of police cars and saw the blinding flash of blue lights filling the floor of the barn.

At the same time her phone flashed a call. 'Where are you?'

It was Detective Constable Alan King. Steady, worried, in control. 'In the barn,' she managed, 'in the hayloft. Korpanski's been shot. We need an ambulance.' At the same time she was wondering how it would reach them, with an armed man beneath them. She tried to give them the information they needed. 'An unidentified man climbed the ladder. I pushed him off it. I've had no response since.' She was aware she was speaking almost incoherently. But her mind struggled to be sane and steady.

So this is what shock is like, she thought. And felt a strange, floating detachment, as though this was happening in a film. That was when she knew she was in danger of losing it.

DC King spoke again. 'Ma'am,' he said. 'The man with the gun. What state is he in?'

She crawled away from Korpanski, heard him groan with a feeling of exhilaration; he was alive.

She peered over the side of the hayloft. The man was sprawled beneath, the gun a few feet from him.

'He appears to be lying still,' she whispered. 'The gun is three – four yards away from him.'

'You know the rules,' King said softly. 'We cannot risk another officer being hurt.'

The word *another* stung her.

She hardly noticed the barn door open. All she felt was a rush of cold air and the softest of creaks. An officer was moving forward, bulky in Kevlar. He reached the gun and spoke into his mouthpiece.

'Safe,' he said.

Joanne felt tears fill her eyes and sank back against Korpanski's body.

The cuffs were on their assailant. Then suddenly all was activity and light, the barn filled with police. Her colleagues. Ambulances backed against the barn and the slim man was carted off, Korpanski strapped to a stretcher and taken gently down to a second waiting ambulance. She climbed down the ladder and followed the stretcher, watched the paramedics slide a drip into Korpanski's arm, clamp an oxygen mask over his face. His eyes were closed and he looked white and vulnerable. It was a picture that would stay with her for the rest of her life.

She touched his hand. 'Thanks, Mike,' she said. 'I owe you one. I won't forget this. Ever.' Then the ambulance drove off, lights flashing, siren screaming. She listened as the sound faded into the distance and the light was no longer visible.

Someone threw a blanket around her shoulders, asked her if she was all right, if she needed medical attention.

Yes to the first, no to the second. She wanted to write down her report in detail before she forgot.

They took her back to the station.

She rang Matthew and told him she was safe but would not be home tonight. And now she had her own demons to deal with. How to tell Fran and her children that she had placed her husband deliberately in the path of danger. She hadn't needed to do this with just him as back-up. She could have done it properly, taken a full team, suitably armed and equipped. At the same time, she knew that Fran Korpanski was fully aware that her husband would have followed Inspector Piercy anywhere – into the jaws of...

No not there. She wouldn't go there. Not

death. Nor hell.

The reason she hadn't followed procedure had been because she had really known so little and she had worried she would never know, that nothing would be proven and that Jakob Grimshaw's murder would remain a mystery.

The gunman was admitted to hospital with a police guard. Initially incognito. It was PC Bridget Anderton who identified him as Tim Bradeley, employee at Farrell's Animal Feeds. And so the link had been uncovered but not the entire story. That would come later. For now she had to face up to it. She was responsible. Colclough would hold her responsible. But not as responsible as she would hold herself.

She recalled Korpanski's moving in front of her, shielding her from the blast of the gun.

Every man wants to be a hero.

Every man wants to be a hero. It would comfort her later when she had to recount every single event that had led up to that terrible night.

Worse, she had to admit to herself that she had made the decision to bring Korpanski along because she was *used* to having him at her side. He was a powerful physical presence that she had used, and whatever she said to the subsequent inquiry, everyone at the station would know it. It was indefensible. Somewhere deep inside her was a fact she did not want to face. She had always known that if she stared down the barrel of a shotgun and Korpanski was by her side, he would risk his own life to save hers. Korpanski would shield her. She had known it and taken advantage of it. That had been why she had brought him along tonight.

But back to that night.

It was seven in the morning when they took her to the hospital where she ran the gauntlet of Fran Korpanski's cold stare. 'I won't forgive you for this, Joanna,' she said. 'He would have followed you to the ends of the earth. Your opinion of him mattered more than anything. Even his life, his family. You wilfully took advantage of him. We could have lost him. I could have lost him. Ricky and Joss could have lost their father. We all still could. The doctors are waiting for his condition to stabilise before they operate.'

Joanna began to apologise but got no further than, 'I'm so—' before Fran Korpanski cut in.

'No apology can make up for this,' she said, her eyes drifting down to her husband's still face. 'Nothing.' Then, 'You can have a couple of minutes alone with him. I'm going to ring the children.'

When the door had closed behind the furious woman, Joanna sat down by the side of the bed and touched Korpanski's hand. 'Mike?' she appealed. 'Mike.' But he did not respond and she felt nothing but a cold silence that seemed to isolate her from the rest of the world.

She tried her old sarcasm. 'Come on, Korpanski, don't try and swing the lead with me. No more sickies.' But the humour had gone from the old teasing.

She heard Fran's shoes clipping back towards the room and stood up. It was time to leave, time to go home, face Matthew's wrath and then...

It was much much later that she could at last do what she had wanted to do for hours, drop her head into her hands and cry.

Chapter Sixteen

It was weeks later that Joanna was finally able to piece the whole case together. Tim Bradeley turned out to have been stunned. Nothing worse. And from his hospital bed he was anxious to explain events.

So most of the gaps were filled in with his help and verified by a thorough search of the barn. The animal feed sacks had indeed contained animal feed. As well as packets of cigarettes, a few thousand at her estimation.

Bradeley's had been a minor role; he had been little more than a carrier. Poorly paid.

'But not as poorly paid as being a driver for Farrell's,' he said grimly. 'My wife and I could hardly afford decent housing, let alone holidays and a car. And we've got kids.'

According to him, the extra money had simply melted away in everyday living expenses. He gave a wry smile when Joanna questioned him about this. 'Put it like this,' he said, 'it made the difference between having the heating on or not, holidays camping in the rain or a fortnight at Benidorm. It didn't exactly buy me a yacht or a private jet.'

'But why risk so much?' She leant in, anxious to discover the truth. 'You would have got a couple of years inside – at most. Not worth trying to kill a copper for.'

Bradeley stared beyond her. 'She told me different.'

'Who told you? What?'

Bradeley's eyes grew stormy and resentful.

'That demon woman,' he said. 'Judy. She said I was the only real link between the goods coming over and their distribution, said that I would be charged as an accessory to Jakob's murder, if not charged with it. She said that the police,' he looked straight at her, 'knew that I'd seen his money and I would be chief suspect, that I'd never see my wife and kids again. I was desperate,' he finished.

It struck Joanna then that Bradeley might not be very bright but Judy Wilkinson and her mother had known exactly which buttons to press and had turned Tim Bradeley from an innocent into a dangerous and desperate man. Put a gun in his hands and he was very dangerous indeed because he panicked.

She charged him anyway.

Even though he'd led her straight to Judy Wilkinson and her mother, Avis.

Arresting both the Grimshaw females gave her one of the most pleasurable moments of her career. And how they talked, each one blaming the other.

Nice family, she thought. Avis, Judy and Jakob. The three of them had deserved each other.

Two weeks later she faced her team and debriefed them.

'It was Avis Grimshaw who hatched the plot five years ago, soon after she moved from Spain to Eastern Europe. She muscled in on a fake cigarettes business run by a Slovakian crime baron who needed a means to get his goods from Eastern Europe into the heart of England and a distribution point from there. The trail was followed back to Bratislava, where the police have made three arrests.' She smiled around the room.

'Avis contacted her daughter.' She scanned the alert faces. 'Not through maternal affection, you understand, but with a business proposition. The animal feeds supplier was ideal. Great big smelly sacks of animal food, lorries driving over here on a daily basis. The farm, too, was ideal. People can come and go without attracting attention:

lorries, cars etcetera. A few sacks of "animal feed" going into a car boot would attract no undue interest. Even we have a low index of suspicion of farms and farmers. The only hurdle was Tim Bradeley, the driver. Luckily, he was poorly paid and with a family to provide for even a few thousand a year made enough difference for him to cooperate. The cigarettes were packed in the animal feeds sacks. All Tim had to do was to make sure that the sacks marked with a certain code found their way into Grimshaw's barns. Judy would see to the rest. And as Bradeley told me, if the crime was uncovered there was always the chance he could plead ignorance.'

A few of the officers started fidgeting. She knew what they were anxious to know. She held her hand up. 'Patience,' she said.

'The trouble started when Brian Young, a small-time criminal recently out of prison, tumbled into the very bar that Mrs Grimshaw, alias Maureen Dudson, had bought and was running with her ill gotten gains. She'd thought she was safe, that she'd "disappeared" completely. How many people from Leek were likely to drop into a bar in Eastern Europe? It was her bad luck that she was recognised. She'd enjoyed

373

being incognito. She quickly realised the danger that Young posed and decided to set him up. In the background, Jakob Grimshaw was ignorant both of the fact that his farm was being used as a premises for the illicit trade and of the true fate of his wife. In fact, he'd been so convinced that she had vanished with another man and would never return that he played a cruel trick on his daughter, planting the evidence, which he knew very well she would find with her talent for nosiness.'

Joanna paused. She could well imagine Judy's giggles, shared with her mother, when she read the letter, detailing Avis's *supposed* fate. 'Judy replaced the letter in the box, both mother and daughter thinking it might come in useful some time later. A little bit of talented play-acting and she could easily convince everyone of her horror at her mother's "terrible death". But then things became increasingly unstable. The farm was running at a loss. Jakob was selling off land; the housing estate was built. He double-crossed Frankwell over the sale of the field and then talked of packing in the farm altogether. And there was always the chance that he might uncover some of the fake cigarettes. Judy and her mother decided he had to go. But they needed a patsy. Enter Young, the garage mechanic just out of prison who was ready to muscle in on the smuggling business, right up to his sweaty armpits, and if he didn't get his way was not above a bit of blackmail. The man with no real motive to kill the farmer suited their purpose only too well. If they could pin the murder on an ex-con and dispose of Grimshaw, it would kill two birds with one stone. And they could always fall back on poor, gullible Bradeley. But oddly enough, the fact that the body lay undiscovered for about a week worked against them. It meant that we didn't know the date or time of death, which in turn meant that carefully laid alibis were useless. Still – it had been worth the risk. Take Jakob Grimshaw out of the equation as well as Young, and Avis could return from the dead and take over the farm, reunited with a daughter who would "forgive" her for playing dead for so long.'

It was DC Alan King who asked the question on everyone's lips. 'So who did kill Jakob Grimshaw?'

'Well,' she said, 'we don't actually know. Avis blames her daughter while Judy says it was her mother. We can't do firearms tests as too much time has passed. They've had ample time to destroy any clothes that might contain forensic evidence.' She paused. 'So we decided to charge them both. The CPS is happy with that. Who knows,' she said smiling, 'they might even be lucky enough to share a cell.'

The dissatisfaction at her initial statement gave way to smiles and finally a burst of laughter.

She joined them, needing some lightness before she faced the necessary inquiry into her behaviour on the night Korpanski was shot. There'd be no offer of Chief Inspector either Piercy or Levin now. It would be a blot on her career, no longer the blue-eyed girl of the Leek police force.

She recounted the same story to Korpanski, giving the sling a cursory look. 'Unfortunately, Mike, although we barked up the right tree...'

He grunted and she continued. 'I put you in danger. Maybe the squad of clumsy-footed coppers wouldn't have been such a bad idea after all.'

Korpanski closed his eyes and she knew the arm was as painful as it looked.

'I'm sorry, Mike.'

He opened his eyes. 'I wouldn't want to be in your shoes when Fran comes visiting.'

'Quite.'

Chapter Seventeen

October

Weddings take a lot of planning. The venue, the food, the dress, the bridesmaids. Bridesmaids?! Honeymoon. Date. Sometimes Joanna felt dizzy with the planning of it all. Her sister and mother, however, were in their element and enthusiastically took her shopping.

The trouble was that none of the wedding dresses was right for her. Unlike many little girls, Joanna had never visualised herself waltzing up the aisle in a float of white netting and pearls. But neither could she picture herself in some of the stiff, cream, tailored dresses that clung to the contour and flared out in a fishtail. As September moved towards October she began to panic. They had only allowed a few months' engagement and she had to wear something.

Veils, tiaras, even hats and fascinators, which failed to do as they'd promised.

Matthew offered no help beyond telling her that Jane had worn a 'traditional' dress and he would love her whatever she wore, which didn't help at all, particularly as Matthew looked quite soft and sentimental as he spoke the words. He was looking forward to being married. He wasn't thinking about the detail at all.

Finally, like all good friends, Caroline came to the rescue. Sporting an impressive baby-bump that seemed to play a non-stop game of football, she took Joanna to a small, exclusive dress shop in Knightsbridge and watched as she worked her way along the rack.

As she glanced through the dresses, Joanna began to feel depressed. The trouble was that she simply wasn't a 'wedding person'. Left to her own devices she might not have wed at all – ever – but Matthew wanted it so very much. He had left his wife and daughter for this. She owed it to him.

She turned to Caroline in despair. 'I don't have to wear white, do I? Or ivory?'

Caroline shook her head. 'But remember, Jo,' she warned, 'Matthew is a traditionalist. He won't appreciate you turning up in red...' her face darkened as she saw the hanger Joanna was fingering, 'or black.'

'Hmm.' Joanna turned again to the rack of dresses until she found one that caught her eye. It was...

For that you'll have to wait for her wedding day.

Author's Note

If you want to share Detective Inspector Joanna Piercy's reading habits try *Second Shot* by Zoë Sharp and you'll see why Matthew had trouble tempting her away from it.

With acknowledgment to Hilary Barnes who paid a princely sum to be a character in this book, donated in aid of the Maer Hills Preservation Society.

This Large Print Book, for people
who cannot read normal print,
is published under the auspices of

THE ULVERSCROFT FOUNDATION

... we hope you have enjoyed this book.
Please think for a moment about those
who have worse eyesight than you ...
and are unable to even read or enjoy
Large Print without great difficulty.

You can help them by sending a
donation, large or small, to:

**The Ulverscroft Foundation,
1, The Green, Bradgate Road,
Anstey, Leicestershire, LE7 7FU,
England.**
or request a copy of our brochure for
more details.

The Foundation will use all donations
to assist those people who are visually
impaired and need special attention
with medical research, diagnosis
and treatment.

Thank you very much for your help.